THE
Rocky Road
TO RUIN

ICE CREAM SHOP MYSTERY #1

By Meri Allen

St. Martin's Paperbacks

First published in the United States by St. Martin's Paperbacks, an imprint of St. Martin's Publishing Group.

THE ROCKY ROAD TO RUIN

Copyright © 2021 by Meri Allen.

All rights reserved.

For information, address St. Martin's Publishing Group, 120 Broadway, New York, NY 10271.

www.stmartins.com

ISBN: 978-1-250-26706-1

Our books may be purchased in bulk for promotional, educational, or business use. Please contact your local bookseller or the Macmillan Corporate and Premium Sales Department at 1-800-221-7945, ext. 5442, or by email at MacmillanSpecialMarkets@macmillan.com.

Printed in the United States of America

St. Martin's Paperbacks edition published 2021

10 9 8 7 6 5 4 3 2 1

This book is dedicated to:

THE STAFF OF KINGSTOWNE LIBRARY and LIBRARIANS EVERYWHERE—Underpaid, under-appreciated, and underestimated guardians of the world's knowledge, you encourage and grow generations of readers and thinkers.

AND YOU, DEAR READERS—Characters are words on a page that only come to life when you read them. Thank you for spending a few hours of your precious time with Riley and me.

xo Meri

Acknowledgments

Many thanks and a mint chocolate chip hot fudge sundae with sprinkles and a cherry on top to:

Bill and Charlotte, my ice cream dream team, for whipping up all the treats and keeping the freezer stocked with good things.

Jessy and David, for encouragement, cheering, and laughter.

Hugh O'Hare, for taking time out at a wedding reception to explain milk and cream mixtures.

The wonderful team at St. Martins. I'm so lucky to have you in my corner.

First reader and editor extraordinaire Barb Goffman, and my wonderful friends at Writers Who Kill, Cozy Mystery Crew, Stiletto Gang, and Sisters in Crime.

And special thanks to Alice Pfeifer, who inherited me, and helps me keep it cozy.

An inconvenience is only an adventure wrongly considered.

—*G. K. Chesterton*

Chapter 1

If you looked up "New England" you'd probably find a picture of my hometown, Penniman, Connecticut. Miles of gray stone walls bordering narrow country lanes? Check. A covered bridge? A town green with a war memorial in the center of the emerald swath of grass? Check and check.

My rented car's engine purred as I drove one of those lanes under the spreading branches of oaks whose leaves would shimmer with crimson and gold come fall. A warm feeling of homecoming washed over me as the car rattled across the covered bridge that spanned the Seven Mile River and swept into the village center.

I took a spin around the green, enjoying the familiarity of the charming boutiques, restaurants, and stately Victorian houses that had been restored and painted to perfection, then parked in front of my dad's used bookstore, The Penniless Reader. The brown clapboard building was shaded by a cheerful red-and-white-striped awning. Two benches flanked the front door, and a reader with a golden retriever at his feet sat there with a book in one hand, a coffee in the other. Golden marigolds and red geraniums burst from window boxes and the hanging basket outside the front door. The last time I'd been home, pine and holly wreaths hung in the windows.

As I got out of my rental, a blue convertible Mustang I'd splurged on, I turned slowly, taking in the green that was the heart of the village. Dad's bookshop was at the north end of the Penniman town green, and a white Colonial-era Congregational church, graceful with tall columns, watched over it from the south end.

The more things changed, the more Penniman stayed the same. Thank goodness.

The retriever's tail thumped as I bent to give him a pat. I'd come home to be with my best friend Caroline Spooner at her mom's funeral, but I had just enough time to stop first to see my dad. I pushed open the door.

"Look what the cat dragged in!" My dad, Nathaniel "Nate" Hawthorne Rhodes, rushed from the front counter and wrapped me in a hug. His words were light but he held me close. "Riley, I missed you, honey."

"I missed you too." I felt a pang as the sunlight streaming through the window highlighted the gray in his curly brown hair and bushy eyebrows. I let my cheek rest for an extra moment against the chest of his blue plaid shirt. Dad was wiry, six feet tall with stooped shoulders, and I fit perfectly under his chin.

My dad had left his teaching job and started The Penniless Reader soon after I was born. My mom passed away when I was two, and for many years it had been just the two of us. Until Paulette.

"Is that Riley?" My stepmother's lovely voice fluted from the back of the shop.

Ten years ago, Dad hired Paulette, a retired nurse, to work part time in the shop. When Dad asked me for my blessing to marry her, what could I say? I'd started taking overseas assignments and I wanted someone to look after him. If only she weren't so perfect. Despite the fact that I was a thirty-five-year-old librarian who did occasional undercover work for my employer, a certain three letter agency in Washington, D.C., had several thousand followers of my own food blog, and traveled the world solo since I was sixteen, Paulette's Stepford perfection always had a way of making me smooth my unruly shoulder-length black hair and wonder if I had spinach in my teeth.

"Welcome home!" Paulette emerged from the local history section, gracefully opened her arms in welcome, and gave me a kiss on the cheek. Though she was sixty-seven (she never mentioned her age, but I looked it up), she had an ageless beauty. Everything about her gleamed: her flawless manicured nails, her silver hair, her diamond-stud earrings. Paulette's elegant cream-colored cashmere top contrasted with the shop's warped linoleum floors, narrow rows of overstuffed shelves, and Dad's goofy homemade signs that read Treat Your Shelves and My Weekend Is Fully Booked. Her lovely cornflower blue eyes swept over me.

"You're tired." Paulette turned to Dad. "Doesn't she look tired, Nate?"

"She's a sight for sore eyes." Dad beamed.

"Jet lag. I couldn't get comfortable on my flight from Rome. I came as quickly as I could when Caroline called to tell me Buzzy'd passed away." Caroline's mom, larger than life Elizabeth "Buzzy" Spooner, owned Penniman's iconic Fairweather Farm and the Udderly Delightful Ice Cream Shop for decades.

Dad's voice softened with concern. "How's Caroline holding up?"

On the phone, Caroline's strained voice had sounded

overwhelmed and exhausted. She lived in Boston where she worked as an art appraiser for an auction house, but for years drove to Penniman every weekend to help Buzzy in the ice cream shop.

"She's holding up. The Brightwoods are a huge help."

"Thank goodness for them," Dad said.

I agreed. Darwin and Prudence Brightwood had run Buzzy's farm for years so she could concentrate on the shop.

Paulette lowered her voice. "I heard there's been fresh tension with Mike."

Her words didn't surprise me. Caroline and her brother had never been close. The little bell over the door jingled as customers entered the shop and I bit back the words I'd been about to speak: *What now?*

"Sometimes people rise to the occasion," Dad said. "I'm sure Mike will support Caroline now that she needs him."

Dad always saw the good in people. I loved that about him, but I didn't share his optimism. I'd known Mike for too long.

I checked my watch. "I'd better get going. The funeral's at two o'clock."

"You and Caroline must come for dinner tomorrow," Paulette said.

"Thanks, Paulette, we will."

Dad hugged me again. "We'll see you at the service."

As I got in the Mustang, I caught my reflection in the rearview mirror and recalled Paulette's words. So I had bags under my eyes. My eyes were the same emerald green as my Granny's—"Green as the cliffs of Moher," she'd say. The lilt in her voice as she put on an Irish accent always made me smile.

I turned the key and the engine surged to life, the rumble and sense of power a pleasure I savored. Dad had always taught me to look for the good in difficult times, that beauty can be a consolation, and I tried to let the charm of the countryside on the short drive to Buzzy's farm wash over me.

It didn't work. What was Mike up to now?

Chapter 2

"Riley, can you believe it?" Caroline said. "Mom always lied about her age. Now she's made it official!"

Church bells chimed as our steps took us from the cemetery behind the Congregational church, leaving the gray marble headstone that marked the spot where Buzzy was buried next to her husband, Charles. I did the math—the birth-date-to-death-date span was eighty years, but underneath was inscribed Aged 29. Buzzy had stopped counting birthdays at 29 and she'd had the last laugh.

"I can't imagine the Gravers approve," I whispered to Caroline. "Gravers" was our nickname for two of Buzzy's part time staff, retired sisters Flo and Gerri. Devoted genealogists, they spent their free time "graving"—documenting graves for a website called Finding Your Dearly Beloved. The name tickled me. How beloved could they be if no one knew where to find them?

Caroline smiled, but took off her thick tortoiseshell glasses to dab her almond-shaped brown eyes. Though petite as a princess in the pre-Raphaelite paintings she loved, Caroline had strong features: a prominent aquiline nose, full lips, and thick brown corkscrew curls. "I need to get back home," she said. I put my arm around her as we walked toward the parking lot, my mind turning one last time to Buzzy.

Buzzy had always encouraged me to see the world and she'd been thrilled that I started a blog, Rhode Food, to document my travels and the food I discovered while on the road. She'd called herself my number-one fan.

Dad and Paulette joined us. "Honey, I'm sorry we have to go. We have an appointment at the shop."

"You're both coming for dinner tomorrow," Paulette said as she brushed away an invisible piece of lint from the sleeve of Dad's jacket.

"Yes, thank you," Caroline said.

I watched Caroline's brother, Mike, shake hands and slap backs as he shouldered through the crowd to join us. He'd left Penniman right after high school, but everyone remembered the tall, dark, and handsome star of the high school football team.

Buzzy had fostered Caroline and Mike, then adopted them, but though they were biological siblings they'd always been different: Caroline introverted, studious, and artistic; Mike a hard-partying athlete. Despite having the square jaw and physique of an action-movie hero, Mike had never been someone you could rely on.

"Mr. Rhodes, Mrs. Rhodes, thank you for coming." He shook hands with my dad and gave Paulette a kiss on the cheek. *Mrs. Rhodes.* I still wasn't used to hearing Paulette called that.

Dad and Paulette embraced me and Caroline. "We'll see you tomorrow." They headed to the parking lot as Mike wrapped Caroline in a careful hug. She hesitated, then closed her eyes and leaned her head against his broad chest.

The last stragglers left the reception in the church hall, including our former high school gym teacher Mrs. Danforth. We'd called her Dandy because on humid days her overbleached blond hair frizzed and reminded us of dandelion fluff. Now her shoulder-length hair was gray and tamed smooth into a bob, another reminder that I'd been away from home too long. She chatted with Mike's best friend, Kyle Aldridge, and Kyle's wife, Nina.

"Mike!" A woman with a waterfall of straight white-blond hair, dressed in a pink suit with a tiny miniskirt edged through the crowd. Though I hadn't seen her since high school, I recognized her immediately.

She took Mike's hands in hers, batting heavily mascaraed blue eyes. "Remember me?"

Mike threw a quick look at me and Caroline, his message clear—*Help me!* "Of course I remember you, Sugar Bear! It's been too long." Sugar Bear was what Mike called all his girlfriends, especially when he couldn't remember their names.

Behind us, Dandy stumbled as she shot that same disapproving look I remembered from high school at the woman's too-short dress. Some things never changed. Kyle steadied her, then Nina said something that made her laugh.

But the woman in pink plowed on, despite Mike's panicked expression and Mrs. Danforth's reproachful look. "Emily Weinberg! You took me to prom!"

I shared a look with Caroline. This should be good.

"How could I forget?" Mike gave her a kiss on the cheek. "You look great."

"Thanks, so do you." Emily tilted her head and beamed.

Was she still crushing on Mike all these years after high school?

"Sorry for your loss, Caroline. Hi." Emily looked at me, then recognition dawned. "Oh, you worked at the ice cream shop too. You don't have glasses anymore."

"Or braces." Inwardly I rolled my eyes but pasted on a smile. "Riley Rhodes."

Emily had been one of the queen bees of Penniman High School and had never given me or Caroline the time of day. Had she even known Buzzy? She was as out of place as her outfit.

I couldn't help it. I glanced down at my sensible black travel dress and Caroline's even longer black pencil skirt and leather flats. I had to agree with Dandy: Emily's outfit was inappropriate for a funeral.

Emily had turned back to Mike, angling her body in front of mine. "You look great, Mike. You know, we could get dinner sometime . . ."

"Sure." Mike's dark brown eyes radiated equal parts sincerity and flirtatiousness.

Emily fished in her purse. "Here's my card."

"Here's mine." He handed her a card and they laughed.

Leave it to Mike to get a date at a funeral.

An engine growled as a red Porsche—be still my heart, a vintage Porsche 911 Turbo—downshifted and slid into an empty parking spot. Heads turned. A tall, leggy woman in a fitted black pantsuit emerged, smoothing her cascade of wavy brown hair. She scanned the crowd and then jogged over to us, her hair flowing in the wind like a shampoo commercial. "Mike!" she called.

"Angelica!" He cast a quick, uncomfortable glance at Emily. "I didn't think you could make it."

Clearly.

The woman smiled, her lips vivid with deep red lipstick that complimented her dramatically arched brows and deep brown eyes. I couldn't help thinking of the song

"The Girl from Ipanema"—the woman was tall and tan and slender and moved with enviable grace. "Turned out I was able to get on an earlier flight," she said as she gave him a quick kiss.

"Everyone, this is Angelica Miguel," Mike said.

"Nice to meet you." Caroline extended her hand. "I'm Caroline."

Angelica took Caroline's hand, then gently embraced her. "So good to meet you." Her smile faltered. "I'm so sorry for your loss. Buzzy sounded like a wonderful person."

Mike turned to me. "Our family's good friend, Riley Rhodes." Angelica and I shook, her grip bone-crushingly strong.

"And this is"—Mike hesitated for a split second—"Emily Weinberg."

The two women nodded as they shook hands.

Nina walked over and put her hand on Caroline's shoulder, her hazel eyes warm. Tall and slim, with her thick, ash blond hair styled in a simple bob cut, wearing a classic black suit and pearl necklace, Nina radiated calm good taste. "Kyle just got a call he has to take and he insisted on walking Mrs. D to her car. Once again, our condolences. If you need anything, please give us a call."

"Thank you, Nina."

"Hello, Riley, nice to see you." Even though we hadn't traveled in the same circles in high school, Nina was friendly to everyone. "Em." Nina and Emily were old friends. "Mike, we'll see you tomorrow."

"For sure," Mike said.

Nina's calm evaporated when she turned to Angelica. "You're Angelica Miguel! We're huge tennis fans from way back." Nina grinned as she shook hands. "I'm so pleased to meet you."

"Nice to meet you too," Angelica said.

"Sorry, I have to run. See you later." Nina gave Caroline a small smile as she hurried after Kyle and Dandy.

Mike wrapped his arm around Angelica's waist. "Riley, can you take Caroline back to the house? I'll show Angelica the way. Nice to talk with you, Emily."

Emily nodded, tossing her waterfall hair as she turned on her heel and stalked off.

So much for dinner with Emily.

As Mike and Angelica strode to Angelica's Porsche, I thought how well suited they were, both strong, tall, and athletic. Mike helped Angelica into her car then jogged over to his sedan.

"His latest?" I asked as Caroline and I crossed the parking lot.

Caroline shrugged. "I guess. She seems like a catch. A pro tennis player."

"Makes sense," I said, "considering his real estate development company builds golf and tennis resorts."

Caroline sighed as we got into the Mustang. "This is a great car." She ran her hands over her leather seat as I pulled out of the parking lot. "You always did like to go fast, Riley."

Her head dropped back and she closed her eyes. "Oh, I'm tired." Lines I'd never seen before etched either side of Caroline's mouth and sunlight picked out strands of gray in her hair. Painting was something she turned to when troubled, and I noticed bits of paint flecked her hands and there was even a splotch of blue paint among the white cat hairs that clung to her black skirt.

"Are you painting?" I asked.

She nodded. "I just started a landscape. I can't resist all the sunflowers on the farm."

"How's Sprinkles?" Sprinkles was Buzzy's cat, an

ageless Persian with the haughty demeanor of a queen forced by a stroke of cruel luck to live with the servants.

"She who must be obeyed?" Caroline brushed at the cat hairs and tightened the knot on a dove gray silk scarf I'd bought her in Paris years ago. "Spoiled beast as always."

Sprinkles had been hiding when I picked up Caroline for the funeral. "I can't wait to see her."

Caroline's breathing deepened as the movement of the car lulled her to sleep. My mind wandered as we drove to the farm where I'd spent so many happy moments riding Buzzy's sweet ponies and playing Capture the Flag after dark. And eating ice cream, of course— as much as I wanted.

Ten minutes later, just outside of town, I joined a slow-moving line of cars. The roads around Penniman had been designated scenic byways, and every summer day brought traffic jams to the narrow lanes. I didn't mind the slowdown. I drank in the scenery: Farmland greened into soybeans or cornfields on both sides of the road. Red barns stood tall beside white farmhouses with black shutters. We passed the gray stone walls and pillars that marked the drive to Moy Mull, Penniman's artists' colony.

Who was lucky enough to live here? For hundreds of years, it had been farmers and then folks who worked at the thread mill. But in the thirties, artists started flocking to Moy Mull, along with actors from New York and Boston who wanted to escape to a country house on the weekends. For years, Penniman had been our little secret.

About ten years ago, an article about Penniman's organic farms put the village on the foodie map. Rich people pretending to be farmers moved in, new restaurants and shops opened. It was great for the town's economy, but it came with a price—traffic, development, and crowds in the summer and fall.

Just past the sharp curve where sunflowers crowded the road, a stopped car startled me from my reverie. I hit my brakes and Caroline started awake. There was a traffic jam at the ice cream shop, just like old times.

The Udderly Delightful Ice Cream Shop had once been a simple farm stand where Buzzy sold the farm's produce, and occasionally homemade ice cream. But Buzzy soon noticed that her ice cream was bringing in more money than the corn and tomatoes. Neighbors helped her expand the stand; Caroline and I helped her paint it her favorite color, a deep eggplant purple; and I knocked together some window boxes for flowers. The sight of the cheerful little building always raised my spirits, but now I gripped the wheel as I watched cars jockey in the crowded parking lot. Horns blared.

"I thought Mike was going to post on social media that the shop was closed today." Caroline fumbled in her pocket for her phone. She scrolled to the shop's site, then huffed. "He forgot. I taped a *Closed* sign to the front door this morning, but I guess it wasn't enough."

"You can't blame people for coming," I said. "It's a gorgeous day, perfect for ice cream."

Caroline rubbed her forehead as I eased past cars and headed up narrow Farm Lane to Buzzy's house.

Farm Lane divided Fairweather Farm into two halves, and two farmhouses faced each other across the lane: Buzzy's white farmhouse to the east behind the shop, and a sprawling red farmhouse and barn across the road to the west. Buzzy's farm manager, Darwin Brightwood, and his family lived in the red farmhouse and ran the organic farm and orchard behind it.

The wraparound porch of Buzzy's small Victorian farmhouse beckoned with red geraniums and ivy spilling from baskets, and yellow daylilies and marigolds ringing the foundation. The view from her porch was breathtaking—over fifty acres of fields, orchards, and woodland.

All Caroline's and Mike's now, I thought.

Caroline craned to look back down the lane to the shop as I parked next to the kitchen door.

I followed her gaze. "Lots of disappointed people," I said.

Caroline chewed her lower lip.

We got out of the car. Some kids ran to the small petting pen where Buzzy usually kept animals, either llamas or miniature goats from neighboring farms. The pen was locked and empty. A little boy kicked the gravel, his shoulders slumped.

"Buzzy would hate this," Caroline said, "but Mike thought it best to close today."

"Of course." We stood, shoulder to shoulder, watching cars back up.

"Riley, are you thinking what I'm thinking?" Caroline said.

I turned to her. "Are you thinking about opening the shop?"

Caroline grinned. "Let's go."

We jogged down to the shop, unlocked the back door, and flipped on the lights. I looped an apron over my head and tied it around my waist. Faces pressed against the broad windows and a buzz of excited voices grew as Caroline and I prepared to open. I hauled tubs of ice cream from the industrial freezer in the back and felt my spirits lift as the dipping cabinets filled with a dozen different flavors. The colors—from the pale pink of strawberry to the soft purple of lavender and honey to the rich brown of mocha almond—reminded me of a box of watercolors. The enticing scent of bittersweet chocolate filled the shop as Caroline started a batch of hot fudge in the kitchen. I glanced outside as a long black Lincoln Continental lurched to a stop right in the middle of the lane before speeding up again.

Moments later, the back door of the shop burst open and the Graver girls hurried in. "Reinforcements have arrived! Give me an apron!" Gerri Fairweather Hunt, former principal of Penniman High School, had a deep alto voice that resonated with authority as she tossed one of her flowy scarves over her broad shoulders.

"Gerri, I told you that with Riley here Caroline was sure to open." Flo Fairweather looped her apron over her head, beaming at me. Flo had been a kindergarten teacher and her voice was gentle and musical, her round face surrounded by soft white curls. While her sister dressed in jewel tones, Flo wore bright primary colors, bright as a new box of crayons.

Mike pushed through the door, his face red. He sidled behind Caroline and said in a low voice, "Caroline, we said we weren't opening today."

"You forgot to put the closing online," Caroline said. "Look at all those people."

Mike folded his arms and scoffed. "You don't expect me to scoop ice cream—"

Angelica slipped through the back door. Her eyes wide, she ran her fingers along the yellow Formica countertop, taking in the bright windows, the yellow gingham curtains, the marble tables, the mural of sunflowers behind the counter. "Oh, Mike, you never told me how cute it is!" She took an apron from a hook and turned to me. "Do I get free ice cream for helping?"

I smiled. "Of course. Flo, will you show Angelica how to make the waffle cones?"

"And"—Caroline squared her shoulders—"everything is free today—in Buzzy's honor."

I couldn't think of anything more appropriate. More times than I could count I'd seen Buzzy give a free ice cream cone to someone who looked like they could use a break.

Flo, Gerri, and I clapped, Flo bouncing on her toes, Gerri's many bangles clanking.

Mike held up his hands. "Free? Caroline—"

"Ready?" I threw open the door.

B y closing time, almost every bit of ice cream in the dipping cabinets was gone.

When people insisted on paying, saying it was for whatever charity Buzzy had named in her will, we took the money and put it in a gallon-size jar that had held penny candy. But the truth was that Buzzy hadn't named a charity. Before the funeral, Caroline had confided that Buzzy had put off making a will, and Caroline wasn't sure she'd even left one.

After we closed the door and I wiped down the counters, I noticed that the money jar was gone. Caroline followed my gaze, her lips turned down. "Mike said he was taking it up to the house for safekeeping." We shared a look.

Wherever the money was, that's where Mike was. Not that I could talk, but Mike had hardly ever come back to Penniman to see Buzzy, even for holidays. Caroline shared a house with some coworkers in Boston, but she spent every weekend back home in the bedroom she'd been given twenty-seven years ago when Buzzy had first fostered her as a malnourished, shy eight-year-old with all her belongings in a single green trash bag.

Caroline stood at the counter, her shoulders bowed, her hands smoothing a folded apron over and over. She looked beyond exhausted and I could feel that the emotional weight of the day was finally sinking in.

"You head up and get a bite to eat. I'll finish closing," I said.

She gave me a quick hug and slipped out the back door. I swallowed the lump in my throat as I made sure the front door was locked.

There wasn't much left to do. Flo, Gerri, and Angelica had whirled through cleanup. I turned off the lights and locked the back door.

Night was falling, the sky behind the farmhouses a gorgeous shade of suede blue. A soft, warm breeze bent the heads of the tall sunflowers that crowded the lane. Buzzy had planted ten acres years ago and now they were a favorite backdrop for thousands of amateur photographers.

It was peaceful, but the night was full of a thousand different noises—dogs barking, small critters scurrying, the wind sighing through the sunflowers. Despite the warm breeze, I felt a chill. There was something in the air, a feeling that hovered around me like a swarm of gnats.

Sadness sure, an emptiness. I couldn't fool myself into thinking that Buzzy would be waiting at the door, smiling in her favorite purple jeans and lucky Patriots T-shirt. But I also felt unsettled, like when I was a little girl watching a storm, counting the seconds between a lighting flash and the roll of thunder that followed. Something made me whip around and peer into the shadows behind the shop.

I felt . . . watched. I scanned the farm and the towering line of sunflowers. They were beautiful but their dark shadows could hide, well, anyone . . . or any thing. I jogged to the back porch of the farmhouse, relief flooding me when I stepped into the pool of light by the kitchen door.

Chapter 3

I went inside, easing the screen door shut behind me, the warm kitchen making me feel silly for my earlier apprehension. *Don't be a drama queen, Riley.*

Caroline sat at the old round oak table, a pot of tea in front of her. It was one of Buzzy's favorites, a Brown Betty I'd sent her from England three Christmases ago. Tupperware containers and foil-wrapped dishes lined the kitchen counter behind her. There were several pies—everyone in Penniman knew Mike loved pie. The scent of flowers wafted from the dining room, where sympathy arrangements crowded every surface.

"So much food. People have been bringing dishes like crazy." Caroline's voice was dull. She hadn't noticed that her scarf had fallen from her shoulders to the floor. I put it on the back of her chair and then hunted through the fridge and filled two plates, putting scoops of her favorite fruit salad on hers. I set the plates down and poured myself a cup of tea.

"Where are Mike and Angelica?"

Caroline shrugged. "In the Love Nest." There was a one-bedroom cottage a quarter mile north of the farmhouse, built for a combative mother-in-law generations ago, which Buzzy occasionally rented out.

"Thank goodness for the Graver Girls." We clinked our teacups.

"Riley, I'm so glad you're here." Tears brimmed and Caroline swiped them with the back of her hand. "Of course, I'm a mess, Mom's gone. But she was eighty and she was content. She said she was going home and that Charles would be waiting for her." Neither of us had known Charles. He'd died years before Buzzy adopted Mike and Caroline.

"It's just . . ." Caroline's voice drifted as she smoothed her skirt, a familiar self-calming motion. "What do I do now? With the shop and the farm?"

"Do you have to do anything?" I said. "Maybe get through the summer and then decide?"

"Mom worked so hard for Udderly." Caroline used our familiar name for the shop. "It's a Penniman institution. I want to keep it open. But I have to go back to work at the auction house and none of the staff here wants to be a full-time manager and—"

A soft knocking at the door made us turn.

Pru Brightwood stepped inside, her wavy silver-gray hair woven into one thick braid. Her husband Darwin followed, hands in his pockets. Last I'd seen him his hair was salt and pepper; now his hair was snow white and so was his beard, but he still wore his jeans held up with bright red suspenders. Behind them came their seventeen-year-old daughter, Willow, with honey blond hair and sea green eyes so beautiful I marveled every time I saw her. Prudence was a midwife who'd thought she'd never get pregnant herself—until she turned forty and Willow made her surprise appearance.

For more than twenty years, Prudence and Darwin Brightwood had run the farm for Buzzy, growing organic vegetables, fruit, and specialty herbs, in exchange for free rent on the property. Darwin partnered with a group that brought in volunteers who worked on organic farms in exchange for experience and room and board. These visiting interns, some from overseas, had delighted Buzzy.

"We hardly got any time with you at the service and reception today," Willow said, throwing her arms around me, then Caroline.

Everyone gathered at the table. I set a platter of sandwiches in the center, then passed everyone a plate.

Willow took a sandwich and passed the platter to her father. "Riley, I can't wait for your next blog. Will you post more about Italy? I want details."

"You've got a fan," Darwin said.

"I haven't had a chance to write." I didn't want to get too specific. Italy had been complicated. "I've been on a leave of absence from my librarian job, so I hope I can do more traveling." I crossed my fingers at this white lie. I was on leave and did hope to travel more, but it hadn't been my idea.

"That sounds more exciting than being a librarian," Willow said. "Even a CIA librarian."

I laughed. Little did anyone know that for the past few years, in addition to my job at the CIA library, I'd had a few undercover assignments. My librarian job as well as my blogging were great cover.

Willow squeezed my arm, her eyes sparkling. "Riley, are you staying here for a while? You have to see the baby goats I'm raising."

"I'd love to!"

"And are you going to help in the shop?" she continued.

"Of course."

Pru said, "Willow and I can help in the ice cream shop tomorrow. I'm between babies."

I gave her a quick smile. "Thanks."

A plump, impossibly fluffy white Persian halted at the entrance to the kitchen, her copper eyes surveying the scene.

Willow swooped her up. "There you are, Sprinkles!"

Sprinkles had been a star on the cat-show circuit, granted, a difficult star, a feline Gloria Swanson in *Sunset Boulevard*. Her owner, Buzzy's dear friend, had passed away and left Sprinkles in Buzzy's hands. She loved Sprinkles, even though she'd been more accustomed to free-wheeling barn cats, not aging stars like Princess Hortense Ophelia Tater Tot, Sprinkles' official name.

A flash of annoyance ruffled Sprinkles' broad face as Willow picked her up. Willow had spoiled her entrance. Sprinkles liked nothing better than to be admired—from a distance. I knew well enough to let Sprinkles come to me. She'd scratched me more than once, but she allowed Willow to pick her up without incident.

"Hey, the gang's all here," Mike said as he and Angelica entered the kitchen. Everyone greeted them as Mike took off his warm-up jacket and set it on the back of Caroline's chair, then gave her shoulder a squeeze. Caroline stiffened, but smiled a greeting to Angelica.

Sprinkles squirmed from Willow's arms and disappeared under the table, looping once around my ankles, then sashayed down the hallway with one sweep of her lush tail.

Mike and Angelica had both changed into something more comfortable. Mike wore gray sweats embroidered with Mystic Spa, a pricey resort near the shore. Angelica wore blue yoga pants and a matching fitted jacket that accentuated her height and toned physique.

"You're Angelica Miguel!" Willow exclaimed.

"Guilty." Angelica shook Willow's hand, then accepted a cup of tea from Pru. Mike unwrapped one of the pies and cut a slice. "Blueberry! Any takers?" He wolfed the slice down as he leaned against the sink.

"It's good to see you, Mike," Pru said. "Where are you living now?"

"Greenwich," Mike said. "Brand new condo with a water view."

Willow and Angelica chatted about tennis, but after a few minutes the conversation dragged. Caroline picked at her food and kept her head turned away from her brother.

Pru shared a look with Darwin, then squeezed Caroline's hand. "We'll let you get some rest."

"Thank you for the snack." Darwin brushed crumbs from his hands and stood. "Well, you know I'm up way past my bedtime."

Mike set his plate in the sink. "Can I talk to you for a second, Darwin?" Mike gestured down the hall to a small parlor.

"Sure." Darwin pushed in his chair and joined Mike.

That was odd. What did Mike have to say in private? Caroline lowered her eyes.

Pru cleared her throat. "You're up at the Love Nest, Angelica?"

"Is that what you call the guest cottage?" A light blush colored Angelica's cheeks. "Mike didn't tell me that. I guess I'll head back up there for the evening. It was nice meeting you all." She stepped out the kitchen door to a chorus of crickets.

Pru and Caroline talked while Willow and I gathered the dishes. I rinsed plates, wondering what Mike had to say to Darwin that had to be said in private. Was he telling Darwin to take care of his sister before taking off with his celebrity girlfriend?

Over the water and clink of silverware I heard the men's voices, not their words but their tone: Mike's low baritone, Darwin's tenor rising at one point. I turned off the water as I cursed the solid wood walls. I still couldn't make out what they were saying.

Darwin came back into the kitchen, hands in his pockets, his back stiff. "You take care now, Caroline. We're here if you need us. Always good to see you, Riley." A rasp of repressed emotion in his voice made my heart drop. Whatever Mike said had blindsided Darwin. One of Buzzy's old Yankee sayings ran through my mind: Beware the anger of a quiet man.

"See you tomorrow," I said. *Wouldn't I? What happened?*

Money. Had to be. It was always money with Mike.

Oblivious, Willow threw her arms around me. "Eleven o'clock at the shop, right?"

I returned the hug. "Come at ten thirty."

She laughed and saluted. "Yes, ma'am."

Pru wrapped her arms around me. "I'm glad you're here." Her words were freighted with extra meaning and I felt the tension in the room build as the Brightwoods stepped into the night.

As the screen door closed softly, I turned to Caroline and Mike. "Okay, what's going on?"

Mike went to the inner door and closed it, cutting off the chorus of crickets. He straddled a chair at the table and tented his fingers, a gesture he'd picked up after watching the *Godfather* movies.

"You can say anything in front of Riley," Caroline said. "You know I'll tell her everything anyway."

Mike turned to me. "Maybe you can talk some sense into her."

Caroline lifted her chin. "Mike wants to sell the farm and the ice cream shop."

Chapter 4

Caroline's words sent a shock through me and I dropped into my chair, listening with growing disbelief as Mike outlined his plan to develop the farm into a high-end residential community. My jet lag and dismay blurred his words. *Buzzy had died only a week ago and now he wants to sell the farm?*

"I have all the players lined up and they're ready to move. This parcel of land is terrific, but there may be others coming on the market," Mike said. "You were in the army once, Riley. When the time comes, you have to pull the trigger, right?"

"That's a very bad analogy, Mike." I ran my hand along the uneven line of my collarbone, a souvenir of the helicopter crash that ended my very short military career. I turned to Caroline. "Caroline, do you want to sell?" I asked but knew the answer.

Caroline shot out of her chair. "Riley, the last thing I want to do is sell. This is my home! The Brightwoods' home! Mom worked so hard to make that ice cream shop work. The town loves it! But I can't do it alone. I love my work at the gallery, and we're about to start a project where I'm the lead. I won't be able to come home on weekends for at least two months." She faced Mike, her chin trembling, her eyes brimming. "And you won't help."

"My life's not here." Mike shrugged.

Buzzy had always wanted her children to get along, but these two had never seen eye to eye. Caroline's absentminded-professor mind was tied to a heart as big as Buzzy's. Mike was a man of action with an affinity for get-rich-quick schemes.

"Come on, Caroline," Mike huffed. "You make me seem heartless. I love this place too."

Caroline crossed her arms. "That's why you're in such a hurry to unload it."

An angry wave of red surged up Mike's neck and cheeks. He clenched his handsome square jaw, took a steadying breath. "There's a lot of money at stake, but we have to act fast. Think about it. I'll see you in the morning." He grabbed his jacket from the back of Caroline's chair and stormed out the kitchen door, letting the screen door bang shut behind him.

"Riley, I could kill him!" Caroline moaned. "What am I going to do?"

After Caroline went up to bed, I turned over the last hour. Caroline and Mike had presented such a united front at the funeral. He'd been so solicitous, so charming. Maybe she thought he'd turned a new leaf. They must have talked about the business deal before I'd arrived for the funeral. Perhaps she'd thought he'd change his mind.

Ha.

As I mulled Caroline's predicament, I went into the guest room, which was Mike's old bedroom. It was now a catchall, with a sewing table on one wall, a bureau and single brass bed on another, and overflowing shelves of colorful fabric in plastic bins on the other two. I smiled at a framed cross-stitch over the sewing machine that declared, "Whoever dies with the most fabric wins."

The remaining shelves were jammed with sports trophies, old yearbooks, crafting materials, and a small TV with a vintage gaming system.

Over the narrow bed hung three framed, almost identical photos taken at the National High School Summer Football Camp, in Derbyshire, Indiana. I peered close at the rows of young men, all with serious faces and padded shoulders, and found Mike and Kyle. They'd attended the monthlong camp in July three years in a row. Both had excelled at football and went to UConn on athletic scholarships.

I scanned the faces in the photos on the bureau and pulled up short when I recognized my teenage self in one of them. The photo was of a pie eating contest at the Penniman High Fall Fair almost twenty years ago. There was Mike, handsome even with a mouth full of pie, and next to him a laughing girl with golden shoulder-length curls. Brooke Danforth, Dandy's daughter. I didn't know Brooke, but I remembered the shock I'd felt when she died. Caroline and I had been at summer camp when we heard the popular cheerleader had taken an accidental overdose of sleeping pills. She wasn't a friend—we moved in different circles—but it was the first time someone I knew, someone my own age, had died.

Next to Brooke sat Kyle, then Nina. Everyone else was spattered with pie filling, but somehow Nina's white shirt was immaculate. There I was in the background, serving pie, and next to me . . . that straight-as-a-pin platinum hair was hard to miss: Emily Weinberg. I set the photo back on the shelf.

One window had an air conditioner, but there was no need for it tonight. I opened the other window and the cool night air flowed in as I leaned on the sill. There was no moon, and beyond the porch light was an inky, absolute darkness that I rarely experienced, having lived and traveled in cities for so many years.

Movement caught my eye as a small animal darted across the yellow pool of porch light. I remembered that I'd left my travel bag in my car. I could borrow Caroline's pajamas, but I needed my toothbrush. I grabbed my keys, stepped into the hallway, and noted Caroline's door was ajar. I could see Caroline sitting at her easel, an almost-empty canvas in front of her, painting to keep her mind occupied and the sadness at bay. I crept downstairs, placing my feet to avoid creaky steps so I wouldn't disturb her.

Soft sounds came from the kitchen. It took me a moment to realize it was Sprinkles meowing, almost as if in conversation. Who was she talking to? I froze.

Buzzy?

No such thing as ghosts, I chided myself. Besides, if Buzzy were a ghost, she'd invite me to sit down for a cup of tea. The thought made me feel safe, protected even. Buzzy wouldn't let anything harm me. What a wonderful ghost to have in my corner.

Sprinkles on the other hand. . . . What was she up to?

I went to the back door, my footsteps loud on the worn linoleum. Sprinkles sat on a table by the window, the light from the porch making her shadow loom almost the full length of the floor. She'd like that—a shadow as big and imposing as she thought she was.

She held a paw to the window and turned her flat face to me abruptly, a rebuke for rudely interrupting her.

"Forgive me, your majesty. Who're you talking to?" I opened the back door and heard a soft thump.

That was no ghost. I peered into the darkness beyond the porch light.

Sprinkles joined me at the screen door, her tail switching, but I knew she wouldn't go outside. She was an indoor cat through and through.

I jerked open the screen door and leaned out, but there was nothing waiting except for the sound of a million crickets. To my shock, Sprinkles slid past me onto the porch. I followed, scanning. I couldn't see anything in the dark beyond the light from the porch, but my skin prickled.

"Who's there?" As soon as I spoke, I felt stupid. If someone was there, they'd have spoken up—unless they didn't want to be seen.

The sounds of the countryside were unfamiliar, unsettling. My imagination switched into overdrive. Skunks, no, *rabid* skunks might lurk. Or coyotes. Or—my heart beat fast—former boyfriends. Or serial killers. . . .

The last made me laugh. *Get a grip, Riley.* The only people who'd be outside here would be teenagers hoping to raid the ice cream shop.

I pulled out my car keys and beeped my car. The interior lights came on, the glow casting pale light into the shadowy yard. Sprinkles gave a forlorn, questioning *miaow*, then threw another irritated look at me as she turned to face the door. My dimwittedness disappointed her. Her expression said, You couldn't get good help these days. I opened the door, and with a twitch of her tail, she went back inside. I eased the screen door closed behind her.

Sprinkles had left me to face any rabid skunks on my own. Warily, I popped the trunk and got my bag. A dark shape darted across the porch and disappeared into the shadows.

A kitten!

Sprinkles glared at me from the window.

I slammed the trunk and ran back into the house. Would wonders never cease. Sprinkles had a friend.

Chapter 5

The next morning, I rose at seven and put on my running gear. Caroline's door was still ajar, and I pushed it open a few inches. Her room hadn't changed since we were girls—still stuffed with books and canvases, art supplies, every wall covered with posters of the Impressionist artists she loved so much. The canvas on the easel was now completely covered with a field of brilliant sunflowers. Caroline breathed softly, her form motionless under a faded blue patchwork quilt.

I headed down the hall. Sprinkles darted out of Buzzy's bedroom as I passed, tripping me. *She'd been lying in wait.* "You beast," I muttered.

I followed Sprinkles downstairs and she slunk into the powder room off the kitchen. I made sure the automatic coffee maker was set, then I opened the cabinet in the pantry where I remembered Buzzy kept Sprinkles' froufrou gourmet cat food. I put out Sprinkles' breakfast, made sure her water was fresh, and headed out the door.

I crossed the yard, drinking in the view of the farm directly across the lane. Behind their sprawling farmhouse and big red barn, Darwin and Pru's handiwork spread in bright green rows and blocks like a well-constructed quilt of organic vegetables and herbs. I turned north up Farm Lane, following the narrow road to the crest of the hill where a gravel road, barely wide enough for a car, crossed from east to west.

If I followed the road east, it cut past the Love Nest and an old barn, through a field of sunflowers, and dead-ended by a pond. To the west the road led through more sunflowers to the apple orchards and another pond, twisting past a centuries-old family cemetery.

Continuing up Farm Lane, the road curved and narrowed as it bisected heavily wooded hills. There were just a few homes back here, shaded by centuries-old oaks and bordered by gray stone walls.

Directly across the gravel road from the Love Nest, behind a virtual screen of towering, unkempt bushes, was a two-level home so overgrown by ivy and laurel it was hard to see the yellow siding underneath. This house was owned by a man everyone called Aaron the Hermit. In true New England fashion, he kept himself to himself.

Across from Aaron the Hermit's house and a bit up the lane was the Danforth home, a red cedar shingled one-level ranch surrounded by lush English gardens. I had no idea my sour-faced high school gym teacher had such a green thumb.

A quarter mile farther up the road I passed the Fairweather homestead. Geraldine and Flo had started life as the Fairweather sisters, born into one of Penniman's oldest families. After the deaths of their husbands, they'd returned to the family homestead, a more than two-hundred-year-old red Cape. Their family had sold the farmland to Buzzy's family generations ago.

The road climbed uphill here and my muscles burned

as I reached the end of the lane where it intersected busy four-lane Town Road. If I turned west, I'd run into town. Turning east, I passed the Penniman Ridge winery and then, a mile past that, the dairy farm that produced the milk for Buzzy's ice cream. I wanted a short route today, so I turned and retraced my steps back to Farm Lane and turned onto the road in front of the Love Nest. The only sounds here were birdsong and the crunch of my footsteps on gravel. Mike's car was parked by the front door of the tiny whitewashed cottage, but Angelica's was not. I slowed my steps.

Had she left already? I glanced at my watch: 7:30. Maybe she'd realized what a terrible person Mike was. She couldn't have missed the tension between Mike and . . . well, everyone after the funeral.

Too bad. I'd especially liked the way she'd pitched in at the shop. It would've been easy for Angelica to beg off of helping out. Certainly it was a difficult situation, the funeral of the mother of a guy you were dating, but she'd handled it well.

Sweat pooled on my forehead and I swiped it away. A small animal darted from the underbrush at the side of the road—the kitten from last night—and I pulled up short.

"Whoa!" The kitten, all black, stopped in front of me with a yowl. I crouched and beckoned to him. "Here little guy. Here."

He tilted his chin and regarded me with wary amber eyes. His right ear was bent and ragged—a cauliflower ear, just like a boxer. Another scar ran across his back; the fur was missing and the skin visible. No wonder he kept a cautious distance. "You poor thing! You've been in some fights, haven't you?"

I scooted closer but he switched his tail and trotted

across the road onto the gravel path leading to the barn.
He looked back at me, then ran to the side door, which
was steps from the kitchen door of the Nest. He was so
thin, I could see his bones move beneath his fur.

"Hang on, I'll take you home." My footsteps crunched
on the gravel as I followed. "We'll get a bite to eat."

He picked his way through the weeds at the door and
went inside.

"Dumb cat, the food is this way," I muttered, but still
I followed him into the dark barn, stepping past a metal
rack jammed with grimy old cans and cardboard boxes.
Rusted tools, pitchforks, rakes, and shovels leaned in a
corner, unused for decades.

The sweet, musty smell of hay surrounded us, and
the dust made me sneeze. The kitten's tiny sneeze answered mine. "See? This is no place for you. Let's—"

There was another scent, one I'd experienced before.
A metallic smell . . .

The kitten yowled, the sound making the hair on my
arms rise.

I hesitated for a few moments, letting my eyes ad-
just to the dim light as a tendril of dread grew in me.
There were two wooden stalls on either side of the barn.
I pressed my hand against the rough wood as I followed
the kitten's cry to the one on the left. Steeling myself, I
edged to the entrance of the stall. A pale shaft of sunlight streamed in a window, illuminating the lower half
of a man's body sprawled on the floor, his muscular legs
clad in gray sweatpants.

My heart thudding, I scanned the area for threats.
There was no sound, nothing moved except for the little
black cat that now brushed against my ankles. I pushed
down my panic as I eased into the stall.

Mike lay on his back on a pile of hay, his eyes closed,
his arms splayed. A pitchfork lay just beyond reach of his

outstretched left hand. He might have been sleeping but for the crimson splotches on his torso and thighs that told me he'd been stabbed more than once. I struggled to make sense of what I was seeing. As I inched closer, my vision telescoped onto Mike's ashen face. A bit of hay had fallen against his cheek. I crouched and gently removed it. I'd seen dead men before but still I held two fingers to his cold neck to check for a pulse.

The cat yowled again. My eyes traveled down to where he sat by Mike's waist. A bit of gray silk trailed from the pocket of Mike's jacket. My stomach lurched as I recognized the pattern of Caroline's scarf.

Chapter 6

I stumbled from the dark interior of the barn into the bright morning sunshine, throwing up my arm to shield my dazzled eyes. I pounded up the steps to the screen door of the Love Nest and yanked it open. The inner door was ajar.

Why hadn't I brought my phone? There'd been a landline here ages ago—there! A black phone was mounted on the wall by the avocado green refrigerator. My fingers trembled as I dialed 911; I took a deep breath to steady my voice as I gave the dispatcher directions. He told me to stand outside and wave down the police cars.

I hung up the phone, realizing too late that he'd probably assumed I called from a cell phone and expected me to stay on the line. My body thrummed with adrenaline as I paced in the small kitchen. *Who killed Mike? Where was Angelica? What happened?*

There were only four rooms in the snug one-story cottage: kitchen, living room, bedroom, bath.

On the oak kitchen table were an empty wine bottle and two glasses. The label read Penniman Ridge Special Edition in gold lettering; it was from the winery just down the road. In the clear light streaming through the lace curtains, I could see the dregs of wine in both glasses, and lipstick on the rim of one glass, deep red lipstick. Angelica's color.

An overwhelming feeling of something missing came over me. What was it? The wooden counter and white porcelain sink were empty. I scanned the living room. There was a brown leather recliner, a plaid loveseat covered with a crocheted afghan, and an old television with a VCR set on a homey, blue rag rug. I turned back to the kitchen and caught sight of a wadded-up piece of paper on the floor next to the refrigerator.

Sirens wailed in the distance. I hurried to the bathroom to get a tissue and used it to pick up the paper. I was messing with evidence, but I couldn't help it. Caroline had mentioned that nobody had stayed in the Love Nest since leaf peepers last fall. This paper must have to do with Mike and Angelica . . . and perhaps, his murderer.

I unfolded the crinkled paper which had been folded into three sections, as if to fit in a business envelope. I scanned the floor but didn't see any envelope; the trash was empty. I turned the paper over, opening it just enough to read the typed message: "Meet me at midnight. The usual place."

The usual place? The barn?

Memories tumbled back to high school. Saying Mike was popular with girls was an understatement. Buzzy always teased him and called him Romeo. Caroline and I had seen him bring dates here to the barn. We knew they weren't just visiting the ponies.

Now Romeo was lying dead where he'd met so many of his Juliets.

A police car pulled up to the cottage. I put the note

back where I'd found it and stepped outside onto the front porch to meet the cops.

watched in disbelief as the peaceful road by the barn filled with police vehicles. Right after I directed officers to Mike's body, I told them Angelica was gone.

The officer questioning me was tall, with a thick head of dark brown hair going gray at the temples and an impressive beard that called to mind sea captains and biblical prophets. He handed me his card: Det. Jack Voelker. Penniman Police Department.

"Angelica Miguel? The tennis player?" The officer's eyebrows rose. "Do you know when she left?"

"No. No idea." My heart rate ticked up. *Was she okay? Did she have something to do with Mike's death?*

I had to tell Caroline about Mike. I tried to tamp down my impatience as I answered the detective's rapid fire questions.

"Name?" he said.

"Riley Rhodes."

"Address?"

I gave him the address of my tiny one bedroom apartment tucked away on a cobblestone street in Old Town Alexandria, Virginia.

"Occupation?"

"Librarian and travel blogger," I said. He didn't ask so I didn't mention that I was a librarian at the CIA. That would definitely complicate things.

"What brings you to Penniman?"

When I answered 'Buzzy Spooner's funeral,' the detective paused his note taking for a brief glance that told me he'd known Buzzy.

He angled his head toward the barn. "How did you know the deceased?"

"Mike's the brother of my friend, Caroline Spooner." *Caroline.* Who was asleep in the house just down the lane, who had no idea her brother had been murdered. "I have to tell Caroline about Mike. He's her brother."

An officer stood behind Mike's sedan, taking down the license number. Voelker flashed a look at his counterpart. I read it clearly: they weren't going to let us alone together, give us time to get out stories straight. Because I'd just told them we were friends. Because we might be suspects. No, we *were* suspects.

My hackles rose and I tried to keep my voice steady. "I told you everything. When I came out for a run this morning, Caroline was asleep in the house. Please, I have to tell Caroline about Mike."

Voelker jutted his chin at his counterpart. "Accompany Ms. Rhodes to the house. Ms. Rhodes, you'll have to come to the station later to sign your statement."

"Yes, of course."

A cruiser pulled up to Buzzy's house as I hurried down the lane with my keeper. Another officer got out of the cruiser and introduced herself but I barely heard her.

I ran up the steps ahead of them. The house was quiet, filled with the scent of coffee and the cloying sweetness of the floral arrangements. I went upstairs, one officer behind me, her equipment belt jangling.

I hurried to Caroline's bedroom and knocked softly on the doorjamb as I pushed it open.

"Riley?" Caroline's voice was groggy. "I took one of Buzzy's sleeping pills and I'm so out of it. Did I hear sirens?"

"Caroline." I hurried into the room, sat on the side of her bed. Sprinkles lay next to Caroline and blinked up at me. Caroline fumbled for her glasses and gasped as she noticed the officer at the door.

"I'm sorry, I have awful news."

The next hours were a blur. Caroline threw on some jeans and a T-shirt and joined the police in the living room. I thought she'd fall apart when she heard the news about Mike, but her reaction was the opposite: she'd gone still, her narrow shoulders bowing as if under an invisible weight.

After Caroline spoke to an officer, I made her a cup of tea and put in a spoonful of sugar. "Try to drink this."

She took the cup but held it in her lap, her face devoid of expression. A volunteer from Penniman Police's chaplain corps sat next to her. He spoke softly to Caroline—I couldn't make out his words, but his accent was lilting, comforting. When she lifted the cup to her lips and drank, the small, normal act sent a surge of relief through me.

The front door opened and another officer came in without knocking. Murder made manners go out the window. A few moments later a yelp came from the kitchen. "Ow!" Sprinkles dashed into the room followed by the officer. "Geez, I tried to pet her and she bit me."

"I'm so sorry!" Caroline set aside her tea, rushed to Sprinkles, and cuddled her. "Bad cat! Don't worry, she's had all her shots."

I put an arm around Caroline's shoulders. "Can she go lie down now?"

The officer shared a glance with the chaplain. "Yes. We'll be back later to ask you a few more questions, Miss Spooner."

"When can I see Mike?" Caroline's voice cracked.

"We'll let you know."

I thanked the chaplain and officer, then accompanied Caroline upstairs where she sagged onto the bed. Sprinkles hefted herself onto a footstool next to the bed and then onto the pillow next to Caroline.

By the window, the canvas on the easel showed sunflowers reaching to the horizon, a mirror image of the scene out the window. Caroline must have spent hours last night working on it.

"Riley." Caroline gripped my arm. "I can't handle this, not with Buzzy gone too!" I held her as she wept.

I called Dr. Gilroy, the Spooners' longtime family physician. He gave Caroline a mild sedative and tucked her into bed. He was a lovely man—he'd set my broken arm when Buzzy's pony Buttercup had bucked me off when I was twelve.

"I'm glad you're here, Riley." Dr. Gilroy shook his head. "This is tough."

I walked him to his car. As he drove off, a white Lexus SUV pulled up. Kyle jumped out and rushed to me as Nina exited the passenger door.

"Riley, how's Caroline?" Kyle's brow furrowed as he looked up the lane toward the police vehicles at the Love Nest.

"Sleeping. Doc's given her a sedative."

Nina's eyes were troubled as she slipped an arm around Kyle's waist and leaned her forehead against his shoulder. He pulled her close with a convulsive movement and my heart caught, remembering that Kyle and Mike had been best friends since high school. Kyle's light blue button-down shirt was wrinkled, his thick gold hair mussed, and he needed a shave. "This can't be real," he muttered. "What happened? What are the police saying?"

Though my heart went out to Mike's longtime

friends, I couldn't bring myself to go through another recounting of finding Mike's body. "I don't know," I said.

"I'll ask Jack what he knows," Kyle said. "Tell Caroline that we're here for her, okay?"

Nina gave me a sad smile, then followed her husband as they got into the car and drove up the lane. From what I'd seen of the taciturn police detective, I didn't think Kyle would learn much.

A crowd gathered around me: Flo, Willow, some of the farmhands, Pru. Shock rippled through them as the news spread.

Though the morning was already warm, Pru rubbed her arms as if chilled. "I have to tell Darwin. He's been working in the orchards since dawn."

I recalled the emotional rasp in Darwin's voice last night. He'd made it clear whose side he was on: Caroline's, not Mike's. I wondered how he'd take the news.

A truck from the dairy farm rumbled into the shop's parking lot. "Oh, my, that's the milk and cream delivery," Flo said. "We have to open so we can get that in the refrigerator."

I felt everyone's eyes turn to me. We all needed to keep moving and stop thinking of the grim line of emergency vehicles parked at the Love Nest. With a police officer just downstairs, Caroline couldn't get much safer.

"Let's get to work." I headed to the shop.

Chapter 7

Not much had changed at the Udderly Delightful Ice Cream Shop since I worked there in high school. The building was rustic and homey looking on the outside, but the kitchen where Buzzy crafted small batches of ice cream was sterile like a lab, with bright white walls, porcelain sinks, a black-and-white-checkerboard linoleum floor, and stainless-steel tanks and mixers. One wall was covered with chalkboard paint, and across the top in a rainbow of slightly smudged letters was one of Buzzy's favorite inspirational quotes: "Bloom where you're planted."

After we'd put the milk and cream delivery into the industrial-size refrigerators, Flo and Willow lined up in front of me, Willow in a swirling sundress, Flo dressed in a sunny yellow T-shirt, jeans, and spotless white sneakers she'd threaded with yellow laces. Her reading glasses swung from a lanyard of primary-color beads. "What do we do now?" Flo said.

What do we do? I wanted to say, *You've been working here longer than I have*, but I stopped myself. Everyone was used to Buzzy, larger-than-life Buzzy, telling them what to do.

"We'll keep things going until Caroline gets on her feet," I said. "We finished all the ice cream in the dipping cabinets yesterday. Willow, will you please restock from the storage freezers in back?"

"Got it." Willow dashed down the hallway, skirt whirling.

A teenage guy ran in through the workroom door. He was about my height (5′ 8″) but seemed to be all arms and legs, with shaggy brown shoulder-length hair and a wisp of beginner moustache. He wore baggy cargo shorts, a neon green T-shirt printed with a picture of crossed drumsticks that read Weapons of Mass Percussion, and a set of expensive headphones looped around his neck. He startled when he saw me and stopped short.

"Hi," I said. "What's your name?"

"Ah, Brandon Terwilliger?" His voice went up at the end of the sentence, as if he were asking a question. I hid a smile.

"Brandon, I'm Riley. I'm helping out today. Please make sure the napkin dispensers are full and the cups and spoons are fully stocked, then start the waffle cones."

Brandon pushed his thick black-rimmed glasses up his nose and dashed to the front of the store.

"You don't have to run!" I took a deep breath. Things were only going to get more complicated and, well, awful, as the days and police investigation went on. Keeping things normal, or as normal as possible, was key.

I considered how not normal my life had been for the last few years. I hated the word "spy"—I know, I know, semantics. Though I understood that the ramifications of my missions were serious, my tasks were simple. Compartmentalizing was key. I'd need that skill here. The busy pace of an ice cream shop would keep my mind occupied and the awful image of Mike's body at bay.

Getting Udderly up and running was something I

could do. I'd worked here many summers as a teenager. The staff just needed someone to take charge until Caroline could hire a manager. I squared my shoulders to project confidence.

Willow pushed a cart loaded with tubs of ice cream to the front of the store.

"Willow, when you're done with those, please write the chalkboards." We listed the ever-changing flavors on two chalkboards—one we set outside, one hung over the counter.

"Got it."

"Flo." I turned to Flo.

"Ma'am, yes, ma'am," Flo saluted.

I laughed. "Can you take a look at what Willow's putting out and what's left in storage? Take inventory? Then we can make a plan for what flavors to make next."

"Right," she said. "And check the special-events orders."

My stomach dropped. "Special-events orders?"

Flo nodded. "Buzzy took special orders for parties."

Ah, the first monkey wrench. "Where did she keep those orders?"

Flo scurried to the office, which, instead of having a door had a beaded-curtain in rainbow colors. She parted the curtain and flicked on the light. I followed, my eyes widening when I realized Buzzy had redecorated her office: the walls were painted purple and angel and cow figurines filled several shelves. An antique rolltop desk was covered with stacks of papers. I flicked through them.

"Are these all," I gulped, "bills?"

Flo shrugged. "I only help at the counter and in the kitchen. Buzzy put special orders on there." Flo pointed to a calendar on the wall, the old-fashioned kind that had a single number on a page that you ripped away every day. My heart caught as I realized the date hadn't been changed since the day Buzzy died. I'd never change it. Ripping off those pages would be like ripping open a wound.

I could tell Flo felt the same way. She stepped back, so I flipped through the calendar. On today's date, in purple ink, Buzzy had written in her looping script: *"Two gallons of margarita for Debra Jo Burnette's bachelorette party."*

My eyebrows raised. "Margarita ice cream?"

"One of her new boozy ice cream recipes," Flo said. "It's really a sorbet she called the Ultimate Frozen Margarita. It's a big moneymaker."

Boozy ice cream? I shook my head. "If we don't have it in the freezer, I hope the recipe is in the *Book of Spells*." That was what Buzzy called her binder of recipes, which was kept on a table by the chalkboard.

Buzzy had reveled in using creative ingredients. "Margarita," I muttered under my breath. "Please take care of that inventory and see if we have the margarita made already." *Please be ready.*

Flo pointed at the lowest drawer of the desk. "Okay, right after I get the cash register ready. The money's in the box."

I pulled open the drawer and lifted a dented metal cash box. "Some high-tech security system here."

"Oh, don't worry, Riley, it's locked." Flo jutted her chin at a lanyard with a circle of metal keys hanging behind the door. "It's the smallest one."

I fitted the key and opened the box. It was stuffed with stacks of wrinkled bills and a few rolls of change. I flashed to the money in the jar Mike had taken from the shop. I hadn't seen it in the Love Nest. That's what was missing.

Where was the money jar? Had Mike been killed for

a few hundred dollars? Had he been killed in a robbery gone wrong? I'd have to tell the police. But wait Riley, then why was Mike killed in the barn? And what about that note?

Flo patted my arm. "You're lost in thought, Riley. Are you sure you're okay?"

"Flo," I said. "You live up the lane. Did you see or hear anything unusual last night?"

She shook her head. "I've been asking myself that over and over. It was quiet as usual. Heard some cars, but Farm Lane's a cut-through. I slept like a log."

I went to the front of the shop and placed the money in the cash register. It was the same one I'd used all those summers years ago. Like so much here, the shop was frozen in time. Even the muffled sound of the customers waiting to come in seemed the same, and the scent of the waffle cones freshly made. . . .

I called, "Brandon, how are the waffle cones coming?"

No answer. I went into the kitchen where Brandon was bopping to music on his headphones as he rolled waffle cones on metal forms. They were all perfectly golden. When he noticed me and jumped, I gave him a smile and a thumbs-up.

Back in the shop, Willow had all the tubs of ice cream open in the dipping cabinets, the flavors arranged in rainbow order, making a wonderfully colorful display. I glanced at the clock. We opened at eleven. Ten minutes to go.

On the chalkboard behind the counter, Willow had used an assortment of colors and stylish lettering to list all the flavors. She'd also decorated the borders with sunflowers and a sketch of a black and white goat. "Nice job, Willow" I said. "That goat's adorable."

"Thank you," she brushed chalk dust from her fingers. "He's one of my babies. We call him Hairy Houdini because he keeps escaping from his pen."

Flo came into the shop waving a piece of paper. "Here's an inventory. We need lots." My heart dropped as Flo continued. "We're wiped out because the shop's been closed and no one's been making ice cream since Buzzy passed. We do have butter pecan, mango tango, pineapple upside-down cake, salted caramel, raspberry chocolate chip, rocky road, cherry dark-chocolate chunk, bourbon-pecan praline, maple walnut, lemonade, and gluten free cookie dough, but we're low on cookies and cream, funky monkey, brownie bomb, chocolate chip, and peanut butter cup crunch." She drew a breath. "We have the stalwarts, thank goodness." The "stalwarts" were chocolate and vanilla. "No margarita, and we need that margarita—remember. They're picking up at seven—and we'll have to get going on sunflower."

"Sunflower?" I blinked.

Willow waved a hand, "Not till next weekend. That's when we have the Penniman Sunflower Festival here on the farm. We'll start making it this week."

A vague memory surfaced. Caroline had mentioned something about a new flavor Buzzy had crafted for the town's sunflower celebration.

"Ready to rumble." Flo looped a purple apron over her head. Printed on the chest was the motto "Will Work for Ice Cream." The clock ticked toward eleven.

Restless customers pressed against the door. I'd figure out the sunflower ice cream later. "Scoops?" I said.

Flo and Willow waved metal scoops.

Brandon carried out a metal rack of crisp, still-warm cones and set it on the counter behind us. The scent—buttery, sweet, with a hint of spicy vanilla—was intoxicating. If I could get through the day without devouring a dozen of these, it would be a victory.

"Okay, Brandon, open the doors and hang up the other ice cream board outside," I said.

Brandon hefted the chalkboard and opened the door. As a tide of ice cream lovers surged through, a man with the broad shoulders of a linebacker lunged to the front of the line. His forehead wrinkled in an intense expression as he pushed toward Brandon. "You work here? Tom Snow, New England News Now. What can you tell me about the dead man in the barn?"

Brandon's eyes went wide behind his glasses. He gripped the chalkboard like a shield and stumbled backward.

All the tension, sadness, and worry I'd managed to set aside as I prepared the shop to open surged back at Snow's words. I turned my emotions to ice as I strode toward the newsman. "Brandon, please put the flavor board outside and then get behind the counter. Mr. Snow, was it? Step outside." I took him by the upper arm and maneuvered him through the crowd.

Once outside in the parking lot past the line of customers waiting to enter, I loosened my grip. Snow gave me an aggrieved look, straightened his blue blazer, and ran a hand across his blond crew cut. "And you are?"

The length of the line surprised me, but so did the scene outside. Fairweather Road was not only lined with customers' cars, but with news vans. An oversized news truck with a satellite rig was causing a bottleneck and horns honked as cars tried to edge around it.

A woman with a video camera stood by the rear hatch of a white SUV marked News Now, and to my horror, started filming.

I angled my body away from her.

Now that the camera was rolling, Snow's behavior changed. His voice warmed and he leaned toward me with a deeply concerned expression. "We've heard that a man was found dead in a barn on Farm Lane. Do you know the dead man?"

I inhaled slowly as I gathered my thoughts.

News had traveled fast. Locals certainly already knew about Mike, and with all the reporters here, it wouldn't be long before the ghoulish and curious flooded into the shop.

My mind flicked through possibilities.

I respect journalists, but this was too close to home and too soon to deal with. Although with every fiber of my being I wanted to kick this guy and his fake concern, I had to stay calm and give him just enough so he'd leave us alone.

"I'm a friend of the family that owns the ice cream shop," I said. "You should talk to the police."

"The police have blocked the road and the spokesman hasn't made an official statement yet. Surely you're in the know, working here." He leaned closer, hoping his flattery would work. "Is the man connected to the Spooner family?"

"You'll have to talk to the police." I turned back toward the shop but Snow stepped in front of me.

"You're opening the ice cream shop? Isn't that a little cold?" He grinned. "Ha, ha, see what I did there?"

I took a steadying breath and narrowed my eyes. The camerawoman shook her head and coughed.

Snow cleared his throat. "Sorry, sorry. We'll cut that." The woman nodded.

"The owner passed away recently and the family wants to keep the shop open," I said.

"Is there a connection between the owner's death and the man in the barn?" Snow said.

"Of course not!" Inside my thoughts churned. A connection? Buzzy had died peacefully in her sleep. Mike, on the other hand . . . I couldn't imagine much worse.

"And the tennis player, Angelica Miguel," Snow said. "Do you know if she's connected to the death? The police are on the lookout for her."

Where was Angelica? Why couldn't they find her?

Could she have killed Mike? Of course. It was obvious. She'd seen him talking to Emily Weinberg at the funeral. That note . . . had it been left by Emily? Had Angelica argued with Mike about another woman? Killed him in a fit of jealous rage?

The pitchfork. Angelica was an athlete with great upper-body strength. She'd be strong enough to wield that pitchfork. Or . . . had the killer murdered her too? And stolen her car?

I shuddered. I'd liked her. Tom Snow stared at me. He was waiting, knowing that I knew more than I was saying, but I wasn't going to be anybody's scoop.

"You'll have to excuse me," I said.

The camerawoman's head swiveled around the parking lot. I'd bored her. Good. "I need to get back to work. Don't bother any of my staff." Could he? The shop was private property, right? "This is private property."

At the end of the line, a lanky man watched us. He wore a black cowboy hat and was dressed in well-worn jeans and a denim jacket over a fitted black T-shirt. Silver gray hair peeked out from under his hat; he had a silver moustache and the warmest deep brown eyes. He was so out of place and handsome I did a double take. He glanced from me to Tom Snow. "You okay, little lady?"

Little lady? Sheesh. "I've got this."

I turned to Tom Snow. "Good day."

Did I just say good day? It felt good.

The cowboy touched the brim of his hat as I strode past. I shouldered through the crowd, ignoring their curious looks.

Was Angelica Miguel a murderer? Or was she a victim of the same person who'd killed Mike Spooner?

Chapter 8

When customers asked questions about all the police cars up the hill, I gave them a polite but firm "I don't know." The staff followed my lead.

When the cowboy reached the head of the line, I watched from the corner of my eye as Flo handed him a sundae of butter pecan ice cream, the scoops twice as big as normal, drizzled with extra hot fudge, a mound of whipped cream, and three cherries.

I didn't blame her. He was undeniably handsome—rugged with dark eyes and a movie-star smile—but talk about a fish out of water. What was this cowboy doing in Connecticut?

Around one o'clock, Caroline beckoned me from the kitchen. I hurried to her.

"What are you doing here?" I didn't say anything, but she looked awful: her skin ashen, her eyes red and rimmed with dark circles.

"I can't stay in bed any longer, I need to do something." She yawned. "I don't like being sedated. The police said it was okay for me to work. Pru came over to check on me and I asked her to help me bring lunch for everyone."

Pru stepped inside and set a basket on the broad worktable. She wore running shoes under her paisley peasant-style dress, but her socks—one bright red, the other burgundy—didn't match.

"How are you doing, Pru?" I said.

Pru glanced at Caroline and forced a smile. "Fine. Here to help."

I remembered the order for margarita sorbet. "Caroline, do you feel up to making some of Buzzy's margarita recipe?"

Caroline's lips lifted in a ghost of a smile as she opened the *Book of Spells.* "I've made it before but it's nice to have the recipe in front of me," she said as she flipped the pages. "I think we have everything I need— oh, except the booze. Orange-flavored triple sec and tequila." Her voice trailed off.

"What is it?" I said. "Do I need to buy some?"

Pru poured batter into the waffle iron. "It's in Buzzy's office. She kept the liquor locked in there, in the closet. She called it the packy."

I smiled. "Packy" was a term for liquor store I'd only heard in New England.

"I'll get it." I could understand Caroline's reluctance to go into Buzzy's office. I pulled down the key ring and unlocked the office's closet door. When I saw the dozens of bottles of alcohol lining the shelves, my jaw dropped. "Buzzy must've planned to make a lot of boozy ice cream."

I grabbed what I needed, relocked the closet door, then handed the bottles to Caroline.

"Riley, you need to eat," Pru said. "I made tomato sandwiches." I took one from the basket and bit in. Pru's was no ordinary tomato sandwich. It was thick with sweet yellow and red heirloom tomatoes piled on garlicky homemade herbed focaccia, layered with soft goat cheese and fresh greens, and sprinkled with tangy red wine vinaigrette. It was so delicious my knees buckled.

As I ate, I watched Caroline work. To my surprise, her movements were precise and unhurried as she measured the ingredients. She double-checked the recipe, shrugged, then poured in the entire bottle of triple sec. "It's a big batch."

"I'm dying to try it," I said.

"Me too," Caroline said. "We're going to your Dad's tonight for dinner, right?"

I registered the circles under her eyes, her pale lips. "If you're up to it."

"I need to stay busy," she whispered. "Let's bring some."

I washed my hands and returned to the front of the shop. The line was so long, staying busy would be no problem. As I grabbed a scoop, I noticed customers hanging back from a tall, thin man in camo pants and a long-sleeved black T-shirt. Despite the heat, he wore a black knitted cap pulled so low on his brow it covered his hair and ears. As he got closer to the counter I understood why people hung back—he smelled of wood smoke and sweat.

Despite unshaven cheeks, he had a gentle face, with large hazel eyes and a wide expressive mouth. "Do you have the sunflower flavor?" He met my eyes then glanced away quickly.

"We'll have some this weekend," I said.

"I'll come back." He pulled his cap lower. "Chocolate and vanilla in a cup, please."

I gave him two generous scoops, channeling Buzzy, who would've thought he was down on his luck. But as he took the cup I noticed two things: his nails were beautifully manicured and his watch was a diving model a friend owned. It cost more than most people's cars.

My interest was piqued. In the spy world, the cover story is of utmost importance. Every detail—clothes, hair, jewelry, behavior—had to fit the person the agent is pretending to be. That watch and that manicure didn't go with the dirty clothes, the unkempt look. Had he fallen on hard times? Or had he found, or stolen, that watch? What was this guy's story?

Willow set a bowl of freshly made marshmallow topping on the counter behind me. She smiled at my customer. "Hello, Stretch."

"Hey," he replied. Stretch put money on the counter, said "keep the change," and scuttled out.

As I put the money in the cash register, I watched Stretch through the window. He took a bite of ice cream, tilted his head back and closed his eyes as he savored the flavor.

"He's really enjoying that ice cream," I said to Willow. "You know him?"

Willow shrugged. "Not really. He started coming in last week, comes in almost every day."

"His name is Stretch?" I asked.

"'Cause he's tall, I guess," Willow said. "If Flo doesn't know someone's name, she gives them a nickname. Stretch tries different flavors every time. I think he's working his way through our list."

At seven o'clock, two women in pink boas and party hats picked up the Ultimate Frozen Margarita, their giggles and excitement a welcome break. It was a relief that they seemed unaware of the day's events and asked no questions about Mike's murder or Angelica's disappearance. I almost dropped the check when they paid and I saw how much Buzzy charged for the boozy treat. *Way to go, Buzzy.*

After some reinforcements from the farm came to relieve us, Caroline and I walked back to the house.

I could just make out the sound of a police radio squawking at the Love Nest up the hill. I cast a glance at Caroline. She hunched her shoulders and ran into the house.

Caroline and I freshened up, made sure Sprinkles was fed, then got in the Mustang and drove down Farm Lane and east onto Fairweather Road. It was a longer route to Dad's house but there was no way I'd drive past the Love Nest and the barn.

I pulled into Penniman proper and turned past the town green onto Church Lane. So many emotions churned through me, but as we approached my childhood home, my heart settled and I saw Caroline's expression relax. No matter what happened, I was always happy to see Dad.

The house I grew up in was one of the most charming houses in a town full of them, a Victorian Gothic painted sunshine yellow with black shutters. White gingerbread accented the peaked roofline, and the porch was broad and welcoming. There was a porch swing with striped-green cushions where I'd spent hours reading as a child. Two urns at the base of the front steps spilled over with red geraniums, white petunias, and ivy.

Right across the street was the back entrance of The Penniless Reader. Dad and Paulette had a great commute.

Caroline gathered her handbag and the container of margarita sorbet as she got out of the car. "It's such a beautiful house. It always makes me think of fairy tales. That's why I'm afraid to ask. Didn't you say Paulette was renovating?"

"Yes, Dad told me she started after the holidays. At least she can't change the outside. The town's Historic Preservation Committee would have a cow." *Thank goodness.*

"Did you say 'have a cow'?" Caroline said.

I groaned. "I've been hanging out at an ice cream shop all day."

"Your Dad will love that pun."

Dad did love a good pun—sometimes too much. I shouldered my bag and followed Caroline up the porch steps where Dad held the door wide.

"Glad to see you, girls."

Caroline handed Dad the ice cream. "Margarita—one of Buzzy's special recipes."

Dad's shaggy gray eyebrows shot up behind his thick glasses. "Well, well, I'm sure it's udderly delicious." He winked. I groaned and Caroline laughed.

We stepped over the threshold and I stopped short.

"Whoa, this is different," Caroline whispered.

She put my shocked thoughts into words.

Although the exterior of the house was the same, Paulette has gutted and changed the interior. The snug wainscoted living room, cozy with old-fashioned William Morris–style wallpaper and overstuffed hand-me-down furniture, had been transformed. The curvy antique settee and arm chairs had been replaced by sleek brown leather furniture and glass-topped tables, and the walls had been painted a buff beige and hung with watercolors in soft hues.

I realized Dad was watching me so I swallowed my shock and managed to say, "Good update. Very modern." I didn't speak my next though out loud—*and probably expensive, like Paulette*. My dad was Mr. Comfortable, who'd never given the furniture a second thought. He'd inherited the house from an aunt and hadn't moved a single lacy antimacassar or cross-stitched sampler. When he wasn't in the bookshop, he liked to hike and bike. I should've seen this coming when Paulette upgraded his decades-old Schwinn to a thousand-dollar model made of some super-strong material NASA had invented for space shuttles.

"Riley! Caroline! How are you?" Paulette greeted us, drying her hands on a towel. She embraced Caroline and rubbed her back.

Caroline gave Paulette a peck on the cheek. "Honestly I'm okay, but would it be all right if we don't talk about Mike?"

"Of course. I made a nice lasagna in honor of your trip to Italy, Riley." Paulette shifted gears smoothly.

"That's so nice of you, Paulette. Oh, that reminds me." I pulled gifts from my bag: a silk scarf of a soft blue that would complement Paulette's eyes and a book I'd found in Rome for Dad.

Dad took the book out of the box with reverent fingers. "*Red Harvest*!" Caroline and I exchanged grins as Dad geeked out on the book. Nobody loved books like Dad, though he'd had little choice, being named Nathaniel Hawthorne Rhodes by his bibliophile parents. He collected vintage detective fiction, and this first edition by Dashiell Hammett was right up his alley.

"Hammett's first. The diamond pattern on the spine—his publisher used that for his books. Nice skull and crossbones on the cover. No dust jacket, but still, firm, some softened spine edges, cloth." Dad opened the book. "Alfred A. Knopf, New York. 1929. First edition. What a great find, Riley!"

I beamed. I loved poking around in old bookshops as much as Dad did. I'd been thrilled to find this book in a dusty antiques shop in Rome, and even more thrilled to have paid only twenty euro. The book was worth more than twenty times that to a collector.

"I'll put this in a safe place for now." He set the book gently on the fireplace mantel, next to some family photos.

I was relieved to see Paulette hadn't removed my parents' wedding photo during her renovation. It was still there, next to several pictures of Paulette's son from her first marriage, an "entrepreneur" named Richard. I never said anything out loud, but I thought of him as Richard the Sponge. He'd stayed at the house for almost a year writing a novel (he said) while he was "between jobs." Thank goodness he'd eventually moved out to Tacoma to take a job as a budtender in a marijuana dispensary.

"Marvelous! Thank you!" Paulette looped the scarf around her shoulders. I flashed back to Caroline's dove gray scarf, peeking out of Mike's pocket in the barn. My eyes went to Caroline, but she reached out to touch the scarf, her expression relaxed. "That's gorgeous on you, Paulette."

I swallowed. Caroline must not even realize her scarf was missing. What would the police do? They had to realize it wasn't Mike's.

"Thank you, honey," Dad said. "How's the travel blogging?"

Paulette said, "I was just saying to your Dad that it was nice that your library job gave you so much time off to travel."

I couldn't tell them what had happened in Rome, but I could tell one undeniable truth. "Rome is magic."

"Oh, Nate, we should go!" Paulette gushed.

We took seats in the dining room where cool evening air flowed in the open windows, gently lifting the new pale yellow silk curtains. Dinner was delicious—a thick lasagna, green salad, and home-baked garlic bread.

Despite her request earlier, Caroline brought up Mike. I sensed she did want to talk about everything that was happening. "And," Caroline said, "I can't believe Angelica's missing."

"She's been all over the news," Paulette said. "You'd think they could trace her car."

"She has a vintage Porsche." I took a sip of Paulette's delicious wine. Maybe Paulette was good for dad. "There's no onboard software to track her."

"Do you think she ran away because she—" Paulette stopped talking abruptly but we could fill in the rest of the sentence. *Do you think she ran away because she killed Mike?*

"They seemed crazy about each other," I said quickly.

"Caroline, tell me what's new in Boston," Paulette said.

The evening had turned cool. "I'm going to grab a sweater from upstairs." I'd left some of my clothes and books behind in my old bedroom.

"Let me show you where they are," Dad said. "Paulette refreshed the bedrooms and some of your things were, ah, moved."

I pushed away a pang of foreboding as we climbed the narrow wooden stairs. If Paulette had ditched my stuff it wasn't really a big deal. I hadn't lived here in years. Still, I took a deep breath as I opened the door to my old bedroom.

Where there'd been a single brass bed with a crazy quilt crafted by my Granny Rhodes, there now stood a queen size-bed with a plaid comforter in soft shades of camel and blue. The walls were no longer covered with travel posters nor were they painted my favorite color, emerald green. Now they were a stylish navy blue and hung with subtle seascapes. The decor was quietly tasteful and impersonal.

I searched my feelings. I truly didn't mind. "I mean it, Dad. It's nice. I shouldn't have left my stuff here. Time to clear it out. I'll go through it while I'm here in town."

Dad's shoulders relaxed and he opened the closet door. Four large plastic bins were stacked with my stuff, including my collection of Nancy Drew and Harry Potter books. My quilt was folded on the top shelf. I ran my fingers along its age-softened fabric, relieved to find it hadn't been discarded.

I popped the top of one box and reached in. With a surge of relief I fished out a navy blue cardigan. A librarian always needs a cardigan.

Dad helped me move two boxes into the Mustang and I promised to come back for the rest. As we stepped back into the house, I could hear Paulette comforting Caroline in the kitchen.

"We'd better go," I said.

As we gathered our things to leave, Paulette said, "Be sure to keep your doors locked. There's talk of bums living in the woods behind the farm. Setting fires! Can you believe it?"

That was right near the Love Nest and the barn where Mike was killed.

Caroline's hand jumped to her throat.

I gave her arm a reassuring squeeze. "The police have been up there. I'm sure there won't be any problems."

"Campfires," Dad said mildly, "probably kids camping and having a bonfire."

Paulette folded her arms. "Those homeless people shouldn't be in Penniman. This is a nice place." My mind flashed to Stretch. Was he homeless?

Dad put his hand on Paulette's shoulder. "My only worry is that we haven't had much rain and those acres of sunflowers are dry. They could go up quickly with just a spark. Keep an eye out, girls."

Chapter 9

I didn't want to show it on the way home, but Paulette's comment about people in the woods behind Buzzy's house unsettled me.

Riley, you are in peaceful Penniman, Connecticut. Shake it off.

How had I gotten so suspicious? *Because you work for the CIA.* I took a deep breath. Barely worked. I'd been put on leave and had a note of reprimand in my personnel file now.

Still, I'd internalized the mindset of my coworkers. Caution kept a person alive. It wasn't melodramatic to be wary, to be careful.

I'd learned this the hard way. I hadn't been wary enough in Rome.

My assignment had been simple. During the day, I helped a group of archivists create a database to inventory the artwork in the embassy and the ambassador's spectacular *palazzo*. For one glorious day, I toured the art collections, then I spent the rest of the time staring at computer screens in my little office down a drab hallway far from the ornate front façade of the embassy. The room had been repurposed from a parlor and retained a few decorative, fussy touches from its earlier function: a gilt edged painting of a forgotten general brandishing his saber, a chair with curvy legs and ruby silk upholstery, and on a dusty shelf, a small marble statuette of a Roman goddess who kept watch as I worked at a battered metal desk.

At night, I enjoyed delicious local food and nightlife with friends. In the morning I had one mission: jog along the Tiber River. Innocuous, right? Despite what we see in flashy Hollywood movies, real spy work is subtle. Messages could be sent in so many ways, ways beyond phone calls or texts or letters. A message could be sent by a card propped in a car window. A book left on the table of a coffee shop. Or even a jogger wearing a particular color on a particular day.

One morning I found a package on my desk, wrapped in plain white butcher paper. Inside was a shirt. No note. No note was necessary. I knew what to do: wear this shirt on my next daily jog. It was red with the word "equipe" across the back, French for *team*.

No doubt I was sending a signal to a watcher on my route, one I'd never see but who'd be watching me. They would see this shirt, this message, and act on it.

I never saw anyone I knew on my jogging route, but that next morning, in the window of a little café, I recognized Paolo, a handsome local who worked in IT at the embassy. He'd waved. He'd never spoken to me before. I had earbuds in but no music playing. I pretended I hadn't noticed him, dismissing the coincidence, but I sped up to lose him in case he decided to try to catch me.

The next morning, a body was found floating in the river by an ancient bridge called the Ponte Rotto, the Broken Bridge. I had no way of knowing if my message had played any part in that, but the embassy buzzed all day with repressed excitement. Paolo stopped by my desk and asked me out for a drink. I accepted.

A week later, he asked me to accompany him after work to the Isola del Cinema, an international film festival on the Isola Tiberina, the tiny boat-shaped island in the middle of the Tiber, not far from the Vatican. Impossible to get tickets, but he had two. Just as he arrived to pick me up, I received a call asking me to come to the human resources office two floors away and in another wing of the building. Paolo said he'd wait in my office. When I got to HR the office was dark, closed for the day. When I ran back to my office, heart pounding, he was gone.

So was the little marble statuette, which turned out to be worth a lot of money.

When Caroline and I returned to Buzzy's house, we found two floral arrangements and a boxed coffee cake on the front porch. I remembered Paulette's warning and glanced up the dark road. Everything seemed peaceful but the quiet and the beautiful gifts didn't dispel my apprehension. Could one of the strangers in the woods have killed Mike? I wondered where Stretch was now. *Leave it to the cops, Riley.*

I turned my thoughts to the farmhouse in front of me and considered how secure it was. Improving our security was something I could do.

Buzzy's home was sturdy, a farmhouse built by one of her great-great-grandfathers in the 1800s. The front door was crafted of solid oak but it had a lock that any ten-year-old with a bobby pin could open. Despite her bad disposition and biting the cop earlier, Sprinkles was hardly a guard dog. Why couldn't Buzzy have a dog? I sighed. Sprinkles probably hadn't allowed it.

Caroline and I carried the flowers and coffee cake into the kitchen and set them on the table, then I went back to the door and twisted the knob, making sure it was locked. "Caroline, where are the house keys?"

Caroline bent over the flowers, inhaling their fragrance. "Keys? I think there are some keys hanging in the mudroom."

The mudroom was a narrow closet-sized space by the front door. One wall was covered with various coats, sweaters, and shopping bags hanging on hooks. I pushed them aside until I found a ring with several ancient-looking metal keys under a yellow rainslicker. Some were skeleton keys, like something that would unlock a wardrobe that led to Narnia. I went back into the kitchen and held up the keyring in disbelief. "These are the keys? Are you kidding?"

Caroline shrugged. "Buzzy never locked the doors. But if it makes you feel better, I'll start." She selected two from the keyring and gave me one. I slid it into my pocket.

I poured a glass of water while she opened the cards with the flowers. One bouquet, lush with pink and yellow roses, scented the air.

"Who's that bouquet from?" I said. "It's gorgeous."

Caroline smiled. "Dandy. They're from her garden. Wasn't that sweet? And she even offered to help in the shop."

"We'll need help in the shop."

"Riley." Caroline's smile faltered and she lowered herself into a chair at the kitchen table.

I steeled myself. This was the moment I'd dreaded.

Caroline's voice was steady. "I want you to tell me

everything you saw. With Mike in the barn. Everything."

L ater that night I lay in bed, trying to find a comfortable spot on the lumpy old mattress, remembering my conversation with Caroline and wondering if I'd held back too much or too little of what Mike's body had looked like. Wondering if I'd done the right thing telling Caroline I'd seen her scarf in Mike's pocket.

I hadn't mentioned the scarf to the police.

I'd reassured Caroline. I was pretty sure Mike had picked up the scarf when he'd taken his jacket from the back of her chair. He'd been so angry I was sure he hadn't noticed that he'd also grabbed her scarf by mistake. But would the police believe me? The police knew Caroline and I were friends. I was her alibi. She was my alibi. But right downstairs in the kitchen she'd said she could kill him and soon enough the police would discover that they'd fought about Mike's real estate deal.

I closed my eyes and let details of the discovery of Mike's body, of what I'd seen in the Love Nest, replay. Angelica's lipstick on the wineglass. The crumpled note. That wasn't from Caroline.

The money jar. I had to tell the police about the missing money jar. I'd go to the police department early, before the shop opened. Or should I call? The card the officer had given me was on the nightstand.

I turned it in my hands. Jack Voelker. He was probably the local liaison to the state police. Like most small New England towns, Penniman wasn't big enough to have its own homicide team.

I scrolled my phone. Mike's murder was news, but

Angelica Miguel was headline news. I pressed START on a video.

Behind the newscaster, a photo showed Angelica holding up a trophy at center court. How vibrant she looked, so powerful, so full of life.

"In our top story, the quiet village of Penniman was rocked by the brutal slaying of real estate entrepreneur Michael Spooner. His body was found in a barn on Fairweather Farm early Saturday morning. Police say one of the most mystifying aspects of the case is the disappearance of Spooner's girlfriend, tennis star Angelica Miguel. Police are looking for her red Porsche, a vintage model, license plate 10IS. Anyone with information on the vehicle is asked to contact the police at the number on the screen."

I shut down my phone and turned off the light, but I tossed and turned, trying to get comfortable, trying to quiet my mind. Of course the police wanted to talk to Angelica. She was probably the last person to see Mike alive. Plus she'd be strong enough to wield the pitchfork. Don't they say that the killer is always the one closest to the victim?

But I'd seen them together and I couldn't believe Angelica would kill Mike. The phrase "golden couple" was made for them.

Could the murderer have kidnapped and maybe killed her too?

Pale sunlight brightened the windows and burnished the old trophies on Mike's shelves just as I fell asleep.

Chapter 10

Nine o'clock! I'd overslept. I dashed into the bathroom to wash, threw on some clothes, and began pulling my hair back into a ponytail as I hurried into the hallway. Caroline's door was ajar, her curtains open, and her bed made. A laptop and a pile of folders covered half her bed. Sprinkles darted out of Buzzy's room, tangling in my feet and sending me sprawling. "Darn cat!" Sprinkles gave me a haughty look and sashayed downstairs. I tossed my hair elastic after her.

"Are you okay?" Caroline called from downstairs.

I eased to my feet—nothing broken—retrieved my elastic, and followed the aroma of brewing coffee down the stairs.

"Sprinkles ambushed me. Again." The little minx sat by her food dish grooming her paw. At her name she looked up, her offended expression saying, *Who, me?*

"Pru called and said she'd open Udderly today with some interns from the farm." Caroline turned down the volume on the small television on the counter. She wore plaid flannel pajama bottoms and a navy blue long sleeve T-shirt. "We don't have to go in until lunchtime."

I poured a cup of coffee and sank into a chair. "That's

so nice of her. I know they must be busy getting ready for the Sunflower Festival too."

Caroline bent over a stack of papers, holding her head in her hands. "Buzzy's bills," she groaned. "I gathered them from her office. Some are from two years ago. She didn't exactly have a system."

I looked around the kitchen. Buzzy's level of organization reflected her level of interest. The spices on the rack were arranged in alphabetical order. Family photos were hung with military precision on the walls. Her plants were watered and tended within an inch of their lives.

Another headache for Caroline. "Are things, ah, okay? Financially?"

"I can't tell." She pushed her thick curls from her forehead. "I wish I were an accountant, not an art appraiser. Buzzy has an accountant, Wilmer Reyes. I don't think he's seen these." She sipped her coffee. "Remember when she had the farm stand? She'd leave a cigar box on the table and people would take their veggies and leave money in the box?"

That was something you still saw on the back roads here. "Is that still her system?"

"Close." She smiled. "She could've used you, Riley. Librarians are so organized."

I returned her smile but busied myself cutting the coffee cake that had been left on the porch last night. She didn't know about my occasional assignments. No one did, that was part of the game. I longed to tell Caroline everything. This was a sign that I wanted a change, I knew it.

I cut a thick slice of coffee cake for Caroline and set it in front of her.

She continued, "I'm going to meet with Wilmer tomorrow. And Buzzy's lawyer."

I took a bite of the coffee cake—divine—and sipped my coffee. "Who's Buzzy's lawyer?"

"Kyle."

I set down my mug. "I forgot to tell you, Kyle and Nina stopped by to see you yesterday, but you were," I hesitated, "sleeping." *When you were sedated, after learning your brother had been murdered.* I scanned Caroline's face. She looked tired and her soft brown eyes were bloodshot, but her pointed chin was firm, determined.

Caroline winced and rubbed her glasses on the hem of her T-shirt. "Kyle and Mike were so close. Buzzy didn't even have a lawyer until a year or so ago. Mike insisted, he even made the appointment for her. One good thing Mike did," she muttered. "Will you go with me, Riley?"

"Of course," I said.

"And . . . I talked to the police on the phone. They can't"—she swallowed—"release Mike's body yet."

Sprinkles materialized by Caroline's chair and Caroline scooped her up. "I took a week off, for Buzzy. Now this. I don't know what to do."

I squeezed Caroline's arm. "You don't have to do anything right now."

"Except deal with the ice cream shop," she said. "All part-time workers. No one wants to be manager."

"You could close . . . until you find someone." A thought began to take shape. I'd worked in the shop. I knew what to do. It would be nice to disappear for a while.

"The shop's the only thing that makes me feel normal. And the Sunflower Festival is coming," Caroline said, "but I'll have to go back to work in Boston next Tuesday."

Staying in Penniman and running the shop was an opportunity. It felt right. "I can run the shop," I said.

"Oh, Riley, you've done so much already!" Caroline shook her head. "And your job"—

I held up my hand. "I have tons of leave." That was true, plus I doubted I'd have another covert assignment after what happened in Rome.

Caroline's eyes shone. "That would be amazing. Of course, you could stay here in the house rent free and we could work out your pay."

I'd always been good at living and traveling on a shoestring. The shop closed October through March. I'd have all that free time to travel and really put my heart into my travel blog. *A fresh start.* Maybe the ice cream shop was the answer.

"I'll do it."

Caroline threw her arms around me. "Thank you, Riley."

Caught in the hug, Sprinkles yowled, jumped to the floor, and stalked into the powder room.

"Don't celebrate yet, okay? My salary will totally bankrupt you." I grabbed my running shoes from the mudroom. "I'm going for a run."

Sprinkles stuck her head out of the powder room and meowled.

"Coming, your majesty." Caroline stepped into the powder room and flushed the toilet.

I stopped short. "Did you just flush for Sprinkles?"

"She prefers the water from the powder room toilet." Caroline avoided my eyes.

"You're serious. She can reach?"

Caroline nodded.

I laughed. "You're nuts."

"No, Buzzy was nuts," Caroline said. "I'm just carrying on the tradition."

As I tightened the laces on my running shoes, I

remembered Sprinkles' friend, the scrappy black kitten. "Have you noticed a little black cat hanging around? Kind of torn up, poor guy, like a boxer who's gone too many rounds. Sprinkles was talking to him the other night."

Caroline shook her head. "Sprinkles has a friend? Maybe she's mellowing. Part of the reason she had to re-tire from the show circuit was because she'd fight with her competitors."

My mind swirled with questions as I jogged up Farm Lane. There was something about the wine bottle in the Love Nest that bothered me. I'd stop at the winery and ask some questions.

As I passed the turn to the Love Nest, I saw a sin-gle police vehicle and a white SUV with a state police shield decal parked by the barn. Yellow tape was strung across the doorways of the Love Nest and the barn.

I shivered and continued up the hill thinking of the news video I'd watched. Where was Angelica Miguel? had become the question, more so than who killed Mike Spooner. The sexy tennis star was nowhere to be found. How could she have just disappeared? Was she a victim or a murderer?

I swung onto the shoulder of Town Road and headed east. As my feet pounded the hot asphalt, sweat damp-ened my chest and back. I wasn't going to look my best when I arrived at the winery.

The man at the counter turned out to be the owner. I introduced myself, but he was so talkative I didn't need to ask questions. "Shame about Mike Spooner and that tennis player. I'll tell you the same thing I told that detective and all those reporters. I work every day and I don't remember either one buying wine. Of course, we do sell to a few other package stores and wine shops, so

they could've bought my wine anywhere." He shrugged.
"Buzzy Spooner did buy some a couple weeks ago. Told
me she was working on a wine-flavored ice cream."

Wine-flavored ice cream? Buzzy had certainly been
thinking outside the box.

I thanked him and resumed my run, heading west
toward the center of Penniman, the steady cadence of my
footsteps helping to clear my mind. I passed the hospital,
then turned toward the historic center of town. The sight
of the white-columned church and the emerald grass of
the green always calmed me. I pushed on, looping onto
curving Fairweather Road, through the covered bridge,
enjoying my footfalls on the sturdy wooden planks. Just
before the turn onto Farm Lane, I cut across onto a narrow road through the sunflower fields.

"Road" was pushing it. Farm tractors used this
path years ago during harvest time, pulling trailers of
peaches and apples to market before Farm Lane was
paved. It led through the peach orchards to a pond.

A nice place to camp.

I was drenched in sweat and my legs felt like jelly
when I arrived at the pond. I bent to the water and splashed
some onto my face and arms, reveling in the coolness.
Then I walked the perimeter of the pond, scanning the
ground. I was halfway around when I found the remnants
of a campfire. A log nearby was probably used as a seat.
A couple of dragonflies skimmed the water as I sat,
stretching my legs in front of me, trying to imagine the
person who'd built the fire.

A precise circle of rocks ringed bits of burnt wood
and grayed coals. There was no trash anywhere I could
see. The person who'd built this fire was tidy, careful. Me-
ticulous, even. I thought of Stretch, how he smelled of
wood smoke. Willow said he'd started coming into the
shop a week earlier. Paulette said the fires had started

about a week ago. I thought of his manicured hands. If he kept building fires and camping in the woods, they wouldn't stay that way.

Behind me, a trail ran past an old cemetery and intersected with the road in front of the Love Nest, less than a five-minute walk away.

I swiped sweat from my brow and thought of Stretch's hat. Wearing a cap in this heat was definitely strange. He was hiding his hair. Why?

Frustrated, I pushed off the log and ran up the trail. Maybe Stretch wasn't camping in the woods. Maybe he was just an odd guy who liked ice cream. A lot. And smelled of wood smoke.

I pushed Stretch out of my mind and scanned the underbrush for the cute black kitten as I jogged back home, but there was no sign of him.

Back home, I showered then unloaded the boxes of clothes and books I'd taken from my old bedroom. I sorted through the clothing, some of which I hadn't worn since high school. The sweaters still fit, not that they'd do me much good in July's muggy weather. The pants, well, I sucked in my stomach, but I'd never see a size six again. Good thing the dress code at Udderly was casual and I could get away with the comfortable tops and miracle fabric travel leggings I'd had in my carry-on. I'd shipped everything else from Rome to my apartment in Virginia.

The detective's card sat on my nightstand. Just looking at it made my palms sweat. Why was I so nervous? I had nothing to hide. I hesitated, my fingers over my phone. I did have something to hide. Even as I pressed the buttons I debated if I should mention Caroline's scarf. "Do it fast," I muttered. Whenever I had an unpleasant task—rip off a bandage, clean Sprinkles' litter box—I'd repeat this mantra. I dialed the police station.

A woman's voice, smoky and rich, answered. "Penniman Police Services."

"May I speak to Detective Voelker?" I said.

"Detective Voelker isn't in. May I take a message?"

Something about her tone—A little too helpful? A little too confiding?—made me hesitate. "This is Riley Rhodes at Fairweather Farm. I'd like to talk to him about something I remembered—"

"About Mike Spooner?" the voice whispered. "I'll relay the message."

I explained that the lipstick on the wine glass was Angelica's shade of red.

"Go on," the voice encouraged. "You can tell me everything."

I froze. Was this legit, leaving a message? The voice made me feel I was gossiping, not sharing information in a murder investigation. "Um, that's all."

The line was quiet for a moment. "Detective Voelker will be in touch to follow up." She sounded disappointed.

"Thank you." I hung up and caught my reflection in the mirror on the back of the bedroom door. "What are you looking at? You didn't like her tone." *You have to tell the police about Caroline's scarf, Riley.*

And the money jar. I smacked my forehead. I'd forgotten.

I ran down to Udderly, inhaling the rich scent of chocolate as I entered. Caroline paced by the *Book of Spells*, tapping her palm with a tasting spoon. "Last year we made one hundred gallons of sunflower ice cream for the festival. Our chiller can do five gallons at a time. It takes about two hours per batch . . . we're open ten hours a day . . ."

Brandon carried an empty ice-cream tub and put it in the sink. "Out of Brownie Bomb. Good thing Flo started the brownies."

"So we need to make five a day for five days," I said as I washed my hands. "The festival is—"

"Saturday and Sunday." Caroline's brow wrinkled.

"And today is Sunday. We have," I gulped, "six days." *Only six days? No time to panic. Stay positive.* "We can do it."

Willow carried a tub back. "Out of lavender honey, and we're on the last fudge ripple."

"Sheesh." I was starting to see the problem. We needed to make not only the extra sunflower ice cream for the festival but also had to replenish all the other flavors. The weather had been hot and sunny—perfect ice cream weather. The shop had been swamped, so swamped that we were running out of flavors quicker than we could replace them.

I pushed up my sleeves. "Then we'd better get started."

Udderly's ice cream was so delicious because of Buzzy's absolute insistence on freshness. "Cow to cone in two days" was her mantra. A free spirit in most respects, she was militant about making her ice cream with no preservatives, no chemicals, and only the freshest ingredients.

The organic dairy around the corner made milk mixtures to Buzzy's specifications. Rich flavors like her creamy vanilla were made with a mix of fresh milk, sugar, and the highest butterfat cream. Mixtures with less cream and more milk were used when a lighter mouthfeel was desired. The mixtures were the canvases for her flavorful creations.

"I'll get to work on Brownie Bomb," I said. One

of the most popular flavors, it melded pieces of fudgy brownies and bittersweet chocolate chips into dark chocolate ice cream.

The chime on the oven rang and I pulled out the pan of brownies, savoring the chocolatey scent. I cut two small pieces and handed one to Caroline. "Quality control," I said. We bit into the still-warm brownies and sighed at the gooey goodness. "Acceptable."

I chopped the brownies into bite-sized pieces as Caroline made a velvety custard base and added Dutch cocoa, a bit of brown sugar, and spicy vanilla extract, then poured the mix into the top of the chiller machine where a dasher spun the mixture inside a refrigeration unit to thicken.

When the ice cream was the consistency of soft serve, we set a tub under what Buzzy called "the spout"—a chute where the ice cream poured out. We alternated pouring a few cups of ice cream with the addition of mix-ins into the tub. Caroline added the brownie pieces and chips to each layer and stirred. When the tub was full, I placed it in the large industrial-size freezer, where it would chill to the proper hardness.

It was almost eleven p.m. when Caroline and I cleaned the kitchen and trudged up to Buzzy's house. My arms ached from lifting heavy tubs of ice cream and my feet were killing me.

The house was dark and only the single light by the front-porch steps was on. Again I bemoaned the lack of security. The outside lights weren't automatic, and no one was home to put them on. I wondered if Sprinkles could be trained to do that for us.

The dim light reflected on a pink Mini Cooper parked in front of the house. A woman spoke from the porch as we approached. "Caroline, I was leaving these for you." Her white blond, straight as a pin hair was distinctive, even in the dark. Emily Weinberg descended the stairs and threw her arms around Caroline. "I brought you some flowers. I wanted to say I'm so sorry about Mike."

The cellophane wrap on the flowers rustled; it was too dark to see them but the scent of roses tinged the air. I couldn't see Caroline's expression as she pushed away from the embrace. "Thank you. Excuse me." She pounded up the porch steps and ran inside, the screen door banging behind her. The door must've been unlocked. This peaceful life was getting to me—I'd forgotten to lock it.

Emily turned to me. "Hi, Riley." *Now she remembers my name.* "I hope Caroline likes the flowers."

Nice way to ambush Caroline, I thought as I gritted my teeth.

Emily swung her hair. "Mike and I knew each other in high school, well, you knew that. When Buzzy passed, I learned that my dad's real estate firm was partnering with Mike's on the Preserve at Fairweather Farm. It was nice to reconnect and it would've been great to work with him."

"Preserve at Fairweather Farm?" That must be the name of the real estate development Mike was planning. I started to see where this conversation was going.

I took a deep, steadying breath. "This isn't a good time to discuss real estate."

Pru and Darwin walked across the lane, the porch light glinting on a tinfoil-covered dish in Pru's hands.

Emily nodded to the Brightwoods. "I see you have company. Stay in touch. Good night." She got into her Mini Cooper and spun in a U-turn back to Fairweather Road.

Darwin stroked his white beard. "Pru figured you two didn't have a chance to eat and thought you'd like some dinner."

"We didn't." I was starving. "Thank you."

"How's the sunflower ice cream coming?" Pru said as we went inside.

"We have a ways to go. Come in and chat for a few minutes."

Darwin helped me set the table while Pru made tea. Emily's flowers lay on the table, still wrapped. I plucked out a business card that was tucked among pink roses and white baby's breath. "Emily Weinberg, Penniman Preferred Properties." *Emily had actually put her business card in with condolence flowers?* My head felt like it would explode. I didn't think Caroline had seen the card so I slid it into my back pocket. *She'll call you when hell freezes over, Emily.*

Caroline came in from the hallway, slipping on a sweater. I couldn't imagine wearing a sweater in the soupy humidity of a Washington, D.C., summer—another reason to stay here in Penniman.

"Pru's spinach-and-mushroom quiche." Darwin unveiled the golden brown quiche and served us. For a moment I thought Caroline wasn't going to eat, but she surprised me and had two helpings. She looked better than Pru and Darwin. He could barely keep his eyes open, and Pru tried to hide a yawn.

"You two are so sweet coming over here with dinner," I said. "I know it's past your bedtime."

"You're the best," Caroline said.

"We wanted to check in on you," Pru said.

Darwin nodded. "The peaches are starting to come in—just right for the peach ice cream."

"Great news," I said, but thought, *Peach ice cream? One more thing for my to-do list.*

Pru and Darwin wished us good night and closed the door softly as they left.

"I don't know how they do it," Caroline said. "They've been helping at the shop even though they need to prepare for their Sunflower Festival open house on the farm."

After we cleaned up, Caroline wished me a sleepy good night and trudged upstairs.

It had been a long day, but I felt wired. As I hung up a dishcloth, Sprinkles padded into the kitchen. I wondered if she'd have a visit from her friend, the little black kitten.

Instead, she threw a look over her shoulder at me, then stood at the door of the powder room switching her tail. I knew what this was—a command.

I folded my arms. "Really? Do you think I'm going to flush for you? You have perfectly good water in your bowl."

Her tail switched again, a whip crack. Her eyes held mine.

"Oh, all right." I flushed and she jumped onto the seat. She looked back at me as if to say, *Give me some privacy.* Understandable. I wouldn't want anyone watching me drink water out of a toilet bowl either.

I stepped into the hall but peeked around the doorjamb to see how on earth she could reach the water. Her maneuvers seemed to contradict the laws of physics, but she really could! If her fancy cat friends only knew. But of course, they were probably compelling their humans to do the same thing. *Cats.*

I put on the kettle and flicked on the small TV on the kitchen counter. The newscast led with video of Angelica, "a person of interest." The way the police were looking for her, it seemed they knew something. Was she guilty of murder? I flicked the TV off as the water in the kettle came to a boil. Where was she? With every moment that passed, I was more and more troubled.

I poured the hot water over some chamomile tea. Down the hall Sprinkles disappeared into the parlor, a room we'd hardly ever used except for sprawling on the floor with a Monopoly or Clue game. I heard a soft thud and hurried after her.

Several magazines were scattered on the floor. Sprinkles batted at a scrap of paper, hauled herself onto a footstool then onto the couch, and then clambered from its arm up to the back. Jumping was too undignified for a cat of her age and girth. I gathered the magazines and set them back on the coffee table, tossed the scrap of paper into a wastebasket, and tidied the couch cushions. Sprinkles settled in front of the window and stared into the inky darkness.

In the distance, a tiny spark of light gleamed on the hill not far from the barn next to the Love Nest. *Was that fire?*

I pulled my phone from my pocket, then hesitated. Was this a campfire set by the "bum" Paulette had been talking about? My mind jumped to Stretch. He seemed quirky, not dangerous. The campsite I'd seen earlier was made with care, but a spark could still fly to the parched sunflowers. It was only a quarter mile or so from the barn to the house. I'd make sure whoever'd made the fire put it out. I headed to the door.

Wait a minute, Riley, think. Mike was just killed! Let the police handle this. Even though I couldn't imagine that Mike's killer was camping by the scene of the crime, I put in a call to the police nonemergency number. If they had someone watching the barn and Love Nest, they could be there in a few moments. I spoke to the operator, then took a heavy flashlight from the mudroom. I slipped out the door, closing it softly behind me, and ran behind the house. I plunged through rows of sunflowers, hurrying as silently as I could toward the fire, glad that I was wearing dark clothing.

Another of Buzzy's sayings played in my mind: *"Curiosity killed the cat."*

I couldn't help it. I'd pegged Stretch as the camper and wanted to know if my suspicion was correct. I crept closer, keeping to the shadows, angling my body to avoid brushing against the dried sunflower stalks.

As I approached the fire, the soft night air carried the mouthwatering scent of frying bacon and wood smoke. I felt a pang of regret at calling emergency services. I should've introduced myself and sat down for a snack.

"Who's there? Penniman Police!" A bright beam swung in my direction, blinding me. I raised my arm to shield my eyes.

"Officer, I'm Riley Rhodes," I said. "I'm the one who called."

"You should've stayed home, ma'am." The officer lowered his beam. "Whoever was here's gone."

My skin prickled; I had that watched feeling again. I wondered if the camper had simply pulled back into the trees or the rows of tall sunflowers. He couldn't have gotten far.

I played my beam along the ground. Just as at the other site, a log had been used for a seat. The fire had burned low, perfect for cooking. The scent of bacon was so strong that I wondered if the camper had spilled grease when he grabbed his skillet and took off.

"I've heard about people camping in the woods," I said, hoping the officer had information to share.

The officer put his hands on his hips. "That, or one person spotted numerous times. We usually find a campsite like this, with the fire dying out. By the time we show up, they're gone." A soft breeze sighed through the sunflowers. "Pretty nice out, actually. Good spot for camping, but it's been dry. Those sunflower fields could go up in minutes if a spark traveled."

"You're right." I thought of Stretch. Was I being unfair to him, just because he looked a little worse for wear? I hated myself for offering him as a suspect, but there'd been a murder. "Have you seen a tall guy, with a black cap, hanging around town?"

He shook his head. "No, but we'll keep an eye out."

"Well, thank you for coming," I said. "I'll head home now."

"I'll give you a ride." It wasn't a question and I followed him to the cruiser. Turns out the officer was a big fan of Buzzy's ice cream. We chatted a bit and he dropped me home. He turned the car back up the hill to his post at the Love Nest.

I scanned the yard, unable to shake that watched feeling. Finally I went inside, locked the door, and tripped on Sprinkles.

Chapter 11

The next morning, I dressed in the thin sunlight and slid carefully out my door so I didn't get ambushed by Sprinkles. Caroline's door was open a crack, and I could see my furry nemesis curled up on the bed, both of them asleep. Good, Caroline needed the rest. I hoped she'd slept well. Maybe I wouldn't even tell her about the campfire up the road last night.

After I'd returned from the campfire, I'd fallen into a deep, dreamless sleep and had awoken thinking of Buzzy's will. I remembered what Caroline had said about not being able to find one. Had Buzzy made a will? If she'd made one, where would she keep it?

Inside Buzzy's room, sunlight gleamed on the frame of the double brass bed. I stepped inside and ran my fingers over the soft fabric of the quilt—cheerful, colorful, just like Buzzy herself.

There was a purple velvet–covered settee in front of the window, with a reading lamp and a basket of knitting. Bookcases ran along one wall, stuffed with books of all kinds—Buzzy was a great reader. On her bedside table was a Bible and a bottle of sleeping pills. Would Buzzy hide her will in her Bible? I flipped through its well-worn pages but found only a few bookmarks and some greeting cards.

I moved to her bureau. The top was covered with bottles of perfume I'm sure she never used—she always smelled like Ivory soap and cinnamon gum. Some of the bottles were expensive brands, probably from Mike. I could see him picking up a bottle and thinking the expensive price tag made it a good gift. On the wall next to a wedding photo of Buzzy and Charles was a cross-stitch that read "Happy the man whose pleasures are cheap." That was Buzzy.

In a corner of the room was a purple velvet cat bed, three feet long and about that high. Sprinkles' bed had carved wooden bedposts and curtains, like something Henry VIII would sleep in if he were a show cat. Now her attitude toward me—and everyone—made sense.

I chuckled as I ran downstairs and laced up my running shoes. I headed up the hill, past the Love Nest where a police car stood sentry. A small blue sedan with Florida plates was pulled up to the cruiser's driver's side window. A rental. The two drivers were deep in conversation. It was no doubt a reporter trying to get the scoop on Mike's death—no, I amended—on Angelica's disappearance.

As I ran, I tried to imagine being Angelica the night of the murder. What if the killer came after her too? Angelica was strong and athletic. She could fend off an attacker, get in her car, and drive away. But if this was the scenario, why didn't she contact the police? Or drive down to the road to the farmhouse for help?

I considered another scenario. Say Angelica saw that note. She's angry with Mike. What if she'd been drunk? The wine bottle was empty. She's drunk and angry and killed Mike. She's desperate. She threw herself into her sports car and drove off. Where would she go?

Penniman was full of twisty back roads, lots of little lanes where Angelica could've gotten lost. What if her car had broken down? Or hit something?

My footsteps had taken me to the intersection with Town Road. Directly across, Farm Lane turned into Woods Road. I waited for a car to pass then jogged across the street.

This road was even narrower and more twisting than Farm Lane, plunging at a steep grade with an almost-hairpin curve. At that curve, a driveway descended to a long-abandoned farmhouse and a pond where generations of Penniman kids skated in the winter.

What if she'd missed that turn?

I hesitated at the entrance to the driveway then jogged forward. Tall laurel bushes and overgrown weeds hemmed in the narrow, rutted strip of asphalt. My footsteps slowed as the angle of the drive grew steeper, then opened into a clearing where an old farmhouse stood. *You're trespassing, Riley.* But there was no sign of habitation in the farmhouse, given its peeling paint, broken windows, and sagging porch. I stood in the clearing, looking over the pond. I remembered skating on the gray ice, cold winter stars pinpricks overhead.

I turned to go. A patch of red by the side of the driveway made me freeze. A Porsche. The car was angled in the gully on the side of the drive—the tall weeds had hidden it from my view. It was tilted onto the driver's side, its nose crushed against a tree.

Oh god. I ran forward, pushed through the brush. I leaned carefully onto the car—the passenger side was now the top—and looked down through the window. My eyes adjusted to the dim interior and I realized with a jolt that I was looking at a body. Angelica. She lay motionless, crumpled against the driver's-side door, her gorgeous brown hair covering her face. "Angelica!" I shouted and pounded the glass. She didn't move, but my pounding made the car rock. I jerked back. If the car fell, it might jar her and injure her further, or kill her if she wasn't already dead.

My hands trembled as I called 911.

"Nine-one-one. Where is your emergency?"

"I don't know the address," I took a breath to steady my voice. "Down by the pond at the curve of Woods Road. There's a car that's run off the road. A woman's inside. She's not responding."

"Don't try to move her. EMS is on its way. Watch for them and wave them down."

I ran to the top of the drive and waited, torn between needing to flag down the police and wanting to find a way to get Angelica out of the car. The police cruiser sped out of Farm Lane, across Town Road, light bar flashing. The blue rental car followed right behind.

"Here!" I waved wildly to stop the cruiser. I ran down the path, skidding on loose stones, the officer on my heels, his equipment belt jangling. He peered in the car, and muttered, "Can't move her. Might injure her more. We're gonna need special equipment."

I tried to calm my breathing. How many days had she lain here? I counted back. The funeral was Friday and it was now Monday morning. How badly was she injured? The car was smashed against the tree. The impact must have been terrible.

Sirens screamed in the distance.

The man from the blue rental car ran up to us. He wore a polo shirt embroidered with the logo of a Boston television station. "Is that Angelica Miguel's car?" He started toward it.

The cop cut him off and herded us aside. "Stay out of the way. Both of you."

A Penniman fire department SUV with Fire Chief in

gold lettering on the door panel rocked down the drive. The man from the Boston station started filming with a tiny video camera, giving a play-by-play. It took me a moment to realize that he was recording notes as he filmed. I held my breath as the sports car was swarmed by emergency workers.

"How'd you find her? Look at this place. You'd never see the car from the road. Was she on the floor?" I realized the reporter was talking to me but I couldn't speak, unable to pull my eyes from the scene.

The newsman tsked. "Tough extraction. Did you see any blood?"

"Yes," I whispered.

"I wonder if she's trapped by the dash," he continued. "They won't break the glass, too dangerous. They'll probably move the car. It's small. Lots of people here. Yep, they are."

The crowd of rescuers surrounded the car and walked it backward away from the tree, setting it down gently. The driver's door and front end were crushed, the windshield spiderwebbed with broken glass. An ambulance inched down the steeply angled driveway.

A team powered up a generator and I jumped at the roar. Two firefighters examined the vehicle, searching for the best way to get Angelica out without harming her further. The noise of the generator forced rescuers to use hand motions to communicate as they worked.

The reporter next to me flagged down a firefighter. "Who owns this place?"

The firefighter shrugged. "Place was condemned a few months back. Nobody comes down here except partying kids or real estate agents showing the property."

The newsman jutted his chin toward the rescue team. "What are they using now?"

"A spreading tool. She's pinned under the dash." The

generator turned off abruptly and someone shouted for a backboard. The firefighter jogged over to assist.

The fire chief leaned into the car, shouting Angelica's name and pausing as if to listen. My heart rose. "She's alive."

"You think so?" the reporter snorted. "After how many days?"

Two EMTs with a backboard raced forward. The fire chief waved everyone clear. I held my breath as they reached into the car. Angelica, limp as a ragdoll, was placed on the stretcher and one of the rescuers gently secured her to the board with straps. I rushed forward but an EMT held me back, so I called, "Angelica!"

Her head turned slightly in my direction.

Angelica was alive!

A crowd had gathered at the top of the driveway. As sirens screamed down Town Road, I felt a tap at my shoulder. Detective Voelker stared down at me. "Are you the one who called this in, Ms. Rhodes?"

My mouth went dry. "Yes. I found the car when I was jogging."

"You jogged down here?" He frowned. "This is private property."

Dark aviator glasses hid his eyes and his mouth was set, but still disbelief and suspicion radiated off him.

And I still had to tell him about the money jar . . . and the scarf.

"Ms. Rhodes—"

"Jack!" The fire chief beckoned.

Voelker said, "I'll be back."

Tom Snow shouldered forward, beaming, no doubt thinking he was getting tonight's scoop. "You, ice cream girl! You saved Angelica Miguel's life. One of the EMTs said she wouldn't have lasted another day if you hadn't found her." Two women threaded toward us, one of them hefting a camera. "Can we talk to you?"

In the crowd of emergency responders, I saw the officer who'd been first on scene talking with a reporter I recognized from CNN. He pointed at me.

"Can you give us an interview?"

There was nothing I wanted to do less. "Sure, give me a sec," I said. "Let's all meet down by the pond? The police detective wants me to talk to him first." At least the last part was true.

The reporters headed toward the pond, exchanging notes as they went.

I mirrored the purposeful energy of the emergency workers around me, avoided eye contact, and slipped into the crowd heading up the hill. I jogged back home. Detective Voelker would be able to find me—Penniman wasn't that big. Finding Angelica was an incredible relief, but I was nearly overwhelmed by a wave of anxiety. The police had one murdered man and one woman who was severely injured, and I was now connected to both of them.

Chapter 12

Caroline wasn't home when I returned. I took a hot shower but my nerves still jangled as I tried to push away the memory of Angelica's crumpled body. I changed into my one pair of jeans and a purple Will Work for Ice Cream T-shirt, then jogged to Udderly. It was just before nine o'clock and no one was there yet. I took three scoops of ice cream—one vanilla, one chocolate, one mint chocolate chip—doused them with Buzzy's secret recipe hot fudge sauce, squirted whipped cream on top, considered the mound of cream and added more, then topped that with three maraschino cherries.

Desperate measures were called for. I rummaged in a cabinet until I found a bag of potato chips. I grabbed a handful and crumbled them over the whipped cream then sat on the stoop outside the back door, hoping no one would talk to me. When stressed, nothing beats a hot fudge sundae topped with potato chips. It wouldn't be long before Detective Voelker showed up and he wouldn't be happy that I'd ghosted him. Was that against the law? Ghosting a police officer?

There are no hot fudge sundaes in jail. I shoveled in

a bite, savoring the fudge, cherries, whipped cream, and salty crunch of the chips.

Caroline and Willow emerged from the Bright-woods' house across the lane, talking intently, their faces flushed with excitement.

Caroline spotted me and they rushed over. "Riley, have you heard? They found Angelica!"

"Such good news!" Willow was practically dancing with excitement.

Caroline's eyes fell on my sundae and her brow wrinkled. "Riley, I haven't seen you eat one of those since you flunked the chemistry final senior year."

I shoveled in another bite, then set the bowl down. "It's great news." I licked a bit of hot fudge from my finger. "I'm the one who found Angelica."

Willow's eyes widened. "Where? How is she?"

We went into the shop's kitchen and I filled them in on everything that had happened—Caroline listening so intently she barely blinked, Willow gasping, her joy playing out across her face. We turned on the small television on the counter and listened for more details as we started prep work.

Willow wrapped her arms around me. "You're a hero, Riley."

There was a soft knock at the screen door. Detective Voelker's broad shoulders filled the door frame. "Miss Rhodes, may I have a word?"

No surprise. Detective Voelker asked me and Caroline to accompany him to the police station. Once there, Caroline went into the interview room first while I waited on an exquisitely uncomfortable plastic bench. After a half hour, Caroline and Detective Voelker emerged from the interrogation room. He bent at the waist and swept his arm down the hallway toward me, a gesture that made me think of a country dance in a Jane Austen TV adaptation. Caroline's lips curved in a smile. How could she look so relaxed coming out of an interrogation?

"Ms. Rhodes?" Voelker straightened and gave a curt nod toward the interrogation room. As I brushed past Caroline, I whispered, "Did you tell him about your scarf?"

"What?" Caroline blinked. "Of course I mentioned it. Shouldn't I?"

I winced and thought, *Not if you don't want to be arrested.* I said, "Of course." She'd just saved me from perjury. I hadn't been sure I'd mention that the scarf on Mike's body was hers unless the police asked. I didn't want to do or say anything that would incriminate Caroline.

The police department secretary nodded to us from her desk, a phone receiver up to her ear. She wasn't talking and I was certain there wasn't anyone on the other end of that line. She was listening to us using a time-honored eavesdropping technique. The nameplate on her desk read "Teresa O'Malley," but I didn't need it. Tillie O'Malley was known as the loosest lips in Penniman and the most flamboyant dresser. Her loose cascade of black curls were highlighted with streaks of blue and corralled by a wide banana yellow head band that matched the fabric in her tropical fruit–print top. Cat eye glasses in the same yellow and fire-engine red lipstick finished her ensemble.

Caroline squeezed my arm and turned to the detective. "Riley's a hero! She saved Angelica!"

Detective Voelker's expression didn't change. "This way, please, Ms. Rhodes."

He let me walk ahead of him into the interview room,

closed the door, and indicated a seat at a table. I took my seat and started to grip the arms of my chair but instead shifted my posture, straightening my back and leaving my hands loose and relaxed in my lap. *Look innocent*, I thought. *You are innocent.* There was something about this cop that made me feel guilty, probably that beard and sweep of almost biblical hair that made me think of the figures painted in the Sistine Chapel.

Voelker took the seat across from me.

"Will Angelica be all right?" I asked.

He scrubbed the back of his head. Without his aviator sunglasses, I could see his gray blue eyes, the color of the ocean in winter. "We have no information yet."

Ah, the stone wall. "But she's alive," I prompted.

He waited a couple of beats, cleared his throat. "Ms. Rhodes, walk me though this morning. You went jogging and decided to run down to an abandoned farmhouse on private property because . . ."

When you put it that way it did sound bad. I took a deep breath. "We used to go skating there years ago. All the kids in Penniman did. I guess you're not from Penniman?"

He kept his look level.

"Okay." I cleared my throat. "I was thinking about Angelica, what she might've done the night of Mike's murder. It's a straight shot from Farm Lane to Woods Road. I thought she might have missed that hairpin turn in the road."

"How long had you known Miss Miguel?"

"I met her for the first time Friday, at Buzzy Spooner's funeral."

He made notes and shifted in his seat. "Did you have a relationship with Mike Spooner?"

"Mike?" I scoffed. "No. He's my best friend's brother. I was his pesky little sister's friend. And after he left for college he never really came back to the farm much at all." A relationship? *Was he developing some theory that I'd killed Mike? Maybe in a jealous rage?*

Then why would I want to help Angelica? I could've left her in that crashed car. I almost said that out loud. If I were jealous I'd want her dead and gone too. Seriously, was he fishing for some kind of soap-opera resolution? Or, I considered, maybe he was keeping an open mind, unlike that reporter who had Angelica killing Mike and running off—though it sure looked that way.

Voelker ran his hand along his jaw. Despite the touch of gray at his temples, his deliberate pace made me think that perhaps he was new to being a detective. He flicked through his notebook. "After you found Mike Spooner's body, how long were you in the guest house before you called the police?"

I blinked. "A few minutes. I had to find the phone. I didn't have my cell with me." *Did they have a witness who saw me go into the Love Nest? Did they think I'd spent too much time in there? You were poking around, Riley.*

Was I a suspect? I swallowed hard, then remembered the wine bottle and the money jar.

"When I was in the house, there was something about the wine bottle that was odd. But I don't know what . . . and the money jar from Udderly was missing. Have you found it?"

Voelker's stony look said *Who's interviewing whom?* "We'll do the investigating, Ms. Rhodes."

After I read and signed my statements—including the one from the morning of Mike's murder, which I'd completely forgotten that I was supposed to do— Detective Voelker had a uniformed police officer drop me and Caroline back at Buzzy's house. We rode in silence except for a quick call to make sure everything was fine at Udderly.

Once we were in the kitchen, Caroline asked, "How did it go?" I still felt unsettled by the interview, but Caroline was relaxed and calm.

No sense adding to her problems. "Not fun."

"Remember you're coming with me to the accountant and lawyer today?" Caroline said as she picked up Sprinkles and gave her a nuzzle.

I'd forgotten. "Of course. But I'd better change."

"I'll heat up some of that quiche Pru made," Caroline said.

I ran to my bedroom and tossed on the black travel dress I'd worn to Buzzy's funeral. I was officially out of clean clothes. All I had in the boxes Paulette had packed were cardigan sweaters and pants that no longer fit. I had thought I'd go to the funeral, then be back home in Virginia in a few days, writing up my next blog. Instead I was in Penniman, Connecticut, where I'd agreed to manage an ice cream shop, one person had been injured and might die, and one had most certainly been murdered.

I recalled a proverb I'd heard from a rug merchant in Morocco: "Man plans, God laughs."

Chapter 13

I pulled the Mustang into a space in front of a sprawling white Victorian on the Penniman green. Buzzy's accountant, Wilmer Reyes, rented an office in what had been the mansion's carriage house. Wilmer had gray hair, gray metal-framed glasses, and wore gray pants, a white button-down shirt, and a gray tie. He hadn't splurged on his wardrobe or his tiny office. On the drive over, Caroline told me the money Wilmer hadn't used for a fancy office or wardrobe had been poured into a magnificent wooden sailboat he kept in Essex.

Wilmer took the box of Buzzy's receipts and didn't roll his eyes, a testament to his professionalism. His news about the state of Buzzy's accounts wasn't good. "Buzzy had invested in an expensive new industrial freezer, which put her in a financial hole. She hoped to grow. Paying taxes was going to be the biggest hurdle." Wilmer put the shoebox on a shelf. "She was talking about turning the farm over to a land trust to help with her tax situation."

"Land trust?" I asked.

"Tax situation?" Caroline gulped.

"Her lawyer can tell you more. Basically, the state wants to preserve open space and farms, but understands that farming's a hard way to make a living, so they encourage putting farmland in a nonprofit trust. It means that you can live on the land and farm it, but the land belongs to the trust and that lessens or eliminates the tax burden."

I leaned forward. "So if the farm was in a land trust, no one would be able to sell it to a developer?" Caroline and I exchanged glances.

Wilmer said, "That's exactly why there are land trusts. Towns don't want to get eaten up by developers."

Wilmer promised to send a report on Buzzy's updated account, and we stood to go.

"You're making the sunflower ice cream, right?" Wilmer held the office door open for us. "I love that stuff. Pray for hot weather," he said. "People like ice cream when it's hot."

As we left the building I muttered, "How much did you pay for that advice?"

Caroline smoothed her skirt and shook her head.

"Caroline, I'm confused," I said. "You were home a lot. Didn't Buzzy talk about financial stuff with you?"

"We never talked about money. Mom always said things were fine." Caroline's shoulders slumped. "I think she didn't want me to worry. I wish she'd told me the truth."

We crossed the green to a white house with tall pillars, the law office of Mike's friend, Kyle Aldridge. Next door was a beautiful white wedding-cake Victorian with a sign on the front lawn that read Penniman Preferred Properties in gold paint. A pink Mini was parked in its lot. Emily was popping up everywhere.

Caroline followed me through the heavily carved door of the law office into a hushed foyer. Sunlight streamed through a stained-glass window onto a gleaming wood floor. The receptionist, a striking redhead in a beautifully tailored blue linen suit, ushered us into a paneled room with soaring windows and a view of the Congregational church. Her diamond watch sparkled as she gracefully waved us to two leather chairs in front of a broad mahogany desk. Kyle must be doing well for his secretary to afford a watch like that, I thought. I sank into the deep cushions, acutely aware of my wrinkled dress.

"Coffee? Tea? Water?" she asked.

Caroline and I declined and she closed the door softly behind her as she exited.

Kyle entered from an inner office. Today he looked rested, his blue eyes bright, his white shirt and charcoal suit perfectly pressed.

"Caroline. How are you doing?" He gave her a hug.

"Okay," she murmured. "How about you?"

"Same. Hi, Riley."

I nodded. Kyle threw a questioning look at Caroline.

"It's okay to talk in front of Riley. She's helping me with, well, everything," Caroline said.

"Sure."

As Kyle and Caroline spoke about Mike, I took in the photos in sterling frames on a shelf behind him. There was a teenage Kyle with his father and grandfather, gray-haired carbon copies of himself, in front of a sign that read Aldridge for Senator.

In another photo, Kyle and Mike posed in Penniman football uniforms, their arms around each other's shoulders, a trophy in front of them. A plaque from a fraternity was behind that, then a family photo—Kyle and Nina and two towheaded children at their lake-front home, all in matching khaki pants and soft blue shirts. Nina, model slim, tanned and beautiful, her thick golden hair tamed with a scarf streaming in the wind, Kyle beaming at her as if he couldn't believe his luck.

"How can I help?" Kyle's words pulled me back from my reverie.

Caroline took a deep breath. "I need to know where I stand so I can decide what to do."

Kyle opened a folder. "Well, we're waiting for the police investigation to wrap up, but that shouldn't affect anything. You have power of attorney with Buzzy's affairs, so business at the shop won't be interrupted." Kyle's smile was reassuring. "Mike's will is simple. You and Buzzy were his beneficiaries, plus there's a small bequest to our fraternity. Now you're the sole beneficiary since Buzzy is deceased." He took a couple of sheets from the folder and handed them to Caroline.

Caroline took the papers, but I wasn't sure she was seeing them. I glanced over and my brows shot up at Kyle's definition of a "small" donation to the fraternity.

A glossy contact sheet of photos on Kyle's desk caught my eye. Campaign signs. My ability to read upside-down print occasionally proved useful. The signs read Aldridge for Senate: A New Generation. So Kyle had decided to take the plunge into politics. No surprise. The Aldridges had three family businesses: a car dealership in Hartford, the law office in Penniman, and politics.

Caroline coughed. "And Buzzy's will?"

Kyle took up an old-fashioned fountain pen as he spoke. "This is where it gets a bit complicated." He tapped the pen on the desk and took a deep breath. "Buzzy didn't make a will."

"But Mike said he brought her here—"

"He did. We talked about her options. She said she wanted to think about some things, and"—he spread his hands—"she never came back."

"If she didn't . . ." Caroline's voice trailed off.

Kyle's voice was reassuring, his smile kind. "It simply means we wait. I'm afraid Buzzy's estate may have to go through probate. Don't worry, Caroline. I'm sure it'll prove to be uncomplicated."

"I was just at Wilmer's," Caroline said. "He mentioned that Buzzy was thinking of a land trust."

Kyle's eyebrows shot up. "Wilmer said that?"

Caroline nodded.

Kyle sat back. "Now that I think of it, it was an option we discussed. But Buzzy was leaning against it. She wanted to leave the farm to you and Mike. She especially wanted to take care of you financially, Caroline. Now don't worry, probate just means that things'll be up in the air for a while. Because Mike is"—Kyle cleared his throat—"gone, and Connecticut law says that relatives inherit, it'll all be okay in the end."

Caroline's hand flew to her throat. "We were adopted."

Kyle's expression softened, radiating reassurance. "That's fine, adopted children inherit. I have all that paperwork. Her estate would've been divided between the two of you. Now you'll be the sole beneficiary."

Sole beneficiary. It sounded lonely. I squeezed Caroline's hand.

"Listen," Kyle said. "I know you're busy with the ice cream shop. I can go to Mike's condo and get his mail, see if he had any other paperwork we need."

"Would you, Kyle?" Caroline said. "Thank you."

Caroline didn't speak as we left the office and got in the Mustang. As I turned the key, she suddenly turned to me. "This car rental must be costing you a fortune."

I laughed. "That's not what I expected you to be thinking about."

"Well, you've been driving me everywhere." Living

in Boston, Caroline didn't own a car. She was an anxious driver and only drove a Zipcar down to Penniman during times traffic was light. "You should use Sadie."

I recalled Sadie, Buzzy's car, an ancient, boxy, orange VW station wagon.

"I know it won't be nearly as much fun as this," Caroline said.

I ran my hand along the Mustang's leather-wrapped steering wheel. No, it wouldn't be as much fun, but renting a sports car had been an expensive whim.

"Sadie should be back on the road," Caroline said. "Let's swing by and get her now."

As we turned into Farm Lane, I remembered the campfire last night and told Caroline what the police officer had said.

"People have always camped in the woods around here," she said. "Like your dad said, my only worry is fire spreading to the dry sunflowers."

A police car blocked the turn for the Love Nest. Caroline went still. I realized that she hadn't been up here since her brother died.

Tillie O'Malley, now clad in a police auxiliary jacket, walked up to the car and peered at us through the driver's window. Her square face and pug nose made me think of a bulldog. She'd changed into a subdued uniform of khaki pants and a blue polo with Penniman Auxiliary embroidered on the chest, but she'd accessorized with a stretchy headband in a pattern of blue Penniman police shields. I was certain that headband wasn't regulation.

"Hey, Caroline, Riley," Tillie said.

"We just saw you at the station. You work"—I hesitated—"in the field too?"

Tillie preened. "Jack, I mean Detective Voelker, encouraged me to join the Auxiliary. It gets me out into the community." She swaggered a bit with her hands on her hips. I gave thanks she wasn't wearing a sidearm.

The loosest lips in Penniman. I didn't know how she held onto her job. Well, actually, I did. Her father had been Penniman police chief, and though he'd retired to Florida, his name still commanded a lot of respect. Tillie had washed out of the police academy years ago—she couldn't keep a secret to save her life. Voelker was wise—it was better to have Tillie out here where she was less likely to overhear confidential information.

Tillie jutted out her chin. "We're keeping the road closed. Lots of news vans have been coming through, using the house and barn for backdrop on the Angelica Miguel story. I can't stop them because Farm Lane's a public road, but this crossroad is on your property so I've blocked it off. Caught one guy trying to sneak into the barn. Creeps."

Tillie would be a gold mine of information. "What have you heard about Angelica Miguel?"

Her radio squawked; she held up a finger, listened, then turned it down. "She's at Eastern Hospital. Hey, you found her, right? Yeah, her leg's messed up and she lost a lot of blood. The doc said she was knocking at death's door but you found her in time. She'll survive."

"Glad to hear it." *I think. Unless she killed Mike.*

"She'll survive to go to jail," Tillie said.

Tillie's words sent a jolt through me. Was she parroting what she'd heard at the police station? Had the police found evidence that pointed to Angelica? The note I'd found . . . was it part of a game she and Mike had been playing? But still, having seen Mike and Angelica together, I had doubts.

Caroline leaned across me and put my thoughts into words. "I can't believe she killed Mike."

Tillie shrugged. "She'll be questioned as soon as she's up to it. Everyone wants to know why she'd kill her boyfriend." She guffawed. "Well, we've all had a few times we wanted to kill a boyfriend, right? Good motive. Who'd want to kill Mike, right, except for all those ex-girlfriends?"

At Tillie's thoughtless comments, Caroline winced and leaned back in her seat. I squeezed her arm but remembered what she'd said in the kitchen the night Mike died. *I could kill him.* I remembered the way Darwin looked that same night.

Caroline leaned across me again. "Is it okay if we take my mom's car out of the barn?"

"I'll have to check," Tillie said. "Might take a while."

"Okay," Caroline said. "Detective Voelker has my number. Please have him call me."

Chapter 14

"Tillie sure is chatty," Caroline said as I drove down Farm Lane to the shop.

"Loose lips sink ships," I said. That was another of Buzzy's old sayings.

"Riley, let's stop a sec. I have to check on Sprinkles."

I parked the Mustang and as we ran up the front porch steps I picked up a grocery bag someone had left by the door. I opened it to find two loaves of banana bread wrapped in tinfoil. I handed her the accompanying card.

Caroline read it. "How sweet. One of Buzzy's customers left the bread for us." She shook her head. "We can't eat all the food we have already. I'll bring them over to the farmhands later."

We changed into work clothes, Caroline fed Sprinkles, and we sprinted down to the shop.

As Caroline went to serve customers, I mentally pushed aside the conversation with Tillie. It was time to compartmentalize and be the manager. I remembered Buzzy's calendar. I'd have to check to make sure there weren't any more special-order surprises.

Brandon was at the ice cream chiller, placing a tub

on a cart under the spout. Brandon's bony shoulders moved back and forth as he bopped to the music on his headphones.

In Buzzy's office, I flipped through her calendar. On tomorrow's page she'd written: Preserve Penniman 7pm. Community Hall. I looked up Preserve Penniman on my phone; the group was dedicated to "preserving Penniman's historic and natural character."

I considered what I'd learned from Kyle and Wilmer. Buzzy was looking into land trusts the whole time Mike was planning to develop the farm. The sale would bring in millions of dollars.

I leaned against the desk next to the empty space where the pile of bills had been and wondered if Caroline had considered how much money the sale of the farm could net. I rubbed my tired eyes. One thing I knew about Buzzy and Caroline: money didn't motivate them.

It motivated Mike.

I'd go to the Preserve Penniman meeting.

I flipped through the calendar to Saturday. Buzzy had drawn a big sunflower around the date: "Sunflower Celebration. D-day!" On Sunday she'd scribbled, "Willow BG for pen." What on earth did "BG" mean? I recalled Willow's sketch of Hairy Houdini. Oh, baby goats. I had to start thinking like a farmer.

I flipped through the rest of the calendar, checking for more special orders. None in August or September or October—my breath caught. There was a big purple heart looping around Halloween and the words "Riley's birthday." *Oh, Buzzy.*

"Uh, help . . . *Help? Help!*" Brandon shouted.

I rushed to the workroom to find Brandon looking wildly from side to side as ice cream spewed from the chiller onto the floor. I ran to the machine, grabbing an empty tub as I went, then slammed my hand onto the on/off button by the chute. The flow of ice cream didn't stop. Brandon pulled aside his overflowing tub and I set mine in its place, sidestepping to avoid the puddle of golden vanilla ice cream.

I yanked the power cord out of the wall and the machine ground to a halt.

"I don't know what happened!" Brandon yelped. "It went crazy! I think it's possessed?"

"Hang on." I turned the power back on. Ice cream flowed out. I tried the on/off button again. This time the machine turned off.

Brandon blushed to the roots of his lank dark hair. "Maybe I pressed it too many times?"

I patted his shoulder. "No, I think it's wonky." Was that a technical term?

Flo hurried into the kitchen. "That machine acts up sometimes. You have to know how to press the button just right." The way she said "just right" made me think of Goldilocks and the Three Bears, and I remembered Flo had taught kindergarten for forty years.

"Let's get this mopped up. I think we can rescue the ice cream. What kind were you making, Brandon?" I asked.

"Ah, sunflower?"

Ah, sunflower. As Brandon mopped, I checked the *Book of Spells* and found the recipe for sunflower ice cream. I double-checked the mix-in ingredients Brandon had gathered by the machine—he had twice as much sunflower seeds and half as much honey as the recipe called for. At least this disaster gave me a chance to correct the ingredients.

Each layer had to be done in a specific order: honey, caramel, and shelled and roasted sunflower seeds interspersed with rich golden vanilla ice cream. It would've been faster and easier to layer in the mix-ins as the ice cream flowed from the machine, but I scooped each layer, drizzled honey and caramel, sprinkled in sunflower seeds, and then carried the heavy tub to the deep freezer. If anything, this job was whipping my arms into shape.

Brandon did do a good job mopping up, I'd give him that, and for the next few hours everything went smoothly. Flo wished us good night as she breezed out at eight. I glanced at the clock. One hour to go. Just before closing, I had to give out the golden ticket, a tradition Buzzy instituted to manage long lines. If the line went out the door, as it did tonight, ten minutes before closing Buzzy gave the person at the end of the line a sign to hold up. That person had to tell everyone who came after them that we were closed. It's funny how well it worked. The golden-ticket holder then got a free ice cream for their trouble.

Flo hurried back in. "You need help closing."

"No, really, go ahead, we can manage," I said.

"I've got this." Flo yanked the sign from my hands and ran outside, then ran back in moments later, smoothing her hair.

It all made sense when the golden-ticket holder stepped in the door—the handsome guy wearing the cowboy hat I'd seen Saturday. Caroline closed the shop door and slid down the shade that said See You ToMOOrow. He touched the brim of his hat as she passed.

I admit I glanced his way as he looked at the flavors board. He had broad shoulders, trim jeans, plus one of those large belt buckles that look ridiculous on most men but on him looked just right.

I scooped maple walnut for the customer in front of me and packed it into a still-warm waffle cone. Flo shouldered past me to wait on the handsome cowboy. Caroline and I exchanged smiles.

"What can I do for you, stranger?" Flo grinned.

He smiled at her warmly. "Good evening." He took off his hat. Though his hair was more gray than brown, it was thick and long enough to brush his collar. His eyes turned to me and he smiled again.

I swear the ice cream in that cone should've melted with the surge of heat I felt. Handsome . . . rugged . . . his eyes were a deep, dark brown, the kind you want to sink into and tell your troubles to, because you knew he'd understand. . . .

"Can I have my cone please?" My customer reached for his maple-walnut cone.

I was pulled back from my reverie. "Yes, anything else?"

Flo chatted with the cowboy and handed him a hot fudge sundae with mint chocolate chip ice cream.

He nodded at the cup. "I notice your mint chocolate chip isn't green, like in many places." His voice was husky and rich and smooth, like bourbon, like amber honey.

"We don't use any artificial coloring or flavors." Flo was cool. I'd be incapable of forming words.

The more I looked at him, the more the cowboy did look familiar . . . but I'd probably seen a model who looked like him on the cover of a romance novel in my dad's bookstore.

The cowboy said, "Thank you kindly," to Flo, touched his hat to me and Caroline, and went outside. I watched him cross the parking lot as I locked the door behind him. He leaned against a long black vintage Cadillac Coupe De Ville as he ate his ice cream, chatting with a couple sitting at one of the picnic tables in front of the shop.

Later, as I swept up, I watched his car pull out. Texas plates. Of course.

Flo hung up her apron, humming "Deep in the Heart of Texas."

"I'm not paying you overtime," I said.

She laughed. "That silver fox is worth every minute. Not often you see a hottie like that."

"Who is he?" Caroline asked, her voice dreamy.

Flo shrugged. "Don't know—yet. My sources tell me that he's been seen in a few restaurants and shops in town. He does stand out."

"In a good way," I said. "My knees actually went weak."

"So did mine." Caroline's cheeks pinked.

Flo grinned. "So did mine. And I've got arthritis."

After cleanup, Caroline said, "Let's drop off the banana bread for the farmhands."

We went down the darkened drive to the Brightwoods' farmhouse. The sprawling house had been built in the 1800s with a deeply slanted back roof in the typical saltbox Colonial style, and a series of whitewashed additions connected the house to the large red barn, additions that ensured that generations of farmers wouldn't have to brave a blizzard in order to tend their animals. A small overhead light illuminated a shingle hung outside a side door: Prudence Brightwood, Midwife.

Warm light glowed from one open window on the first floor of the farmhouse and I remembered that Pru and Darwin had a bedroom near the kitchen. Every window was dark on the second story, where the interns bunked. Even the teen volunteers adopted the early-to-bed rhythms of farm life.

"I don't want to disturb Pru and Darwin," I said.

Caroline whispered. "I'll just put the breads on the table. The door's never locked."

"What is it with you people never locking your doors?" I joked. Growing up in Penniman, I'd never locked my door either. Living in cities for so long, not to mention my occasional assignments as an operative, had made me jaded and security conscious.

We cut through the small kitchen garden, the scent of basil, rosemary, and thyme rising as we passed. I followed Caroline into the kitchen, holding the screen door behind me to ease it shut.

A single light glowed over the sink. Despite the hum of the refrigerator and the gleam of the stainless-steel stove, Pru's kitchen always made me feel that I'd stepped back in time. A long wooden table set with homespun place mats and flanked by long benches ran almost the length of the room. A wooden turned bowl filled with peaches was set in the center on a mat woven in harvest hues. A brick fireplace blackened by the cooking smoke of centuries and tall enough for petite Caroline to stand in loomed at the far end of the kitchen. A rocking chair stood by the fireplace, a basket of knitting nearby. How did Pru find time to knit along with all her farm chores and midwifery?

A clock ticked over the fireplace mantel as we set the wrapped breads on the table. The sound of voices in quiet conversation came from the hallway. We tiptoed out and Caroline slowly closed the door to keep it from banging shut.

As we crossed the garden, Pru's and Darwin's voices suddenly streamed from the window.

Pru's tone was pleading. "Help me understand, Darwin. Why didn't you say something to the police?" She lowered her voice but I made out one word clearly. "Mike."

I pulled up short and Caroline bumped into me.

Darwin replied, "I didn't want Willow to know. I know, I'm a fool. I ruined everything and I've dragged you all with me. I can't lose everything we've worked for. I couldn't take that chance."

Pru's response was muffled, but I heard, "You did what you had to do."

Darwin's voice: "He wasn't worth it, Pru."

With a low cry, Caroline covered her ears and ran home.

He wasn't worth it? He. Mike? I ran through the shadows after Caroline.

Chapter 15

The next morning, I dragged myself downstairs, rubbing my eyes. I needed a run. I'd tossed all night, Darwin's words playing in my mind. He'd been working this farm for over twenty years and I'd never known him to be anything other than what he appeared to be—kind, hardworking, decent.

But all night an uncomfortable apprehension grew in me. Who had a lot to lose if the development became a reality? Darwin. Who'd argued with Mike the night he was killed? Darwin. Those words—"he wasn't worth it." Did that mean that Mike had asked him to do something that wasn't worth Darwin's self-respect?

I knew one thing for sure. Caroline had cried all night. I'd tried to talk to her about what we'd overheard but she insisted she wanted to be alone.

Sprinkles mewed softly from the kitchen, where she again sat at her perch by the window.

She jerked her head around as I entered. She blinked once then jumped down in front of the door, turning her flat face and copper eyes to me again with unspoken command.

I obeyed and opened the door. The little black cat I'd

met at the barn sat on the welcome mat, looking at me as if to say *What took you so long?*

"Well, hello!"

Sprinkles looked at me, then the kitten, her demand clear.

I held the screen door wide. "Oh, for heaven's sake, come in."

Sprinkles blinked, as if granting permission to enter into her royal presence. The little guy sprang inside, his tail high.

As the kitten curled around my ankles, a deep purr coming from his throat, I could see the bones working under his fur. "You're too thin, poor thing!" Sprinkles moved to sit by her food bowl and looked up at me again. Evidently, in addition to her meal, I was to prepare one for our guest.

I fed Sprinkles, then shook some dried food into a bowl for the newcomer and added a tiny bit of Sprinkles' froufrou food. I didn't know what this little guy had been eating but I didn't want to hit him with anything too rich. He drank from Sprinkles' water bowl without incident. I crouched and reached out my hand. He curled his head under it and let me pet him.

Then at an unspoken signal from Sprinkles, they trotted down the hallway together.

Caroline leaned over the banister as she came downstairs. "Hey, where'd you come from?"

We followed the cats as they went into the parlor. Sprinkles groomed a paw as her new friend sniffed the furniture. "We have a guest," I said.

"He's adorable!" Caroline crouched to get a better look at him, then whispered, "And look how nice she's being to him."

There was something so loveable about the little guy. His ear, bent and torn, gave him such a rakish, devil-may-care look. His eyes were gold and bright, with an uncanny expression that made me feel that he could understand everything I said. Plus, is there anything more adorable than a kitten?

But I didn't like the scar on his back. "I think I'll take him to the vet. Listen to me, like I have a vet."

Caroline laughed. "Sprinkles' vet is Liam Pryce, the hottest vet in New England. Word is he did some modeling to pay for school and was very successful, but instead he has dedicated his life to taking care of animals, which only makes him more attractive. Maybe we should both go to the vet." She tilted her head. "This guy needs a name. Midnight? Shadow? Inky?"

"Let's avoid the typical black-cat names. He's a fighter," I said. "I've got it. Rocky. Like the boxer."

"Perfect. And he's yours, so he's Rocky Rhodes." She laughed.

I groaned. Perfect for me now that I was president, CEO, and chief mechanic of the Udderly Delightful Ice Cream Shop.

I found the number for Dr. Pryce on a handwritten list posted by Buzzy's vintage wall-mounted phone and punched it into my cell. I spoke to the receptionist. There'd been a cancellation, and could I be there in a half hour? I could.

Caroline dangled a toy and the little kitten rocketed after it. Sprinkles watched, her tail swishing lazily. "There's an extra litter box in the mudroom," she said. "I'll set it up for Rocky. We have lots of stuff that Sprinkles never uses. Buzzy never threw anything out. I'll get that all set up while you're gone, then I'll head down to the shop." Caroline practically bounced into the mudroom, completely taken with the little guy. I'd wanted to talk about last night and what Darwin had said, but she looked so happy I decided it could wait.

Chapter 16

Dr. Liam Pryce was indeed handsome. He'd come to Connecticut for veterinary school but still retained the lilting accent from his home in Jamaica. I'm a sucker for guys with accents, but it was mostly seeing the gentle way he held Rocky that made me melt.

"No chip." He examined Rocky's ear. "Some programs will spay or neuter strays, and farmers use them for barn cats to keep down mice. They notch the ear to show they're in the program. But this guy's ear is too ragged to have been clipped by a professional. Looks like he was born in the wild. And he's older than you think. He's just undersized because he's malnourished. His muscle development is quite good." Dr. Pryce slid on tortoiseshell reading glasses, which only highlighted his chiseled features and deep brown eyes.

His eyebrows flew up when I shared how Sprinkles had invited Rocky into the house. "Very unusual. Usually an older cat has problems with a new younger cat." I resolved to keep an eye on the two new friends, in case Sprinkles decided to revert to her old tricks.

We set up another appointment so Rocky could be

neutered and get his vaccinations. I couldn't wait to return to see Dr. Pryce, a feeling evidently shared by all
the pet owners in the standing room only waiting room.

I put Rocky back into Sprinkles' car carrier. Thank
goodness the little cat was curious. I placed a new toy
in the carrier and he slunk in, his graceful movement
making me think of a ninja. Silent, watchful. Maybe I
was projecting. Rocky's confidence was impressive but
getting into a cat carrier was probably a piece of cake
compared to what he went through scraping a living in
the woods.

As I drove back to the house, I passed Eastern Hospital. I wanted to talk to Angelica but there was no way
I was taking Rocky to the hospital with me and leaving
him outside in the car on such a hot day.

Willow was sitting on the front porch and jumped
to her feet as I parked. "Caroline told me you have a
kitten!"

I got out and set the carrier on the porch. "Meet
Rocky." As Willow crouched by the carrier, I told her
how I'd found him, omitting the part about him leading
me to Mike's body.

Willow made those sounds people always make
when faced with an adorable pet. "Oh! Can I play with
him?"

"Sure. I was just dropping him off."

"I could watch him for you," Willow said. "I have to
do some social-media stuff for the Sunflower Festival,
and I can do it on my tablet here."

"That's great," I said. "Thank you. He just got some
shots, so I don't want him to be alone. Plus, I'm not sure
how Sprinkles will behave, though her royal highness did
invite Rocky into her castle."

Willow laughed. "Hey, did you bring the banana
bread last night?"

I froze. Had Pru or Darwin seen me and Caroline outside their window? "Yes."

"It was gone in about two seconds." Willow was so distracted by Rocky, she didn't pick up on my hesitation. "Mom figured it was you two."

I breathed a sigh of relief as a delivery truck from Penniman Petals rumbled to a stop in front of us. The delivery man greeted us, checked a clipboard, and set three arrangements on the porch, each bigger than the last.

"They're gorgeous." Willow dipped her head to inhale the fragrance of a white rose.

I signed for them and slipped a tip into the deliveryman's hand. He honked as he drove past Dandy and Nina, who were power walking down the lane.

From a distance, they could've been sisters, or mother and daughter. Despite the difference in their ages, the two women had similar tall, slim builds, shoulder-length light-colored hair, and both moved with athletic grace. Even their outfits were similar: skorts, polo shirts, sunglasses, and golf visors. Nina's shirt had "Sunflower Festival 5K" embroidered on the pocket.

I searched my memory. Nina had been best friends with Brooke Danforth in high school. It must've been a comfort to both women to keep their bond after Brooke's death.

"Good morning, girls." Dandy smiled, but I felt the same frisson that I remembered from high school whenever the formidable teacher assigned push-ups.

"Hi!" Willow smiled, and I remembered she was homeschooled. She hadn't ever had a gym class with Drill Sergeant Danforth.

"I saw you jogging, Riley," Dandy nodded. "Good for you. It's excellent exercise."

"I enjoy it." I remembered it was Dandy who'd

encouraged me to join the cross-country team. Even though I'd only lasted two seasons, I realized now that she'd sparked a lifelong love of running in me.

"How's Caroline?" Nina took off her sunglasses, concern radiating from her hazel eyes.

"She's doing well, thanks." Though I thought Caroline was coping as well as anyone could with two tragedies right on top of each other, I didn't want to talk about it, especially with Willow here.

Nina's smile was warm. "Kyle and I are always happy to help."

I wanted to change the subject. I nodded toward Nina's shirt. "Are you running in the Five K?"

"Yes, and I manage the event with Donna's help every year." Donna? It took me a moment to remember Dandy's first name was Donna. "I'm hoping it will top the fundraising numbers we got for the Memorial Day Half-Marathon."

"Good luck," I said.

"Look at Riley's new cat," Willow gushed.

The women bent down to peer into the cat carrier and made those same cute kitty noises Willow had. Dandy straightened and her pale blue eyes fell on the flower arrangements. "Oh dear." She pointed to one with lilies and roses in a white basket. "Lilies are toxic for cats. Those flowers will have to go."

"I had no idea," I said. "I'll put it in the shop."

"Good." Dandy's concerned gaze shifted from the cat to me. "I'm so glad you're here for Caroline. She's gone through a lot."

Nina glanced at her sports watch. "We have to get going. We're going to get some ice cream before the Garden Club meeting." They waved and walked off.

"I had no idea those flowers are toxic." I took the

carrier into the house, then jogged into the parlor and dining room, which were full of flowers in vases and baskets. "Sprinkles hasn't paid them any mind, but this little guy is so curious." I was relieved to see no lilies in the other vases of flowers.

Willow brought in the other two arrangements, then let Rocky out of the carrier. Sprinkles emerged from the mudroom.

I pulled the quiche Pru had made from the refrigerator. There was enough left for two servings. "Have you had lunch?"

"Yes," said Willow as she followed Rocky down the hall. "You eat and I'll work in the parlor." Sprinkles brought up the rear.

I heated the quiche and gobbled it down, then went into the parlor. Willow sat on the couch working on her tablet, Sprinkles dozing on one side of her and Rocky on the other. I waved and left for the shop, carrying the basket of lilies and roses.

A mom and her son leaned over the fence of the empty pen where Buzzy had kept baby goats, llamas, and sometimes miniature horses for kids to pet. My heart dropped at the sight of their disappointed faces.

"Are the ponies coming back?" the little boy said.

"I hope so." I gave him a reassuring smile. "We'll have baby goats here on Sunday. There are some across the way." I saw one of the interns and waved him over. "Can you take them to see the goats?" He nodded, and the mother and son followed him across the lane.

Another item for my mile-long to-do list. Bring in more animals for the petting pen. Get more picnic tables set up. Make ice cream.

Visit Angelica. More than anything I wanted to hear her version of events from the night Mike was killed. I'd liked her, and I didn't want to believe, as Tillie did, that she was guilty of murder. But I didn't want to believe that Darwin was guilty either.

Caroline was washing a bowl in arm deep soapy water when I entered the shop kitchen. She gasped. "Oh, the flowers are lovely!"

I set the arrangement on a counter behind the *Book of Spells*. "Three arrangements came today. Good thing Dandy was walking by. She told me lilies are toxic to cats."

Dark shadows circled Caroline's eyes. She toweled her hands and took the card from the arrangement. "It's from Mike's office. His boss called, a really nice guy, asking about a memorial service." Her voice drifted. "Riley, come with me. I have to talk to Darwin."

"Now? Are you sure?" I was afraid Darwin would say some things Caroline could never unhear. Darwin had poured his soul into the farm. Mike would've sold it in a heartbeat.

Caroline read my thoughts. "Did Darwin kill Mike?" She smoothed her apron over and over. "Ridiculous. But I have to ask him. I have to hear it from him."

She wasn't going to change her mind. "Who's working?" I asked.

"Gerri and Brandon." Caroline took off her apron. "It's kind of slow now. I'll tell them to keep an eye on the chiller. I'll be back in time to add the mix-ins. Let's go."

Caroline's hunched shoulders straightened as we walked up the lane. When we turned into the driveway to the farm, a Penniman Police cruiser was driving out. Darwin Brightwood sat in the back seat, his head bowed.

A shock ran through me as Caroline gasped and clutched my arm. We watched as the cruiser turned onto Fairweather Road.

Pru stood at the gate to her kitchen garden, tears streaking her face. Caroline and I ran to her. "What happened?"

Pru swiped her eyes. "Come inside." I turned to look up the hill to Buzzy's house. Thank goodness Willow wasn't outside to see her father taken away in a police car.

Pru walked unsteadily into the kitchen. I steered her to a bench and she dropped onto it as if she were a marionette whose strings had been cut. Caroline sat next to Pru and put an arm around her shoulders while I filled the kettle with water and put it on the stove.

"I've been married to that man for thirty years. Never has he hurt another human being." Pru grabbed Caroline's hand. "But he hasn't been himself lately."

I made Pru a cup of tea, set it in front of her, then took a seat on her other side.

"The night of the funeral," Pru swallowed. "You saw how upset Darwin was. Mike had called him a few weeks earlier, telling him about this great real estate project. How we could all work together to make sure Buzzy was well cared for in her old age."

Caroline and I shared a glance. Mike had the development in the works before Buzzy died, and had figured an angle that would strike Darwin Brightwood right in the heart.

"How the development would 'honor the past.'" Pru made air quotes. "Darwin kept asking where all the new houses in the development would go. Mike said it would be a green project that maintained open land.

"Then the night before Buzzy's funeral, Mike sent a group email that had the plans attached—I don't think he realized he'd sent it to Darwin too. The farm would've been cut down to a tenth of its size, most of the orchards ripped out, Buzzy's house gone, ice cream shop gone. Mike had led us to believe that the development would have apartments or townhouses, something very eco-logically responsible. But the plans were for estates—massive homes, each on two acres."

Pru took a sip of her tea.

"I've never seen Darwin so furious," Pru said. "He felt betrayed. You saw how upset Darwin was after he talked to Mike."

"Yes," Caroline whispered.

"After we left your house"—Pru hesitated—"Darwin did some chores. I know he was trying to keep his mind and hands occupied. Then we went to bed but neither of us could sleep. Sometime around midnight, Darwin said he was going for a walk. I watched him head up the lane toward the Love Nest. I knew he was going to confront Mike."

The note in the Love Nest had said "Meet me at midnight."

Caroline bowed her head.

Pru's shoulders sagged. "He came back about a half hour later. Said he'd walked around a bit trying to calm down but he couldn't. Angelica's car was gone so he banged on the door of the Love Nest. But then a black cat jumped out of the dark and scared the heck out of him."

Rocky. Caroline and I shared a glance.

"He felt foolish being scared by a little cat," Pru's voice trailed, "so he came home."

"Did he tell the police he'd been at the Love Nest?" I asked.

Pru jumped to her feet and paced. "No. I still can't understand it. We talked about it again last night. He promised he would today, as soon as he finished the morning chores, but then the police showed up anyway."

I remembered the land trust. "Did Darwin talk about a land trust with Buzzy?"

"He penciled in a meeting about it on the calendar." Pru's voice was dull. Her eyes moved around the kitchen, from the rocking chair to the fireplace, out the window into the garden. I wondered if she was thinking that this could all be taken away.

"What did the police say?" Caroline said in a low voice.

"I overheard one of them say they got a phone call with an anonymous tip that placed Darwin at the Love Nest the night Mike died."

My mind leapt to Angelica. *Had she been able to talk to the police? But Darwin said her car was gone when he got there. And think, Riley. If Angelica was the tipster, the police wouldn't call it an anonymous tip, would they?*

Pru leaned against the sink, her arms wrapped around her stomach. "Darwin told me that when he was leaving the Love Nest, a car was driving up the lane."

"What kind of car?" I asked.

She threw up her hands. "He was so preoccupied he didn't notice. He said a small car."

Farm Lane was a cut-through, Flo had said. Anyone could've driven there.

I thought of the neighbors. Gerri and Flo shared a house and Dandy lived next door to them just up Farm Lane. I'd seen Gerri driving a boat-sized Lincoln Continental. I had no idea what the others drove. Aaron the Hermit? His house was the closest of all to the Love Nest. Did he even notice what happened beyond his wall of weeds and trees? None of the neighbors had reason to be anonymous, did they?

A thought struck me. The driver could've been the killer, trying to pin blame on Darwin.

Caroline stood. "I have to tell you the truth, Pru. I always have."

With a look, I begged her to stop. Pru had had enough.

"Riley and I came by last night"—Caroline cleared her throat—"to drop off the bread. We heard you and Darwin arguing. I heard what Darwin said about Mike."

Pru's face crumpled. "He said some hard things."

Caroline took Pru's hands in hers. "I'm sure of one thing. Darwin could never have killed Mike. Never."

Chapter 17

I wish I shared Caroline's certainty. I'd seen people, desperate people, do things their friends and families would swear they'd never do. We're all capable of anything when our backs are against the wall.

Caroline calmed as we returned to Udderly. To my surprise she went into Buzzy's office. I followed.

"Riley, I feel better." She sat down on Buzzy's chair and burst into tears.

"I thought you said you felt better!" I rushed to her and put my arms around her.

"I do." She sniffled. "I figured something out. Why I feel so bad about Mike. We were never close. Never. When I cry for Mike it's like"—she groped for words—"I'm crying for what I didn't have. I didn't have a good relationship with him, no, honestly, I don't know if I had any relationship with him. When I cry for Buzzy it's because I miss her. I still love her. I don't know if I ever loved Mike."

She grabbed some tissues and stood. "Now I'm going to make ice cream. The sunflower blend should be ready for mix-ins."

I took a deep breath. This was a lot of emotional truth for one day. I needed an ice cream cone.

As Caroline started working, I grabbed a waffle cone and stuffed it with cherry vanilla ice cream. Buzzy's cherry vanilla used black cherries that she'd candied in sugar, lemon juice, and a touch of almond extract. I sprinkled slivered almonds on top and took a bite. Heaven. I sat at Buzzy's desk in the office and gobbled it down.

Sitting at a desk made me think of my librarian job back in D.C. I loved my work but had been itching for a change. That's why I'd taken on my undercover work and even after that, for several years, I'd spent more and more time wishing to travel. I weighed the commuting and stress of life in Washington, D.C., against the peaceful beauty of Penniman and the chance to spend more time with Dad. This was my chance to make a change—for good. I took a deep breath and called my supervisor at the library.

The conversation wasn't comfortable, but we worked it out. She didn't want to lose me, but I gave notice and asked her to send the paperwork. As I hung up, I felt lighter than I had in years.

Just then, I heard a harsh grinding noise. Caroline shouted, "Help!"

I darted into the workroom. In a repeat of yesterday's disaster, ice cream mixture spilled from the machine as Caroline hit the unresponsive on/off button on the chute. I slung a tub toward her, then yanked the power cord.

"Thanks. Look, it's not chilling properly either." Caroline swirled the runny vanilla mixture in the tub.

"I hope it's under warranty." Back to the Rolodex, where I found the number for the ice cream supply company. They promised to send a repairman tomorrow between nine and five.

Thanks for narrowing that down. I bit my tongue.

With four days until the festival, they'd better be able to fix the machine. Nothing I could do about it now. I had to focus on something I could control.

I remembered Buzzy's note on the calendar. Darwin had promised baby goats for the petting pen on Sunday afternoon. I needed some animals for Saturday, the biggest day of the festival.

I flipped through the cards of Buzzy's Rolodex and phoned Magic Minis. "I'd like to see if I can book some of your ponies for this Saturday afternoon, please?"

A woman's voice rasped, "They're not ponies. They're miniature horses."

"I stand corrected."

"Hold please, I'll check the schedule." She put me on hold and came back a few seconds later. "Lady Mirabelle and Bob can squeeze you in from two to four in the afternoon."

"Perfect."

Good thing Lady Mirabelle and Bob could stay for only two hours because the price she quoted made my toes curl.

I remembered that Caroline had mentioned a Facebook page for the shop. I opened Buzzy's laptop and realized I didn't know her password. I flipped through the Rolodex. On a card labeled Password, I found "ABC123." Good grief.

The shop's social media needed updating. I found some photos of Lady Mirabelle and Bob and posted them to our page, and before I signed off had ten Likes.

I walked into the deep freezer to check inventory. We were low on so many flavors.

Everything would be okay if I could get the machine fixed on time . . . and if we made ice cream nonstop between now and the festival. I took a deep breath, the chilled air adding another uncomfortable jolt.

I needed more staff, especially staff that would work for free. Pru said interns from the farm would work the counter during the festival, but I didn't trust them to make ice cream. Did I know someone who was a good cook and might work for free?

Paulette. My Stepford stepmother. I started to call her but considered. This favor was best asked in person, with my dad nearby. She'd say no to me, but not in front of Dad.

I told Caroline my plans to see Angelica and Paulette, then go to the land trust meeting. She nodded. "We're fine here and don't worry, I'll go check on Rocky at dinnertime."

I stepped outside into a warm, sunny, perfect afternoon. The parking lot was full. Cheerful crowds thronged rows of sunflowers taking pictures, enjoying the views across the rolling hills, and gathered around the farm stand where the interns sold organic herbs and vegetables.

As I headed up the hill I saw Flo at the stand buying a quart of tomatoes, and I hurried over to her.

"Flo, did the police question you about the night of Mike's murder?"

"Yes, they came to the house. Donna's too." At my puzzled look, she said, "Donna Danforth." *Ah, yes, Dandy.* "But none of us saw anything that night. We all go to bed early."

"What about Aaron the Hermit?"

She shrugged. "Don't see him much, only driving by or when he walks his dachshund, McGillicuddy. But we'd have heard if the police had arrested him."

Pru waved me over to the kitchen garden.

"What is it, Pru?"

"Darwin's back," she whispered. "The police let him go."

I gave her a hug. "I'm so glad. What happened?"

She turned worried eyes toward the red barn behind the house. "He wouldn't say much. He's fixing the tractor down in the barn."

"I'm going to talk to him," I said.

Just then my phone buzzed. Caroline. "I just heard that Darwin's back. Is it true?"

"Yes, but—"

Caroline hung up, and moments later she ran from the shop. When she reached us, she was out of breath and holding her side.

Pru put a hand on Caroline's shoulder. "Are you okay?"

"Just out of shape." Caroline dashed ahead. I ran after her and easily caught up. We stopped at the entrance to the barn where Darwin bent over a tractor engine.

Caroline caught her breath. "Darwin."

Part of me wondered how truthful Darwin would be with Caroline.

His blue cotton shirt was open at the collar and he brushed sweat off his forehead as he faced us. "I guess you heard where I've been."

I looked to Caroline, and she nodded. This was now about the two of them.

"Someone told the police that they'd seen me up at the Love Nest. It's true. I—" He walked over to us, wiping his hands on a rag, his voice soft. "I'm sorry, Caroline, sorry I didn't talk to you. I was so angry about Mike wanting to develop the farm.

"I swear I didn't see Mike that night. I never opened the door to the Love Nest and I never went into the barn. But someone driving by saw me leaving." He flung the rag to the ground and folded his arms. "I know how bad it makes me look." His forearms bulged with muscle. I couldn't help but flash to the pitchfork used to kill Mike, how easily I'd seen Darwin yield one, how strong farm work had made him.

"Do you remember the kind of car?" I said.

He shook his head and gave me a wry smile. "You sound like the cops, Riley."

"I watch too many TV shows." I tried to keep my tone light, but my mind reeled. Means. Motive. Opportunity. Darwin had all three.

My heart constricted as I considered all he had to lose: twenty years of work on the farm, twenty years building the internship program. Everything.

Something inside me shifted. Pru's confusion and sadness were so palpable, so naked. They'd been married so long. If Darwin had killed Mike, would she cover for him?

"I believe you, Darwin. I know you'd never hurt Mike." Caroline gave him a hug. Darwin's face crumpled as he fought for control of his emotions. He patted Caroline's back and managed to whisper, "Thank you, Caroline."

I lowered my eyes, hoping they wouldn't notice my apprehension. Caroline might've decided Darwin was innocent, but I was sure the police still considered him a suspect.

Chapter 18

Caroline returned to the shop and I dashed up the hill to the farmhouse, composing my face, willing myself to show Willow none of the tangled emotions Darwin's words had evoked. I found her sitting cross-legged on the kitchen floor, dangling a toy mouse for Rocky to stalk. Sprinkles sprawled on a plush sheepskin-covered cat bed, watching.

Rocky pounced on the toy, but his little paws slipped on the linoleum floor and he tumbled. He righted himself and went right back at the toy.

"The mighty hunter." I said.

"I love this little guy. I'm sorry I have to go." With a sigh, Willow set down the toy, sprang to her feet, and gathered her things.

"Thank you so much for watching them, Willow."

"I'll cat sit any time." Willow headed to the door but stopped with her hand on the knob. "Though Sprinkles is getting weird. She keeps meowing at the toilet. See you tomorrow!" She waved and dashed down the stairs.

My smile faded as I imagined Willow's distress when she found out her dad had been questioned by the police. Poor kid.

The thought of Darwin in jail, what it would do to Willow and Pru, was too much to contemplate.

I dug into one of the boxes of my old stuff and found a plain white T-shirt and a pale green cotton cardigan. Blues and greens were good colors for me—they worked with my black hair and green eyes. This was lucky because I'd gone through an Irish phase when I was in high school and had a lot of green sweaters.

I dug up a pair of travel pants that were still presentable, barely, and brushed my hair.

In the mudroom, I found a litter box set up for Rocky. I corralled him in with it and closed the door. "Sorry little guy. It's just until Caroline gets home."

As I drove Town Road to the hospital, I considered Darwin and Angelica as suspects. I shook my head and set aside Darwin, mostly because it hurt too much to think of him in jail.

One detail kept tugging at my mind. The crumpled note I'd found in the kitchen, the one talking about the "usual place." Angelica'd seen Mike flirting with Emily at the funeral. Emily had passed her business card to Mike—could she have also slipped him that note? The note had been crumpled, but it looked like it had been folded. I shook my head. The paper was eight and a half by eleven—so big I would've noticed Emily slip it to Mike. Still, she could've left it in the Love Nest some time while we were working in the shop, or when Angelica and Mike had come to the farmhouse.

Maybe finding that note had set Angelica off. Her deep red lipstick certainly hinted at passion. I didn't follow tennis, but you had to be driven to compete at the professional level. She was a woman who'd take matters into her own hands and was certainly strong enough to wield that pitchfork.

The scenario made sense. Why didn't I want to believe it?

When I asked to see Angelica at the hospital welcome desk, the receptionist and her coworker exchanged glances.

"I'm the one who found her," I said, hoping that would carry some weight. "Riley Rhodes."

She scanned a list. "I don't see that name here. We've had a lot of people claiming to be the person who found her. Some newscasters tried it ten minutes ago. Sorry, no visitors."

Drat. I got in my Mustang and revved its engine. How could I get in to see Angelica? Paulette materialized. She'd been a nurse. Maybe she had connections with her nurse friends that could get me in.

My stomach growled. I needed some vegetables to counteract all the ice cream I'd been eating. I pulled into the parking lot of a small vegetarian bistro near the hospital where I made myself eat a salad then I headed to the green and the Preserve Penniman meeting.

How unusual this little town was, how different from the cities I'd lived in. How many places had a town green? Some kids and a golden retriever chased a soccer ball on the lush grass as their parents watched from a bench near the memorial to Penniman's war dead.

Across the green, chattering shoppers crowded through the door of The Penniless Reader. My heart glowed. How many happy hours I'd spent there. I longed to join them, chat with Dad, and pick up a used Vicky Bliss paperback for a dollar.

I found a parking space in the lot behind the Town Hall next to the modern wing that housed the community center. Through the windows I saw people gathering in a conference room, a whiteboard at the ready. A woman in a pink dress with a cascade of blond hair brushed it off her face with a swing that tilted her whole upper body. Emily Weinberg. She was chatting with Kyle Aldridge.

My footsteps slowed as I considered their presence at the meeting. Across the green I could see Kyle's law office right next door to Emily's real estate firm. They were next-door neighbors. How cozy.

A black Lincoln Continental squealed into the parking lot. Gerri waved, peering at me over huge, round, white Jackie-O sunglasses.

She angled the Lincoln into a space, then got out and flung her peacock blue scarf over her shoulders. Gerri wore her hair in a dyed-black bouffant, highlighted by jeweled pins. Her clothes were always jewel tones, dramatic and deep like her voice.

"Hi . . ." Though she worked at the shop, I still didn't feel comfortable calling her by her first name.

"Hello, Riley," Gerri said. "I'm glad you're here. I'd originally planned to attend this meeting with Buzzy. Where's Caroline?"

"She's working." I didn't mention that she was still fragile and that I hoped she'd soon be home cuddling with the cats.

Gerri made a noncommittal sound as she popped her sunglasses into her purse. Her deep set black eyes made me think of crows, and I remembered that they're considered the most intelligent of birds. She walked with a cane topped with a silver eagle head. Despite the cane and her broad-shouldered build, Gerri moved quickly.

I opened the door for her.

"Thank you, dear. Let's move so we can get a seat." We followed the sound of conversation to a door at the far end of the hallway. A sign next to it read "Quarterly Planning Commission—Public Comments."

A podium was set up at the front of the room and most of the forty or so seats were full. As we entered, Gerri acknowledged murmured greetings with a regal tilt of her head.

Emily and Kyle spoke together at the front of the room and when she saw me, Emily's eyebrows popped up. Gerri and I took seats in the last row. There was only one empty seat left, directly in front of Gerri.

When my bottom hit the metal folding chair, uncomfortable and hard as it was, I felt myself relax. I hadn't realized how tired I was. I wasn't the only one. The man in front of me started to breathe deeply, his breath droning into a snore.

Gerri jabbed his shoulder with her cane and the man jerked upright.

Not wanting to suffer the same fate, I straightened my back. A woman handed out small paper cups of coffee and I took one with a grateful smile. Gerri waved it off and made notes with a fountain pen in a leather journal.

The head of the Planning Commission announced that much of the information to be discussed tonight was also available on the town website. I resolved to read it when I was more awake and allowed my attention to shift to the crowd. It was evenly divided between locals on the side of keeping things the way they were, some wearing Preserve Penniman pins, and on the other side many in expensive business attire—those in favor of the development.

"Time for public comment," the head of planning said. "Mrs. Hunt, I believe you signed up to speak first."

Gerri didn't go to the podium. She stood and waited for the room to quiet. People had to turn to see her, and I wondered if this was some public-speaking trick to keep the audience on its toes.

"Thank you." Deep rolling vowels reminded everyone that she'd taught the elocution portion of the high school public-speaking class. "Let us be mindful of the myriad reasons we love Penniman. Why you developers want to build here. I will not stand by as the land I love is defiled! It's desirable exactly for the things that will be destroyed under the treads of the rapacious bulldozer of greed."

There was passionate applause from our side of the room as she resumed her seat. A voice called, "You tell 'em, Gerri."

The head of planning turned to Emily. "You're next, Ms. Weinberg."

"Thank you." Emily gave him a smile. "I represent Penniman Properties and the Preserve at Fairweather Farms."

"What a pretentious name for a development." Gerri sniffed.

"Preservation is right there in the name." Emily clicked a button on a laptop and a map of Penniman appeared on the board behind her. "Development and history can coexist in harmony. Careful, thoughtful, re-spectful development can meld the needs of the present with the desire to preserve the past."

The snorer nodded. Gerri jabbed his shoulder.

"Kyle will tell you more," Emily said, stepping to the side.

Kyle rose, buttoning his jacket as he did. "Preserva-tion," he said. "That's why our plan is so perfect."

Our plan. I knew it.

Kyle continued. "You don't want some developer rolling in here, one who doesn't have skin in the game, who doesn't have history here. My family's been here for over one hundred years. As some of you know, I was working on this with Mike Spooner." He pressed a button on the computer and the image onscreen changed to a map of Fairweather Farm.

Fury built in me. Mike had suggested that Buzzy use Kyle for her lawyer. Talk about a conflict of interest.

At Mike's name, sympathetic murmurs filled the room. "Mike was all for it," Kyle said. "The plan preserves so much of what we love of Penniman. Even Mike's mom was in favor of the plan—"

Gerri whacked her stick on the back of the empty metal chair, just missing the man in front of us, and the sound rang like a bell. She used the cane to lever herself to her feet. "Balderdash! How dare you put words in Buzzy's mouth! She was not in favor of this plan. I won't stand for this benighted dog-and-pony show." She whipped her scarf over her shoulder, whispered "excuse me, dear" to me, and marched out of the room.

I watched her go, my mouth open. A man in the back clapped with a slow, sarcastic motion. I narrowed my eyes at him. He wouldn't have dared do that with Gerri in the room.

"Well, now that we're all awake," Kyle said. "We know how dramatic Mrs. Hunt gets." Kyle chuckled and there was some nervous laughter, but it died quickly.

There were a few other speakers, but I hardly registered what they said. I was too busy thinking how angry and hurt Caroline would be when she found out Mike and his best friend not only planned to move ahead with the Preserve at Fairweather Farms, but that Kyle was telling everyone Buzzy had been in favor of it. Before I knew it, the head of planning adjourned the meeting and I headed for the door.

Emily ran after me. "Riley, can I talk to you for a minute?"

Impatience rose in me, and wariness. I didn't trust

this woman. At first I'd thought she was just one of Mike's old girlfriends carrying a torch, but now that I knew she was working on the real estate deal? This was no flighty flirt. Mike was gone, but the deal was still in play. That's why she'd come to the house and had the nerve to give Caroline her card in that bouquet of sympathy flowers.

"How's Caroline?" Emily said in a soft, warm tone.

I kept walking.

Seeing that approach wouldn't work, she raised her hands and jogged after me. "Listen, I'm so sorry about Mike. Turned out that his firm was working with mine here on the development. I didn't find out until after, you know. Do you think Caroline would mind if I came over to talk to her?"

"She has your card," I called over my shoulder. "She'll call you if she's interested." *Which will never happen.*

I pushed through the crowd leaving the building and got in the Mustang. What a mess. So many lies. I took a deep calming breath and turned the key. I'd go visit Dad. He always put me in a better mood.

The engine purred to life and once more I realized that I really had to return this expensive rental. If only I didn't love driving it so much. I'd have to ask Caroline if the police had given her the okay to get Buzzy's car out of the barn.

I drove around the green and swung into a space in front of The Penniless Reader.

As I stepped into the welcoming atmosphere of the familiar shop, I felt my tension ebb. The sweet mustiness of old books mingled with the aroma of coffee. Two readers enjoyed cups of the rich brew Dad preferred in overstuffed chairs next to the fireplace where a fire crackled all winter. Now the fireplace was filled with a dried arrangement of golden sunflowers and purple coneflowers. The shop felt like home. I even laughed for the thousandth time at the sign my dad had hung over an old wall phone mounted by the coffee maker: Call Your Mother.

"Come to do some shelving, Riley?" Dad joked but his eyes were full of concern. "What's happening at the farm? How's Caroline?"

I filled him in. When I mentioned Darwin being questioned by police, his eyebrows shot up over the slightly bent metal frames of his glasses. "I know Jack Voelker's a by-the-book guy, but Darwin Brightwood's as guilty as I am." He shook his head. "Everyone's talking about Angelica Miguel—"

"That she's guilty as sin." Paulette bustled over and set a stack of cookbooks on the counter.

"Hi, Paulette," I said. "Actually, I'm going to the hospital to see her."

Paulette read me right away and pursed her lips. "Well, if she wants to see you, your name will be on a list of approved visitors at the front desk." Her expression said, *That will never happen.*

I took a deep breath. One favor would be all I'd get tonight. I smiled at Dad then turned the smile to Paulette. "I was wondering, Paulette, if you had time, if you'd like to come over to the shop for a few hours and help make ice cream. You're such a good cook." *Flattery never hurt.*

Dad could read me too. "Should be quiet here Thursday evening. I bet you'd have a lot of fun making ice cream."

Paulette beamed at Dad. "Of course. I'll come by Thursday. Six o'clock, though usually at that time I'm fixing Nate his gourmet meal, but it's for a good cause." She patted Dad's arm. "You'll have to settle for leftovers, honey."

Chalk one up for love. "Perfect. Thanks!"

Chapter 19

Back at the house, I took a moment to stand on the porch, enjoy the view, and just breathe. Buzzy's property rolled softly to the dying crimson sunset like a gold and green quilt on an unmade bed. Acres were bright now with sunflowers and just over the ridge, apple and peach trees grew, white with petals in the spring, leaves russet in the fall. The scene embodied a kind of peace that was so rare, that sank into my bones.

No way I'd let Kyle and Emily spoil this view.

The lavender gingham curtain twitched by the window. Sprinkles and Rocky watched as I went inside and picked my way through a minefield of stuffed cat toys.

The aroma of pizza scented the air and my stomach growled. "It smells divine in here." I swooped up Rocky and nuzzled him under my chin while Sprinkles trotted to her food bowl. Rocky struggled and I set him on the floor, where he immediately pounced on the toy mice.

"Pizza from Supreme—half-veggie, half-pepperoni." Caroline smiled down at Rocky and popped the cork on a bottle of red wine. "Rocky let me give him a bath. He's into everything but he's easy to feed. Sprinkles is so fussy she won't eat anything that doesn't come in a pretty can with an enormous price tag." Sprinkles raised her head from her dish and shot a hurt look.

Caroline poured me a glass of the wine as I sat at the table and took a slice of pepperoni. "How was the meeting?"

I savored a bite and took a sip of wine. "Tell me about the shop first. Everything okay?" I didn't want to spoil the meal by telling her what I'd learned. We enjoyed a couple of slices and glasses of wine while we watched Rocky play.

Maybe it was exhaustion or the wine, but when I told Caroline what I'd learned at the meeting, she took the news calmly.

"Gerri made a speech," I said. "You should've seen her."

Caroline smiled. "She's a character."

Rocky wove around my ankles and I lifted him to my lap. He purred and let me stroke his soft fur.

"I made some decisions about Mike's memorial," Caroline said. "A lot of his football buddies and fraternity brothers have reached out to me. I'll have a gathering in the fall at the frat house in Willimantic." She swirled the wine in her glass and her voice took on a casual tone. "Detective Voelker said you can use Buzzy's car."

"Good." I smiled to myself. Other people would probably tense at the mention of law enforcement, but Caroline relaxed whenever she said the detective's name.

"Flo said she'd drive up with you to turn in your rental. Sad to say goodbye to your Mustang?" she teased.

Trading a sports car for a rusty forty-year-old station wagon? The pizza and wine made me philosophical. "All good things." We clinked wine glasses.

As I brushed my teeth before bed, Rocky watched with that disconcerting feline detachment that made me feel I was the subject of an anthropological study. He watched me put my toothbrush in the glass and switch off the light, then he trotted into Buzzy's bedroom instead of mine.

"Wait a minute. You're not sleeping with me?" Rocky glanced back at me, then yawned. "Really? You're choosing Sprinkles over me? Sure, she wanted you in, but I'm the one who opened the door. And I feed you!"

I couldn't imagine Sprinkles sharing the royal bed. Rocky sauntered past Sprinkles' bed to a box lined with a piece of cozy sheepskin and cat toys. Willow must've made it for him when she was cat sitting. I sighed. I never stood a chance.

But then Rocky jumped up onto a footstool and clawed himself onto Buzzy's bed. So Willow's bed wasn't good enough either. He circled, the sound of his nails on the fabric making me wince, then he settled. He looked at me and blinked. I was dismissed.

"Darn cat. Okay. Good night. You know where to find me."

Neither Caroline nor I closed our bedroom doors all the way. She left hers ajar so Sprinkles could visit; I kept mine ajar so I could hear Caroline. Now I hoped Rocky would visit.

I went into my bedroom, changed, kicked aside a pile of dirty laundry, and flopped into bed, making the old box springs creak. I was so tired I felt my bones become one with the mattress. Finally, I mustered the strength to raise my arm and turn off the light. Tomorrow was going to be a long day. A lot of ice cream had to be made, and I planned to try again to visit Angelica at the hospital.

Caroline believed that Darwin was innocent, and so did my dad. Both were excellent judges of character. But why was Pru so upset? Didn't she believe her own husband? Or was there another reason for her worry?

A sound by my door, softer than a whisper, drew my attention to a shadow moving to the bed. Glowing eyes reflected starlight from the window as Rocky climbed onto my bed and curled up next to me. I stroked his soft fur as I drifted off.

I recalled Darwin's words: *"The cat came out of the darkness."* Seemed likely Rocky was an eyewitness to Mike's murder. If only he could tell me what he'd seen.

Chapter 20

When I entered the ice cream shop kitchen on Wednesday morning, Flo and Gerri were already there doing prep work. The broken chiller sat idle. Caroline was up at the house, where she'd be on a conference call for work all morning.

It was shaping up to be a perfect day for ice cream: low humidity, temperatures predicted to be in the low eighties, not a cloud in the robin's-egg blue sky. My stomach lurched as I looked at the flavor board. There were chalky smudges where so many flavors had been erased.

Flo hummed as she sliced fresh strawberries. "You won't believe what happened last night, Riley! I should've called you but I was too . . . entranced, too . . ."

"High on your rodeo Romeo?" Gerri gave her sister an indulgent smile, put on a purple apron over an orange tunic with matching scarves and necklaces, and started a batch of caramel sauce. The apron was printed with a cow wearing a beret and the word "cone-oisseur."

"Oh, I'm not going to lie, I was. And I think I still am," Flo said. "Riley, Cadillac Ranch brought his guitar and he serenaded us as we cleaned up."

"Cadillac Ranch?" Did Flo have a nickname for everyone? "The good looking guy with the cowboy hat?"

"Handsome and so talented," Flo sighed.

"So he comes in here and flirts with you, serenades you, and doesn't tell you his name?" I said.

Flo's cheeks pinked. "His name's Jasper Yeaton. Isn't that perfect? He's a painter, staying at the artists' colony at Moy Mull for some classes. He's getting away from it all in order to recharge his artistic batteries."

A musician and artist. I didn't think it possible, but now the man was even more attractive.

I looked at the schedule. Buzzy had been pretty relaxed about scheduling. It looked like she let people sign up for whatever shift fit their schedules. No one had set hours. I sighed. Somehow it had worked for her, but I really liked schedules.

Flo and Gerri were scheduled for the morning. Pru and Caroline were coming in the afternoon. The repairman was supposed to arrive sometime between nine and five. I'd have to wait for a quiet spell to visit Angelica.

Words Detective Voelker had spoken surfaced in my mind. *The only people who went down to the house where Angelica had been found were partying kids and prospective buyers.* Real estate. Was the house where I'd found Angelica a clue to who murdered Mike? Though it didn't fit into my scenario for what had happened with Angelica the night of Mike's murder, a quick bit of internet sleuthing wouldn't hurt.

"Ladies," I said, "I'll be in the office for a few minutes."

I opened Buzzy's practically brand-new laptop and did a search of Penniman real estate listings. The house near the lake was listed with Evergreen Realty, not Penniman Properties. Putting on my researcher hat, I dove into tax records. The house had been owned by the same family since 1900—the Larkins. I closed the laptop and went back into the kitchen.

"Do either of you know the Larkin family?"

"You mean the people who own the house where Angelica was found?" Flo said.

Inwardly, I laughed. I should've just asked Gerri and Flo. They knew everything about everyone in Penniman.

"Good people," Gerri said. "House has been empty since Ruth Larkin died five years ago, wouldn't you say, Flo?"

"Yes, I think that's right."

"There was only one distant relative, a nephew," Gerri said. "He's listed the property at an ungodly price and he's letting it sit there and crumble until someone pays his princely sum."

"Did the family have any connection to Mike, Angelica, or the farm?" I asked.

Gerri shook her head and Flo said, "I don't think so."

A dead end.

Gerri poured the fragrant caramel sauce, the color of a bright copper penny, into a stainless steel warmer, then we went to the front of the shop. Flo unlocked the front door as a red sedan pulled into the lot. She held the door wide and greeted the driver, a slim Black guy in a preppy plaid button-down shirt and dark-wash jeans.

"Good morning," he said. "I'm looking for Riley Rhodes."

"Hi, I'm Riley."

"I'm Jay Cannon, one of Angelica Miguel's assistants," he said. "She'd like to speak with you, if possible. Would you have an hour to go see her? I'm here to drive you."

Flo and Gerri didn't even pretend to not listen. They looked from the preppy guy to me.

Did I want to talk to Angelica? Absolutely. I turned to the sisters.

"Go, go." Their eyes were avid as I read their minds: *Come back and tell us everything.*

"Would you like some ice cream, Jay?" Flo said.

Jay smiled and shook his head. "Not now, thank you."

"Take some for Angelica! When she was here she told me her favorite was Rocky Road." Flo packed a large cup as Gerri pursed her magenta lips with disapproval—another vote for Angelica's guilt.

I assessed the situation. Was this too good to be true? Really, what were the chances I'd be kidnapped by a handsome guy who claimed to work for Angelica Miguel, and offering to take me exactly where I wanted to go?

I removed my apron and handed it to Gerri, took the packed ice cream from Flo, and followed Jay.

As Jay opened the door of the red compact car, he read my mind. "Unfortunately, Angelica's Porsche was totaled in the accident."

"How is she?" I said as I settled in the passenger seat.

Jay closed my door then got in and pulled onto Fairweather Road. To my surprise he headed away from Penniman, away from the hospital. My guard flew up. *Riley, you got into a car with a total stranger! This was too good to be true!* I readied myself to open the door and roll out at the next stop sign. I took a breath to steady my voice. "We're not going to the hospital?"

"Angelica's not at the hospital anymore," Jay said. "She's out of ICU. Too many reporters were trying to sneak in and get photos. She's at Farrow."

I leaned back in my seat and observed Jay. He held the wheel lightly and looked like he was enjoying the scenery. *Relax, Riley. Sometimes people are exactly what they claim to be.*

I'd heard of Farrow, a pricey private rehabilitation institute, but had never been there. The place had its own helicopter pad. Occasionally, there would a celebrity sighting of one of its clients in Penniman village, at my dad's bookshop, or one of the more upscale restaurants and boutiques.

"Angelica's in a private cottage," Jay said. "The security at Farrow's much better than at the hospital."

Jay drove through ivy-covered stone pillars topped with lanterns into a narrow driveway—there was no sign. We stopped in front of a crossbar at an imposing gatehouse. Jay waved and the guard let us through. As we passed, I could see that the gatehouse bristled with high-tech cameras, screens, and communications equipment. We went up a steep drive that opened onto a manicured lawn and parked in front of an ivy-covered gray stone building with two wings. The building would've been at home on the campus of any classic New England college.

Jay jumped out and opened my door. "This way please." I followed him along a paved path behind the building into the woods to a brown, cedar-shingled cottage. Angelica sat on its patio in a wheelchair, one leg extended in a cast. She looked up from a magazine as we approached.

"Riley. Thanks for coming." Angelica's words were slurred as she reached out her hands and took them in mine. "Sorry if I'm hard to understand. My jaw was pretty banged up in the accident."

I didn't know if this woman was a killer or not, but her battered face shocked me. The left side was mottled with bruises from her collarbone to her forehead and both eyes were circled with purple. I tried to keep my expression neutral as Jay held a chair for me at her side.

"I know, I'm a mess." Angelica winced as she settled

herself. "It'll be a long road back, but I lived through an accident the docs said should've killed me." Her lashes lowered and her voice trembled. "Riley, if you hadn't found me when you did, they said I wouldn't have made it. Thank you."

Jay set a tray with a crystal carafe of lemonade on the table between us.

I didn't know what to say. I squeezed her hand again. The words "Did you kill Mike Spooner" were stuck in my throat. Instead of speaking, I handed her the cup of ice cream.

She laughed. "Flo remembered! Have some with me, Riley." She waved for Jay. "You have to try this, Jay. It beats anything in the city."

Jay took the ice cream into the cottage and returned with two bowls. He set them on the table and then faded back to a chair on the edge of the patio.

Angelica took a bite. "Oh, this is so good. The hospital food was awful."

I took a bite of ice cream, taking stock of her injuries. "What do the doctors say?"

Her shoulders sagged and she winced again. "Cracked ribs, my leg's a mess, but I'll mend." Her jaw tightened and I saw a flash of the will that had made her a champion. "I hit my head, so my memory's fuzzy. Riley, how did you find me? How did you know where I'd crashed my car?"

I didn't tell her I was imagining where a scared or unhinged killer had gone. "I was out jogging. It's not far from the farm." I told her about skating on the pond when I was a child. "I went there with Caroline and Mike," I lied. Mike hadn't ever gone with us, but I wanted to turn the conversation to him.

Her eyes shimmered with tears. "You have to believe me. I really cared for Mike. I still can't believe this happened. What does Caroline think? Does she blame me? Does she hate me because Mike died and not me?"

"No! She doesn't know what to think." I had to be direct. "What happened that night, Angelica?"

Angelica called to Jay. "Jay, please go inside. I'll be fine with Riley."

Jay hesitated for a moment, then headed inside, giving the woods around the patio a quick scan before he shut the door.

"Jay's part assistant, part bodyguard. He's a great guy." Angelica's voice softened. "So was Mike."

I kept my expression neutral. My opinion of Mike was more mixed.

"Mike and I met a few months ago. I was doing an appearance at a resort Mike's company built in upstate New York. We clicked right away. Usually I don't move that fast, but I went sailing with him the following weekend. It was Memorial Day and he took me to Block Island, showed me all the funny little lighthouses on the way there. On the way, the weather was rough. I got very seasick, and he took care of me."

She took a shallow breath. "This is going to sound odd, but I had so much fun with Mike the day of the funeral. I loved working in the ice cream shop and he told me so much about Buzzy, and Caroline, and you, Riley, how you're Caroline's best friend and how you travel all over the world. He was so proud of you and Caroline."

Hearing this was unbearable. I shifted in my seat. Mike sounded like a nice guy. It hurt that he was nice only to people far from Penniman.

Angelica rubbed her forehead. "But I knew something was going on with the farmer."

"Darwin."

She nodded. "Mike had big plans for the farm. He knew that Buzzy couldn't run it anymore. He wanted to be sure she was financially secure." This chipped away at my frozen heart, but I knew Buzzy would rather be penniless and keep her farm than have money and lose it.

"The financials weren't good for the farm," Angelica continued. "Mike said that Buzzy was disorganized and was making bad decisions."

I shifted uncomfortably. Hadn't I heard this from Wilmer and Kyle? Why hadn't Caroline known? Because Buzzy told her everything was fine. Mike and Kyle dug into Buzzy's financial situation without including Caroline.

Angelica reached for her glass of lemonade. I held it out to her and she took a sip. "Thanks."

She fell back against the cushions. She was tiring but I kept her talking. Fatigue makes it harder for liars to keep their stories straight. "So that night . . ." I prompted.

"I went back to the Love Nest before Mike but didn't go in until he got there. It was a nice night and I sat on the porch catching up on phone messages. When he came back we went inside.

"This is where it gets fuzzy." Her brow furrowed. "We drank some wine. I started getting a headache. I saw a paper crumpled on the floor by the trash. I looked at it when I picked it up to throw it away and Mike, I don't think he wanted me to see it. It said something about meeting him at midnight.

"I knew he'd played the field in the past. He'd been honest with me about that. But I thought we had something. I was furious but also—disconnected. So angry, but tired . . ." Her voice trailed off. "He'd really let me in, introduced me to his family, and then it turned out he was meeting another woman."

Angelica pulled the collar of her robe tight, and I noticed her knuckles were bruised. "He told me the note was nothing. It was from a long time ago, before he knew me." Her eyelids fluttered. "No, that's not right, sorry, that wine really hit me—I know I shouldn't have gotten in the car. But I got in the car and drove and then everything turned black."

My skin prickled. Leaves rustled in the woods behind me, then a branch snapped. I rose to my feet as the cottage door burst open and Jay ran out full speed, another man close behind him. They dashed into the woods.

A woman in a nurse's uniform hurried from the house. "Let me take you inside, Ms. Miguel." She undid the brake on Angelica's wheelchair and rolled her into the cottage.

"What's going on?" I scanned the woods where the two bodyguards had run. I could hear shouting and just make out two figures cutting through the trees ahead of Jay.

"More vultures with cameras," the nurse said. "Let's get some rest, Ms. Miguel."

"Riley, come back later," Angelica whispered.

I followed them into a combination dining room/kitchenette.

"Please wait here," the nurse said. She wheeled Angelica down the hallway and I turned to the window.

More shouts came from the woods, but I couldn't see anyone. The nurse returned and said, "I've called a driver to take you home."

Ten minutes later, a driver pulled up in a white sedan and I got in. As we pulled between the stone gates, I saw a News Now SUV parked in the trees off the road. Jay and the other bodyguard were escorting two men, one with a camera, to the vehicle.

Reporters had bushwhacked into the woods to find

Angelica. I hoped they hadn't overheard any of our conversation or taken any pictures.

I let my head fall back against the padded headrest and closed my eyes. It had been so much easier to see Mike as the self-centered jock he'd been in high school. Was it my loyalty to Caroline that was blinding me to Mike's good qualities? Angelica had seen a different side of him. Of course, all of Mike's girlfriends did. He was charming, attractive, caring too, if her story about her seasickness was true. Maybe he'd grown up.

But her story about the night he died. . . . Was any of that true?

The part about the note—that was true—I'd seen it myself. But had Angelica really run away before Mike was killed? Or had she and Mike had a fight that took them into the barn and then escalated into murder?

Chapter 21

When the driver dropped me back at Udderly, I was more confused than ever but I had no time to think about what Angelica had said. A line stretched from the door into the parking lot.

I ran in, washed my hands, and threw on an apron. For the next few hours I scooped ice cream, built sundaes and banana splits, and made milkshakes nonstop. Flo heard my stomach rumble and mixed me a chocolate milkshake that I sipped when I could. I could tell Flo and Gerri were dying to hear what Angelica told me, but we didn't have a spare minute. It was all hands on deck.

With every swipe of the eraser on the flavors board, my anxiety rose. I had gallons of ice cream to make. When would that repairman get here? It was almost two o'clock. I vowed to learn how to fix an ice-cream chiller.

"We're out of cookies and cream. There may be a riot," Flo said.

The shop's old wall air conditioner droned, but still I wiped sweat from my brow as I baked the chocolate chip cookies for the cookies-and-cream recipe. On one side of the room was the dormant ice-cream chiller and a worktable, on the other was a stove, a double wall oven, a regular refrigerator, and a prep sink. Pantry shelves ran along the hall facing the large walk-in freezers where we stored the ice cream as it hardened to the right consistency. Ice cream was all about keeping the product cold, and Buzzy's electric bills proved it.

A half hour later, a cheer burst from the shop. Flo led the repairman into the kitchen and struck a Vanna White pose. "He's here!"

His cheeks reddened behind his bushy black beard as he blushed at the welcome. He was slight with tattooed arms, a keychain swinging from the pocket of his jeans, and Tony embroidered on the pocket of his shirt.

"Thank goodness you're here." I showed him the problem and he set to work. As I pulled a tray of cookies out of the oven, he sniffed appreciatively and I set aside a plate for him.

"Thank you," he said. "I need a part, but luckily I have one in the truck."

A few moments later he was back, fitting the new part and running the machine. "Should be fine now. Here's the invoice."

The cost made me gulp. "It wasn't under warranty?" I said.

"Just expired."

"Thanks," I squeaked. "Can I pay later?"

"We'll bill you. Thanks for the cookies." He waved as he left.

Caroline came into the kitchen balancing a tinfoil covered tray. "I brought you some leftover pizza. Sorry my meeting went over."

I grabbed a slice. I was dying to tell Caroline about my interview with Angelica.

Pru joined us and gave me a tired smile as she switched places with Flo. Flo took a piece of pizza and said, "I heard you want to return your rental car. I'll take you as soon as I finish this."

"Thank you, Flo." I pulled Pru aside. "Are you okay?"

She shrugged and forced a smile. "The police have been interviewing us since, you know. Everyone. All the interns. They're digging." She bit her lip. She didn't have to tell me what they were digging for—evidence against Darwin.

Caroline gave me the key to Sadie then Flo followed me to the airport in Hartford in her cute yellow compact car. At the car rental, I bid the Mustang a wistful goodbye. With longing, I watched a plane roar into the sky. How permanent would my move be? I'd cut ties with work. So many changes, so fast. *Get through the summer; heck, Riley, just get through the Sunflower Festival.*

Flo and I talked about Angelica on the drive back from the airport.

"Everyone's saying she can buy her way off with all the money she has," Flo said as she gunned onto the highway and cut off a semi. "Everyone's saying she killed Mike in a fit of passion, but I don't buy it. She was a good girl. I could tell." Flo drove like a bat out of hell, but seemed a good judge of character.

I gripped my seat belt. "She liked you too."

"Some people have good hearts, even if they don't look that way on the outside."

I remembered the customer Flo called Stretch, the contradiction between his ragged clothes and manicured hands, his expensive watch and dirty cap, and the way people stood clear of him. "That guy, Stretch. What do you know about him?"

"Boy, does he love ice cream. I call him the cone-noisseur." She chuckled. "He's been coming in since just before Buzzy passed. He never talks about himself, but he talks about ice cream in detail, always asking us about things like fat content and flavorings."

"Has he mentioned where he lives?" I squeezed my eyes shut as Flo took the exit ramp at double the speed limit.

She shook her head. "It's been too busy in the shop to have a real conversation."

I wondered where Stretch was now.

Chapter 22

Flo parked next to Mike's car at the Love Nest. Yellow police tape sagged across the doors of the Nest and the barn.

"Are you okay going in there, Riley?" Flo said softly.

"I think so." We got out of the car and walked to the far end of the barn. I swung open the doors (unlocked, of course) revealing Sadie, Buzzy's 1970s era VW station wagon. I took stock. The orange paint was faded and rust spotted the finish, though the tires looked new.

Flo jutted her chin toward the other end of the barn. "That's where you found Mike?"

"By the hay bales in the stall by the door," I said.

Flo skirted Buzzy's car, walked through the darkened barn and into a shaft of light streaming in through the stall window. She folded her hands and bowed her head. I hesitated, then joined her. After a few moments, Flo looked up, her eyebrows knitted together. "Who do you think killed Mike?"

I shook my head, not wanting to go into my suspicions. "I don't know."

"We all know the police talked to Darwin." Flo turned and we edged past Buzzy's car out of the barn.

"But almost everyone who lives on Farm Lane was against Mike's development plan. Me, Dandy, Gerri, the Brightwoods, all the kids on the farm. Aaron the Hermit, who knows? Construction would destroy the views. Nobody wants all these new houses popping up." She gave me a rueful smile. "I know, what do they say? First-world problems."

I had a momentary vision of all the neighbors trapping Mike in the barn. Would any of them kill Mike to stop the development?

"Well, Mike's murder won't stop people from wanting to develop this land." I remembered what Kyle and Emily said at the Preserve Penniman meeting. With Mike gone, so was any pressure he'd put on Caroline to sell. It was all Caroline's property now. No wonder Emily wanted to represent her.

"I remember talking to Buzzy about the land trust . . ." Flo's voice faded.

Emily. She'd dated Mike. Mike used to meet high school girlfriends in the barn. "The usual place," I whispered.

"Did you say something, Riley?" Flo said.

Could Emily have done it? She'd been upset seeing Mike with Angelica. Was she jealous and upset enough to kill him?

I shook my head. "Sorry, I'm a little distracted."

"It's okay, honey. We'll talk later." Flo patted my arm then got in her car and drove off.

The cops had to talk to Emily Weinberg. Was she even one of their suspects?

Sadie's door opened with a creak of complaint. I eased into the sagging driver's seat and turned with dismay to look in the back. The backseat, the passenger seat, it was all full of stuff.

Sheesh. Buzzy had definite hoarder tendencies. The

back seat was piled with cardboard boxes. On the passenger seat was a stack of books with Penniman Library stickers on their spines, many cozy mysteries with cats on the cover. I made a mental note to return them.

The arm of a handknit white cardigan sweater trailed from under the books. Carefully, I pulled it out. Buzzy had knit many sweaters, always with pockets. I held the soft fabric to my cheek then folded it on top of the books.

I turned the key, wondering if the car would even start. The engine coughed a few times but sprang to life. I heaved a sigh of relief as I pulled out and stopped. As I jumped out to shut the barn doors behind me, dust motes danced in the beam of sunlight streaming into the stall.

I was dying to talk to Emily Weinberg, but I had to make ice cream. How did the amateur sleuths in the mysteries Buzzy read always have time to investigate and interview suspects? Listen to me—as if I were the investigator. I'd call Detective Voelker and tell him about Emily. Sleuthing was his job, not mine.

Still, with my background, I loved nothing more than digging to find the answers to tough questions. My librarian instincts were piqued. This was the toughest question I'd ever encountered. It mattered. Someone had killed my friend's brother and was still out there. The police were focusing on Angelica and Darwin, but I just couldn't buy it.

Listen to yourself, Riley. Just because you like someone, doesn't mean they're innocent.

I'd learned that the hard way in Rome with Paolo.

I drove down the lane and parked Buzzy's car by the kitchen door. The clothesline fluttered with laundry and I recognized my Washington Capitals shirt and another I'd bought in Italy.

Inside on the kitchen table was a note from Caroline that said "I caught Rocky peeing on your pj's so I threw everything in the wash."

Rocky slunk in and blinked at me. "Thanks a lot, Rocky." I picked him up for a quick nuzzle but he was not having it. He went boneless and slipped from my arms. He leapt onto the table by the window and swished his tail, glancing back at me expectantly.

How well cats communicate without words. I stood behind him looking out over the farm. It had been his playground, his home, and now he was indoors, his metaphorical wings clipped. I'd have to let him out to explore, but my heart twisted every time I saw the scar on his back, his bent little ear. It was a big, bad world. Rocky was a survivor, but I wasn't ready to let him out just yet.

Sprinkles sat by the powder-room door, flicking her tail. I sighed and flushed for her, hoping she wouldn't teach Rocky that trick.

I ran upstairs and picked up Detective Voelker's business card. A jolt of adrenaline made my hand shake as I dialed. Why was I so nervous? *Because you're a secretive woman who doesn't want anyone prying into your life.*

It was almost six o'clock. Would he still be at work?

"Penniman Police."

I recognized Tillie O'Malley's voice.

"I'd like to speak to Detective Voelker, please."

"He's in a meeting," Tillie replied.

I almost lost my nerve. I knew how law enforcement felt about amateurs sticking their noses into investigations. "Hi, Tillie. This is Riley Rhodes at Fairweather Farm. I'd like to speak to him when he has a moment."

"About?" She drew out the vowels. She knew what it was about.

"Mike Spooner's"—the next word stuck in my throat—"death."

"What would you like to report?" she whispered. "May I take a detailed message?"

I rolled my eyes. "Tillie, you know this stuff is confidential. I'll tell Detective Voelker."

"Fine." She took my name and number, then hung up abruptly.

I hurried downstairs and out the front door. Cars jockeyed into the parking lot as I ran to Udderly.

The Gravers stepped out the back door as I entered.

"Hot date?" I said.

Flo laughed. "I wish."

Gerri said, "Tonight we're teaching a class on genealogy at the Historical Society."

"Have fun, ladies." I went inside and checked the work schedule. Caroline, Brandon, Pru, and I were on tonight. Four people. Thank goodness.

Caroline ran into the kitchen. "I just saw Pru. She had to leave. She has a baby coming."

Three people would have to do.

A horn blared from the parking lot as customers jammed into the shop. "How about calling in some interns from the farm so we can make ice cream?" I asked. Now that the chiller was fixed, I didn't want it sitting idle.

Caroline shook her head. "Darwin, Pru, and all the interns are being honored tonight at Town Hall. The farm won the Penniman Prize for fostering relationships in the international farming community. Pru's going to miss it unless that baby hurries up."

We were slammed with customers, and a few grumbled when they learned their favorite flavor had run out, but everyone eventually left happy. Who wouldn't be happy with a three-scoop maple walnut sundae drizzled with the shop's special warm salted-caramel sauce and covered in fresh whipped cream and a sprinkling of finely chopped walnuts? Or a crisp waffle cone stuffed with mint chocolate chip ice cream full of chunks of bittersweet chocolate? After Brandon went home at closing, slurping a cone stuffed with six different flavors he called The Game of Cones, Caroline and I kept working, cooking different ice cream and sorbet mixtures, the scent of lemon, lavender, caramel, and cinnamon filling the shop kitchen. I told her everything about my conversation with Angelica.

"I like her," was all she said.

At two a.m., Caroline and I headed back to the house.

Neither of us had the energy to eat. I went up to my bedroom, tossed my phone on the bedside table, and reached for the oversized Washington Capitals shirt I wore to bed. Darn! It was hanging on the line with the other laundry. I flopped onto the bed, too tired to go down and get it.

Rocky followed me into the bedroom and sniffed where the pile of laundry had been. I knew exactly what he was thinking.

"No!" I leapt from bed, picked him up, and ran for the litter box.

Chapter 23

The next morning, I woke to a tickling under my nose. As I pried my eyes open, Rocky's tail whipped across my face.

"Good morning to you too." I sat up and looked at my phone. Dead. I'd forgotten to charge it. As I plugged it in, the time flashed: 9:00.

"Time to make the ice cream," I groaned. Rocky looked out the window with the unnerving focus that cats have, then he turned back to me with a little yowl. His meaning was clear. Get up, lazy human. I have important things to do.

"Five more minutes, you beast." With a groan, I rolled over and closed my eyes.

Thud. Crash.

I sat up. Rocky had climbed onto the bookcase. He sat very still, held my eye, reached out a paw, and knocked another photo off the shelf.

"Rocky!"

Undeterred, he slid onto the bureau and knocked my hairbrush onto the photos. I scrambled as he started to nuzzle a lamp.

"All right, I'm up." I grabbed him and set him on

the floor. He sauntered away from me with a dismissive swish of his tail. "You've been spending too much time with Sprinkles."

Caroline stuck her head in the door. "What's all the noise?"

"Rocky decided it was time for me to get up." I looked for something to wear, then realized most of my things were on the clothesline. "Thank you for doing laundry."

She nodded. "That naughty little beast was busy yesterday." She scooped Rocky up and nuzzled him. "Weren't you, cutie pie?"

Rocky looked back at me as if to say, *Look what you're missing! If you were quicker to obey, you'd get to nuzzle me.* Sprinkles came in and wove around Caroline's ankles with a purr.

"I'll start breakfast," Caroline said, and they all headed downstairs.

Chopped liver. That was me.

I picked up my brush and ran it through my hair a few times then stacked the photos back on the shelf, stopping at one of Mike and Kyle sitting in a Mustang, Kyle holding up keys, squinting in the sun. I sighed, still envious. I remembered that car, Kyle's eighteenth-birthday present. It helped to have an uncle who owned a car dealership. I ran downstairs where Caroline was breaking eggs into a bowl.

"I'm going to pull in the clothes." Tucking the basket on my hip, feeling like a real farm wife, I went out to the clothesline and looked out at the waving fields of sunflowers. Already people were moving through the fields taking photos, enjoying the relative cool of the morning air.

I folded a pink top and placed it in the basket. The color made me think of Emily Weinberg. *Meet me at midnight. The usual place.*

Had Emily left that note? Had she gone to the barn to meet Mike? That would be pretty nervy, with his girlfriend right there, but they'd exchanged business cards, had each other's numbers. Emily could've slipped in; Mike and Angelica left the Love Nest twice that night, once to help in the shop, once when we gathered in Buzzy's kitchen. But why a note? Maybe Emily'd worried Angelica would see a message on Mike's phone.

A black police SUV pulled up in front of the house and Detective Voelker got out carrying a small paper bag. Tillie must've given him my message. I hadn't been entirely sure she would—from what I'd seen, the words "Tillie" and "professional" didn't belong in the same sentence.

I picked up the basket and went to meet him. I wasn't at my best—no shower, still in yesterday's clothes, and no breakfast. My hand flew to my hair. At least I'd brushed it.

"Good morning, Detective."

"Good morning, Ms. Rhodes. I've been trying to return your call."

"I'm sorry, my phone battery died. I was so busy making ice cream yesterday I forgot to charge it." I went up the steps. "Please come in."

Caroline stood at the screen door, smoothing her hair. "Good morning." As she opened the door, Rocky shot out.

"Rocky, no!" I yelled.

Sprinkles stood at the open doorway and gave a plaintive yowl but Rocky streaked across the road and disappeared into the field of sunflowers.

"Oh, no! I should've known he'd try to get out," Caroline moaned. "I'm so sorry!"

"They always come back at dinnertime." Voelker said.

My heart fell as Rocky disappeared. "I hope so."

Voelker took off his sunglasses and smiled at Caroline, his expression and voice gentle. "How are you doing, Miss Spooner?"

"Fine, thanks," she said. "Please call me Caroline."

Is this a social call? Who was he here to see? Me or Caroline?

"You'll have to excuse us," he said. "I need to talk to Ms. Rhodes."

"Call me Riley," I said, but I was sure he wouldn't. Caroline got the smile and the charm. "Caroline can hear anything I say."

Sprinkles didn't move, so we all edged around her. Her head swiveled between Voelker and the porch, where her buddy had just escaped. I almost felt sorry for her. I could imagine her thoughts. *Ingrate! How could you leave after all I've done for you?*

Leaving Sprinkles pining at the door, Voelker and I sat at the kitchen table while Caroline took mugs from the cabinet. There was a steaming pan of scrambled eggs and toast on the counter.

"I'm sorry to interrupt your breakfast," he said.

Would Rocky come back? I'd lost my appetite. "They'll keep."

"Coffee?" Caroline said as she covered the eggs. I shook my head, too anxious to drink anything.

"Thank you." Detective Voelker accepted a cup and took out a notepad as Caroline slid into a seat next to me. "Ms. Rhodes, you called."

"Yes—"

Caroline jumped in. "We've been busy, making ice cream, well, not making ice cream until yesterday. We'll have our special sunflower ice cream for the festival."

"Sunflower? I'll have to try it," he said.

Can I get a word in? "I've heard that an anonymous source told you Darwin Brightwood had been seen near the—" I almost said crime scene—"barn. I think I know who that person is."

"We can't divulge the identity of our sources, Ms. Rhodes," Voelker said.

I leaned forward. "So you know who it is?"

Voelker rubbed his hand across his forehead. "I, we—"

"Emily Weinberg," I said. "She was at the funeral and she and Mike were flirting. Maybe she was mad that Mike was seeing Angelica. Emily dated Mike in high school, right, Caroline?"

Caroline nodded.

"Do you think she carried a torch for, how long would you say it was that Mike and she graduated from high school, fifteen, twenty years?" He sipped his coffee and for the first time he looked at me with something other than his professional stone face. Was he trying to hide a smile?

"She has a small car," I persisted. "A Mini. Darwin said a small car passed him that night."

Voelker set down his mug. I could read his thoughts. *A lot of people have small cars.*

"This is serious," I said. "You have to question her."

"We'll look at everyone connected to the crime." He hesitated but then wrote Emily's name in his notebook. *Good.* He looked at Caroline. "Again, I'm sorry for your loss."

Caroline lowered her eyes and nodded. I wondered what would've happened if I hadn't been there. There was so much chemistry sparking between these two I could practically feel the heat.

He cleared his throat. "We'll also have autopsy

results as soon as possible and then we'll be able to release the body." *Maybe not so romantic, Voelker.* "Was there anything else, Ms. Rhodes?"

I shook my head. He flipped his notepad closed and set the bag on the table. "These are a few of your brother's effects."

Quiet settled on the kitchen. I craned to look inside the bag as Caroline opened it, and saw a ring, a cell phone, and car keys.

Voelker's phone buzzed and he looked at the screen. "Excuse me, I have to go." We all stood and headed for the door, where Sprinkles was still moping. She hissed, and the detective stepped carefully around her. "Have a good day."

Caroline waved as he got into his SUV and drove down the lane.

"I hope you're not falling for a man who might arrest me for wasting police time," I said.

Caroline rolled her eyes at me but smiled. We returned to the kitchen and her smile faded as she looked toward the bag of Mike's things. "What do I do with these?"

I pulled out the items one by one. "His class ring, keys to his car . . ."

"Maybe you can drive his car instead of Buzzy's," Caroline said.

It was a nice car, but I knew I'd never feel comfortable driving it. "I'll stick with Sadie."

Caroline picked up the phone and I wondered if the police were able to access its contents. I remembered that anything found at the scene of a crime is evidence that the police could use. How I wished I knew what they'd found.

She pressed ON and the screen brightened.

"It's locked," Caroline said. Her eyes met mine and I knew she was thinking the same thing I was. For years, we'd played Mike's computer games whenever he wasn't home. His password hadn't been hard to guess—his high school football team and the number one.

Had he kept the same password all these years? "Bobcat one?" I said.

Caroline put it in and the screen unlocked. Together we bent our heads over the phone. "Let's look at his pictures. . . ." She hesitated then handed the phone to me. "You do it."

I swiped through the photos. Most were of the farm, probably taken to include in his real estate sale brochure. I swiped back further and stopped at a photo of Angelica on a sailboat, silhouetted against a cloudy gray sky, hunched in a sweatshirt. She did look green around the gills, just as she'd told me earlier about their trip. Going through the photos was like replaying a film in reverse. Angelica and Mike traveled back across the Sound to a charming seafront hotel on Block Island I recognized from a bike trip there a few years earlier.

I swiped again, and there was a selfie of Kyle and Mike on a golf course, then shots of a magnificent seaside home. I wondered if they'd stayed there or if it was a property Mike had planned to list. In another photo, taken on a restaurant patio, Angelica raised a glass to a spectacular sunset. Another hand, a woman's, held a drink in the frame. I flicked through and didn't see any photos of Nina.

"Look at that," Caroline said. "Can you make the photo of Nina's hand bigger?"

I expanded the photo of the women toasting the sunset.

Caroline pointed at Nina's diamond watch. "I saw a watch like that once at an auction. Very pricey."

It looked pricey. "Kyle must be doing well to buy that for her."

Caroline took the phone, placed everything back in the bag, and put it on the counter next to the TV, then cleared Voelker's empty coffee cup from the table. A small smile softened her features.

"Let's eat those eggs," I said. "When you're done mooning over that cop, we have ice cream to make."

Chapter 24

After a quick breakfast, a shower, and blessedly clean clothes, Caroline and I hurried down the lane to Udderly. Pru waved from the farm stand.

"Mom and baby okay?" I called.

She held her hands shoulder-width apart. "Big boy. Nine pounds! Mom was a trooper."

Once inside the kitchen, I pulled down the schedule clipboard. Scheduling was one thing I'd definitely change. "Who's on the schedule this morning? Oh. One intern. And us. All day. Every day. Through eternity."

Pru burst in, her colorful paisley-print skirt twirling, her hair tied back with a red bandanna. "I forgot to ask if you're ready for strawberries. The hands picked them this morning."

"Yes!"

Caroline carried a five-pound bag of sunflower seeds from the pantry. "Did the baby keep you up late?"

"Nope, he came fast. Surprised mama and me for sure," she smiled. "I was in time for the ceremony at Town Hall."

"Congratulations. I wish I could've been there," I said.

"Me too," Caroline said. "It's a wonderful honor."

"It was so good to see Darwin recognized for his work with the interns. He's been going full throttle, trying to keep his mind occupied." Pru's smile faded. "He's waiting for the other shoe to drop. He's not sure if the police are through with him."

We reassured her, but still her eyes were troubled.

"You don't want to miss the ice cream making party tonight," I said. "Everyone wants to come. Even Paulette'll be here."

"Paulette?" Pru's eyebrows flew up. "Well, well. Red-letter day."

A little furry black head peeked in the screen door of the kitchen. "Rocky!"

As I approached the door, Rocky turned tail and scampered off. I looked down on the steps to see a dead field mouse—well, more accurately, half a field mouse. "Ugh."

Pru and Caroline joined me at the door. "Ah, a present! He loves you!" Pru teased.

After clearing away Rocky's love offering and giving thanks that the health inspector wasn't there to see me do it, I washed up, switched places with Caroline, and took over making the sunflower ice cream. I couldn't help but dip in a spoon to sneak a taste of the creamy vanilla ice cream with honey and caramel set off by the salty, nutty crunch of sunflower seeds. Delicious.

The screen door in the kitchen swung open.

"The cavalry has arrived," Flo said. "I brought you lunch." She handed me a tray with sandwiches and a pint of ruby red strawberries, then pointed toward the door. "You two have to take a break. Go sit outside at that picnic table and eat, and I mean it."

"I'm afraid if I sit down I won't be able to get back up again," I said.

But we did as Flo told us and dug into turkey sandwiches with thick slices of tomato and lettuce, then devoured the sweet, just-picked strawberries. The food, the warmth of the sun, and the view worked together as a mini vacation. Caroline looked as relaxed as I felt.

A black sports car rolled up Farm Lane to the house. I shaded my eyes and watched Kyle get out and carry a cardboard carton to the porch.

Did lawyers make house calls? My cynical self thought, *They do if the client is sitting on several million dollars' worth of real estate.*

"I'd better see what Kyle wants." Caroline walked up the hill, smoothing her apron—her nervous tell. I gathered our trash and went back into the kitchen.

Flo joined me as Pru brought in an enormous flat of strawberries. "Picked this morning. Darwin had some of the hands wash them." Pru had removed the bandanna and now her hair was pulled back in a tidy ponytail that showed off sparkling silver earrings. "I saw Caroline go up the hill. Is she okay?" Pru asked.

"Kyle Aldridge brought her some things from Mike's condo." I washed my hands, grabbed a cutting board and knife, and started prepping the strawberries.

"His dad was a good man, God rest him." Flo poured batter into the waffle iron.

"Sorry, I have to run." Pru waved as she left.

Flo said, "Pru's going to a memorial luncheon for her friend Martha Woodley. She and all the area midwives do it every year."

I looked up from the cutting board. "Who's Martha Woodley?"

"She was practically a mother to Pru. Trained her to be a midwife," Flo tsked. "Killed in a hit-and-run and the police never caught who did it. What a sad summer that was. It was the same summer Brooke Danforth died."

Brooke, Dandy's daughter. "I remember. Caroline and I were away at camp, but that's all people were talking about when we came home."

"So sad," Flo sighed. "She took an accidental overdose of sleeping pills."

I searched my memory. "She had bulimia."

"Yes, her eating disorder may have contributed to her death. She was a tiny thing. What a sad time." Flo brought the freshly made cones to the front of the shop while I continued to slice strawberries, my mind turning over memories of that summer. I certainly hadn't moved in the same circles as Brooke, a popular cheerleader, but I remembered the shock I'd felt when I learned of her death.

Twenty minutes later, Caroline returned.

"What did Kyle want?" I said.

Caroline shrugged and washed her hands. "Same spiel about selling the farm, the great opportunity. He gave me a box of papers and mail from Mike's condo. I keep forgetting that he and Mike were such good friends. Remind me to send him that photo of them from their trip to Block Island." She squared her shoulders and repositioned her glasses. "There's too much to think about. I need to stay busy."

"No trouble with that."

Caroline went to the counter as I continued to prep berries. My thoughts shifted to Detective Voelker. I hoped he'd take my tip seriously and get to work investigating Emily.

I was convinced Emily had gone to see Mike the night of the murder. She had a distinctive small car. I wondered if Emily had used an untraceable burner phone to make her anonymous tip. She'd probably called the police department's general, nonemergency number. I knew someone who answered the phone at the police department. If I was lucky, the same person had answered the anonymous tipster's call.

Loose Lips Tillie O'Malley.

At six o'clock, Paulette swept into the shop, her hair pulled into a high bun that showcased her elegant jawline and diamond earrings. Leave it to Paulette to wear diamonds to make ice cream on a farm.

Flo gave her an apron printed with exercising cows and the words "Mooove It."

Paulette pinched it between her fingers. "Funny." She smiled gamely and put it on over her designer jeans and white linen tunic.

Once I walked her through the ice cream-making process, from the *Book of Spells* to the chiller to the freezer, Paulette dove in, measuring and moving with confidence. You only had to show Paulette how to do something once. I actually warmed to her.

Flo and Gerri insisted on staying after closing to bake peanut brittle, chocolate chip cookies, and brownie mix-ins as Paulette whipped through several more batches of sunflower ice cream. Caroline, Willow, and I sliced strawberries, stirred custard, hauled tubs of ice cream to the freezer, washed bowls and equipment, and mopped and cleaned.

"So, Willow," Paulette said. "Are you going to college next year?"

"I'm taking a couple of gap years to work and save money," Willow said as she wiped down the table. "I want to go to art school."

"I love what you do with our chalkboards," I said.

We all bumped into each other in the small space, but we laughed, and joked, and filled the freezer with enough ice cream to get us through the weekend. Paulette charmed everyone, and to my surprise she offered to come back and help another time. "I had so much fun," she said.

I think she meant it.

When Caroline and I returned to the house, Sprinkles and Rocky were sitting in the kitchen, Sprinkles mewling pitifully next to her empty bowl, Rocky peeking out from a cardboard box on the kitchen floor. Papers were scattered everywhere.

"Rocky!" Caroline and I scrambled to pick up the papers and stack them on the table.

"I fed you guys before I left," Caroline said. Without being commanded, I flushed for Sprinkles and poured a bit more food in Rocky's bowl.

"So Rocky came back when you were here with Kyle?" I said.

Caroline shook her head. "He must've snuck in when I opened the door to let Kyle in."

"You missed me, right?" I nuzzled Rocky. He purred for a bit, then slid from my arms and went to the window. I put on the kettle and made tea. Rocky remained at his perch, alert, his tail swishing back and forth.

"I think he's longing for his old life," I said. "I'm tying him down."

Caroline bent her head and said in a small voice, "Riley, that's how I feel—like I'm tying *you* down."

"Oh, Caroline! Don't be silly." I took a deep breath. It would feel good to tell someone the truth about the disaster in Rome. "Sit down."

Sprinkles stalked back from the powder room and mewed. Caroline picked her up and stroked her long, silky fur.

"Caroline, when I was in Rome . . . Remember I told you I met a guy?"

"Yes, Paolo," she said. "The guy you said looked like a model. He worked at the embassy, right?"

"In the IT department." I took a deep breath. "Turns out, he was a thief. An antiquities thief."

Caroline's eyes widened.

I told her the whole story, leaving out the part about my undercover work. "I'd fallen for him. And he used me."

"Oh, Riley!" She squeezed my hand.

My throat closed up, but I swallowed my tears. I wasn't crying over him anymore.

"Thank goodness they had him on camera, because otherwise the embassy might've thought *I'd* stolen the statue." Paolo had disarmed a security camera, unaware that there were two in my office. "The statue was small but very valuable. Even though I was innocent of the theft, it tarnished my reputation. Now everyone thinks I'm a foolish woman who let her heart get in the way of good sense."

"Riley, I'm so sorry!" Caroline said in a small voice. "About work and about . . . everything."

"It's okay," I said. "Being here, running the shop, it's been good to have something new to do so I can re-group. Well, there you have my sad story."

"I'm really sorry, Riley." She put her arm around me and I rested my head briefly on her shoulder.

"I have Rocky now and Sprinkles, right?" I went to

pet Sprinkles and she hissed. "Sweet." My eyes fell on the cardboard box. "Anything important in there?"

Caroline looked at the gathered mail. "Not really. I'm not sure why Kyle bothered."

"Bills?" I said.

She handed the stack to me. "All Mike's bills were paid electronically. Kyle's going to send me a report."

I flipped through a sailing magazine and three brochures from art colleges. "Was your brother going back to school?"

"Not that I know of," Caroline said. "It wouldn't be for art. He had no interest at all."

I sorted envelopes. "Junk mail. Family Finder? That's the company that helps you find your ancestry through DNA? Was Mike interested in genealogy?" I handed her the envelope.

"Not in the slightest." Caroline tore it open. "I mean, we were adopted and there's no way he'd want to link up with our biological parents." I didn't ask for an explanation. I knew the years before foster care and adoption had been difficult.

"That's odd." Caroline read, "'More results will be sent via email.'" She handed a paper to me and I scanned it.

I saw why she was confused. The results were for Elizabeth Spooner. "Was Mike helping Buzzy with her ancestry?"

She shrugged. "No idea. And more results via email? Have you seen a computer in this house? Buzzy didn't even have a cell phone. I mean, I got her one, but she never even turned it on."

"There's a laptop in her office. I've used it."

"Mike bought it for her for Christmas. He set it up for her but she never touched it."

I read the results, which listed several nationalities and ethnicities.

"No surprises," Caroline said as she returned the papers to the box. "Buzzy always said she was one-hundred-percent American mutt. I should toss all these papers, but . . ." Her lips turned down.

"I understand."

She stood and stretched. "Well, I'm off to bed. Or maybe I'll paint a bit."

"Sounds good."

Rocky padded down the hallway and Sprinkles jumped down to follow him.

I boiled some hot water to warm up my tea, turned off the lights, then poked my head into the parlor.

Sprinkles and Rocky sat erect on the back of the sofa, looking out the window with uncanny attention. A feeling of foreboding kindled as I came up behind them. "What's so interesting, you two?"

A tiny spark of light flickered up the lane. It was across Farm Lane to the west, close to the old Fairweather family cemetery, instead of behind the barn to the east like the other night. Still, the fire burned close to a field of parched sunflowers. *Too close.* "Not again! Caroline! Fire! Call nine-one-one!" I shouted.

Caroline pounded down the stairs.

My tea sloshed as I set it on the table. I ran out the door, pushing the screen door so hard it banged against the house.

My footsteps pelted on the lane and then sank into the softer earth of the paths through the sunflowers. Years ago I could have run through these paths blindfolded, directly to the opening in the stone wall that ringed the cemetery. Now I thrashed through the sunflowers hoping I was going in the right direction.

"Riley!" Caroline panted behind me. "I called nine-one-one! They're coming. Wait!"

I slowed. Caroline was right. What was I going to do? I had no firefighting equipment. Still, I had to see who was setting these fires.

Frustration surged in me as I pushed through the sunflowers, trying to find a direct path to the cemetery. Their heads nodded gently, unconcerned that their dried leaves tore at my arms, that the darkness disoriented me.

"Riley, wait for me!" Caroline continued to call behind me. I stopped, breathing heavily, and caught the aroma of cooked garlic and mushrooms.

A siren wailed behind us and tires crunched gravel as I crept closer through the sunflowers, following the scent. As I reached the wall, a shadowy, angular figure shrugged a backpack onto its shoulders and cut away into the woods that hemmed the cemetery.

"Stop!" I shouted, but the figure disappeared into the trees. Was it Stretch? There wasn't enough light to tell.

Heavy footsteps pounded toward us and a bright flashlight beam dazzled my eyes.

"Police! You two, stop!"

It took me a moment to realize the police were talking to Caroline and me. Voelker rushed into the clearing and played his flashlight over a campsite and the surrounding trees. A fire burned low in a cleared ring of stones and dirt, and a skillet was set on top of a grate over the fire.

"We're the ones who called. He went that way." I pointed and headed off.

Voelker grabbed my arm as two officers jogged through the graveyard and were swallowed up in the shadows of the tree line. "Let the officers do it."

Adrenaline pumping, I shook off his hold. "I can catch him."

"Let the officers do it." Voelker's voice was quiet, but his tone brooked no argument.

I swallowed my irritation and turned my attention to the campsite. "Is it just me or does it smell really good here?"

"It does." Caroline came up behind me and clutched my arm.

My heart rate slowed. The fire had been built by a camper making dinner. Again.

The crimson lights of a fire engine swirled around us as it pulled up on Farm Lane. Two firefighters pushed through to the cemetery and conferred with Voelker.

I turned my attention back to the campfire. The site was immaculate, the grate set on a neat pile of rocks, all debris cleared away. A mound of dirt was set to one side, at the ready to put on any stray embers.

"It's creepy thinking of someone camping up here in the graveyard." Caroline, clad in flannel pajama bottoms and a T-shirt, hugged her arms.

One of the officers returned, panting. "Lost him, sir."

"Probably just some Scout doing some camping," Voelker said.

A firefighter said, "Not a good idea with how dry it's been, but this guy looks like he knew what he was doing. We'll put it out."

Voelker turned to Caroline and said, "I'll have someone drive by a few times tonight, make sure everything's okay." He threw me a hard look, evidently wondering how such a nice girl like Caroline had such a loose cannon for a friend.

The second cop returned, and bent over, hands on knees, sucking wind. "He's gone."

I bit my tongue. I could've run faster and might've caught the guy. I shook it off and made a point of thanking the firefighters and police officers.

Voelker turned to us. "Best you go home." It wasn't a suggestion.

Caroline tugged my arm. "Come on, Riley."

Chapter 25

The next morning, I rose early and jogged back to the clearing in the cemetery. I picked my way through the headstones, looking for clues, trying to remember which way the camper had run.

I threw my thoughts back to high school, those years before Caroline and I had driver's licenses, when we'd been content exploring myriad paths in the woods around the farm. The camper had had his choice of escape routes through acres of rolling farmland and forest.

Parts of the land on this side of Farm Lane belonged to the Danforths and part to the Gravers, er, Fairweathers. I didn't know where the property lines were. Everyone had coexisted amicably, and the families represented in the cemetery had intermarried for years.

The sound of a distant lawnmower accompanied me as I took the path that led to the small pond, scanning the ground as I ran, searching for any trace of the camper. I found nothing and returned to the cemetery.

The shade of towering old oaks and massive stands of laurel provided a respite from the gathering heat. Most of the stones in the cemetery were weathered and covered with green lichen, so worn that any names on them were illegible. Except for one. I picked my way closer to a shiny stone of pink granite in the northernmost corner of the cemetery and shivered as I read the words carved on it: "Brooke Danforth. A Rose Barely Bloomed."

The grave was beautifully tended, the headstone flanked by yellow rose bushes that seemed to hold the stone in a protective embrace. Some daisies had been planted recently, the earth around them loose and dark. I brushed away a leaf on top of the highly polished granite.

Approaching footsteps made me turn.

Dandy, dressed in a pristine white Penniman Golf Club top and jeans, emerged from a path behind the headstone. She carried a watering can and a basket of gardening tools, the sinews standing out on her tanned arms. A golf visor held her thick hair in place. Surprised, she stopped short when she saw me.

"Mrs. Danforth. Hello." Here I was, thirty-five years old, still calling her Mrs. Danforth.

She smiled. "Hello, Riley. I didn't expect anyone to be here."

I stepped away from the grave. "Beautiful flowers."

She set down the basket and sprinkled water over the just-planted daisies. "Thank you. My hobby." I wasn't sure if she meant gardening or caring for her daughter's grave. Probably both.

"Did you see the fire last night?" I said.

"What a commotion! I didn't see anything but I did hear someone running through my backyard. Flo told me about the firebug"—her lips turned down—"camping here. Disrespectful. I hope the police put an end to that nonsense."

"Would you mind if I checked your yard?" I asked. "I wonder if the person dropped anything."

She tilted her head. "I didn't notice anything, but

you're welcome to look." I followed Dandy through the laurel to a path that looped from the cemetery, through her backyard and out toward the lane, passing the open doors of an elaborate garden shed that was almost as big as the Love Nest. Inside were gardening tools and shelves of equipment, all organized and immaculate. A lawnmower was parked next to it, the scent of gasoline and newly cut grass telling me she'd just been mowing.

My eyes widened as we went into her backyard, a lush paradise of flowering trees and beds at odds with Dandy's outward no-frills appearance and no-nonsense personality. Water trickled into a koi pond under a flowering pergola. Wrought-iron furniture with striped pink pillows decorated a stone patio. "Your yard's beautiful."

A smile lit her face. "Thank you."

I walked quickly through the yard, scanning the ground, feeling more and more ridiculous, until I skirted along the back of the house. I saw a piece of dark canvas by the roots of a boxwood.

I picked it up, my heart thudding with excitement.

"You found something!" Dandy exclaimed.

The thick black canvas was rolled, heavy, and its contents shifted as I set it on Dandy's picnic table. I unrolled it, revealing a set of knives, ranging in size from a butcher knife to a small paring knife, all with dangerously sharp edges.

Dandy looked over my shoulder. "That's a gourmet set. Very pricey."

"I should take it to the police." I could pump Tillie while I was at the station.

"Nonsense. Don't you watch *NCIS*? They'll want to see it *in situ*. Come in and get a drink of water. You must stay hydrated in this heat."

Maybe she was right. "Thanks."

"I think this is important," Dandy said as we stepped

into her kitchen. "What if this fire bug had something to do with Mike's death?"

The thought stopped me in my tracks. I'd thought of the person in the woods—well to be honest, Stretch—as a camper, a drifter. "Firebug" put a different spin on him.

What if the firebug murdered Mike? What if he'd seen Mike's and Angelica's expensive cars? What if he'd been sleeping in the barn? Maybe Mike surprised him and he lashed out. My stomach turned. Was it that simple, that awful?

The roll of knives was heavy in my hands. Here I'd been thinking of the firebug as a camper, as—what did Voelker say?—a Boy Scout. I practically threw the roll onto Dandy's kitchen table.

But the note, I thought. *There was the note*.

Dandy went to the refrigerator and poured a glass of water. "It's a terrible thought, that this stranger was here, so close." Dandy handed me the glass.

"Thank you." As I drank, I read one of those inspirational posters with a sunrise on the wall above her kitchen table: "Perfection is not attainable, but if we chase perfection we can catch excellence."

Dandy picked up her phone. "I'll call the police and let them know. There's a bathroom down the hall if you need it."

"Thank you." The thought of making small talk this early in the morning was not appealing, and finding those knives rattled me. Even though I didn't need it, I went down the hall to the powder room and washed my hands.

As I stepped out of the powder room, I could hear Dandy speaking, but now she was speaking very loudly, almost shouting. "—the fire in the graveyard."

I couldn't make out his words, but I could hear a man's voice answer.

Dandy continued, "We found knives—"

Directly across from me was a bedroom with soft yellow walls and a white canopy bed. Who has a canopy bed anymore? Dandy's and the man's voice faded as the room pulled me in. There were posters of gymnasts and impossibly thin models next to band posters on the walls, bands that had been popular when I was in high school. There was a full-length mirror next to a desk, and on the desk was a vintage computer with a huge monitor. It was probably a valuable collector's item now, but when I was in high school, it had been the latest model. This was Brooke Danforth's bedroom, and it hadn't been changed since she died.

Above the computer, a program for the Penniman High School Players Spring Production of *Brigadoon* was tucked on the shelf with a dried bit of heather. I blinked. I'd painted scenery for that play.

A stack of books drew me. On top was a paperback copy of *Tess of the D'Urbervilles*, a Summer Required Reading sticker on the spine.

My heart rate ticked up. I ran a finger on the desk but there wasn't a bit of dust. Suddenly I was sure that Dandy had kept everything exactly where Brooke had left it when she died.

A Penniman HS gymnastics jacket hung on the back of the desk chair, State Champions embroidered on the sleeve.

On the bed, a pile of silky pillows. There was a denim-covered book on the nightstand, Diary embroidered in yellow stitching on the cover.

There was a sudden silence. The phone call had ended.

"Riley?" Dandy joined me, her face drawn. I'd crossed a line.

"Oh, sorry," I stammered. "I was lost in thought about the guy with the knives. This room faces the backyard." I pointed weakly at the window. "I wonder where he went."

"A real firebug from what Aaron said," Dandy frowned.

She'd been talking to Aaron the Hermit?

She reached past me and shut the door. "We're going to talk to the police outside."

I felt terrible having invaded what she must consider sacred ground. My stomach fell when I realized Brooke would be a woman my age now. The kitchen gleamed with updated appliances, but Brooke's bedroom was frozen in time.

Chapter 26

Dandy and I exited the gate of her white picket fence enclosed front garden as a stocky man emerged from the overgrown yard across the lane. Aaron the Hermit swayed from side to side on sandaled feet as a dachshund waddled behind him on a blue leather leash. Aaron's stringy gray hair was swept over his head in an ineffectual comb-over, and thick dark hair covered tattoos on his beefy forearms. He wore thick metal-framed glasses, and another pair dangled from a leather lanyard around his neck.

I'd heard stories about the Hermit of Penniman and now here he was. I didn't have a preconceived notion of what he'd look like, but I did find his gold necklaces and three heavy gold rings surprising, as was his cute little pet.

Dandy said, "Aaron, this is Riley Rhodes. She's a friend of the Spooners."

The dog whined and Aaron picked it up. "McGillicuddy, say hi to the lady." McGillicuddy had sweet glossy black eyes. A blue bone-shaped tag swung from a matching blue leather collar. Aaron smacked a big kiss on his head and then set him gently down. "Rough business with Mike. I'm sorry about Buzzy. What a great gal."

"She was, thanks," I said.

"How's Caroline holding up?" Aaron asked.

"She's okay. I'm going to help her with the ice cream shop."

"What's that?" He cupped his hand behind his ear.

I repeated what I'd said more loudly.

"That's great," he grinned. "Is that big real estate deal still going through?"

I didn't like the glitter in his deep-set eyes. "No."

"It will. Everyone has a price," Aaron chuckled.

"Have you been contacted about selling your property?" I asked.

Aaron rubbed his finger along his nose. "That's my business."

Before I could ask him more, a police SUV parked on the road next to us and Detective Voelker got out.

"Good morning, Mrs. Danforth." Detective Voelker's eyebrows shot up when he saw me. "Ms. Rhodes. Mr. Tuthill."

So, Aaron the Hermit had a last name.

Aaron said, "I'm going to take McGillicuddy for a little walk."

Dandy led Voelker through the gate and her lush garden of rosebushes into the house. I followed.

In the kitchen, Detective Voelker opened the roll of knives. "You're sure it's from the person camping in the cemetery—"

"Who else's would it be?" Dandy scoffed. "I cleared weeds from that area yesterday and there was nothing there. People don't just traipse through my yard."

"I'll have my team look for footprints," Voelker said.

Oh, great, they'll definitely find mine. Inwardly, I groaned.

I remembered that Gerri and Flo lived next door to Dandy. I wondered if they'd heard anything. I'd ask when they came into work.

We went back through Dandy's front yard and out the gate. Voelker gave me a resigned look, got in his SUV, and took off.

Dandy closed the picket fence gate behind me with a firm click. From here I could see the Love Nest down the road, with Mike's car still parked in front.

Aaron and McGillicuddy hadn't gone far. I'd probably not get another chance to talk to the Hermit of Penniman.

"Aaron, did you see anything the night Mike died?"

"Nope," Aaron said. "Like I told the cops, I feel bad I forgot to turn on my security cameras that night. They don't go as far as the barn anyways. Just here on the road."

He'd forgotten to turn them on the night of Mike's murder? What a disappointment for the cops. Even filming cars coming down the road would've been valuable for their investigation.

I couldn't help but glance into his thickly treed lot. Had I been filmed every time I went for a run? Everyone had cameras. My handlers had taught me to always assume you'll be on video.

McGillicuddy wrapped his leash around Aaron's legs, lunging at something only he could see.

"Wish I had turned them on that night." Aaron scratched his belly and raised his voice. "Quiet night. I walked little McGillicuddy here, but didn't see anything, right, Donna?"

Donna. Dandy's real first name. Dandy was busy deadheading the rose plants in her front yard, and I'd forgotten she was there. She called, "Sorry, I missed what you said."

Aaron continued, "I said I didn't see anything the night Mike died, after McGillicuddy and I went in. I stopped for a chat here with Donna over the fence like we often do around eight o'clock. Then I went in."

"I saw nothing and heard nothing out of the ordinary." Dandy bent to pull a weed. "Most of that night I was in the potting shed behind the garage." She pointed down her long driveway to a weathered freestanding garage, where a blue minivan was parked. "I worked quite late preparing for the Garden Club booth at the Sunflower Festival."

Aaron picked up and nuzzled McGillicuddy. "Sure hope they catch the guy who did it. Or gal. That tennis gal's a looker. Shame if she's the killer."

His thin lips curved in an ugly smile. I said goodbye and ran back home, mulling over what I'd seen. So much bothered me. The way Dandy had turned her daughter's room into a shrine; Aaron's evasiveness when I asked if he considered selling his property; the fact that some drifter was carrying not just one knife but a set of knives. I shuddered thinking of those sharp blades. I'd make sure the door was locked.

After a quick shower I dashed out of the house with an apologetic pat on the head for Rocky. There was so much to prepare for the Sunflower Festival and I had no time to play. I dashed back to secure the door, again shaking my head at the flimsy old lock.

When I got to the shop, Caroline already had the chiller running and a custard cooking on the stove. "When you didn't come home I figured you were here. I was worried!" she said.

I filled her in as I set hot fudge to warm. Her hand crept to her neck and her eyes widened as I described the set of knives I'd found. "Why does someone carry something like that around with them? Is this guy really dangerous, like a serial killer?"

I'd thought the same thing, but resolved to stay cool. I said, "It's just some guy camping." I hesitated, wondering if I should mention Stretch. Was it fair to him that I had pegged him as the camper? But when others called him a firebug, it didn't seem right. He'd seemed a gentle person. I said, "But to be safe, I locked the door."

Her voice faltered. "What if that guy in the cemetery killed Mike?"

"I don't—" I was going to say I didn't think Mike was killed by a stranger, but that was worse. "As far as that camper, I bet this place is too crowded for him. The police are doing the best they can." I gave her a sidelong glance. "Especially the cute guy who's crushing on you."

Caroline hit me in the shoulder with a towel, a smile curving her wide mouth. It was good to see her smile. "I wish we could go into town for the festival on the green."

"Me too. I'd love to go browse the bookshop and visit Dad," I said.

"I insist you take off on Monday," Caroline said.

"We'll see." I wouldn't mind stopping by the police station and chatting up Tillie.

The crowds were steady and festive. A brief shower swept through around three o'clock, but it was soon a memory. I thought of the camper and hoped the rain had given him a good soaking.

So many people asked me about the petting zoo that I found some poster board and markers in Buzzy's office and made a sign to post on the pen outside: "Saturday 2–4 Lady Mirabelle and Bob, The Miniature"—I stopped myself from writing "ponies"—"Horses. Sunday 12–5: Baby Goats." I went outside and taped the sign to the pen.

Flo joined me. "Dandy told me about the knife guy."

Great, now he was "the knife guy." "Don't say that

around Caroline. She's talking about him being a serial killer."

"Probably just someone who wants to enjoy the night air." Flo always looked on the bright side.

"Did you see or hear anything unusual last night?" I asked.

She shook her head. "No. I was watching my shows. I wish I had."

Later, as I mixed another batch of ice cream, I flipped on the TV on the counter. I grimaced when I recognized Tom Snow in front of the Farrow Center.

I wondered if Angelica had any news. She should've been questioned by now. How I longed to know what was happening in the investigation. I checked the schedule. Flo and Gerri were here with Brandon and Caroline. The Farrow Center was only fifteen minutes away.

I pulled off my apron.

Caroline came into the kitchen carrying an empty tub. "What are you doing?"

"Going to speak to Angelica."

She set the tub in the sink. "I'm coming with you."

Chapter 27

There were now two security guards at the entrance to the Farrow Center. A TV reporter was doing a standup at the drive as Sadie chugged past. I expected the media would be here, which was why I'd instructed Caroline to wear a hat and sunglasses. Reporters would be swarming the facility, looking for any angle. I didn't want them to see the sister of the man Angelica may or may not have killed coming to visit. Of course, if the reporters were savvy they'd trace my (Buzzy's, actually) plates. That's why I'd smeared mud on them while waiting for Caroline to get her sunglasses. I might not work for the CIA anymore, but I still had a few tricks up my sleeve.

I'd borrowed one of Buzzy's Red Sox caps. I lowered my sunglasses to speak to the guard. "We'd like to see Miss Miguel, please."

The media swarm had thinned the woman's patience. "Sorry. No one's allowed to see her."

"I'm a friend," I said. "Please call Jay, her assistant."

Caroline took off her sunglasses and leaned toward my window. "Hi!"

The guard leaned toward the car, then smiled. "Oh hi. Caroline, right, from Udderly Delightful?"

"Yes, hi! I recognized you. My friend Riley here's the one who found Angelica and saved her life."

I wasn't sure if it was the connection to the ice cream shop or my role in Angelica's rescue, but the woman made a call and waved us through.

"Ice cream saves the day," I said.

Another security guard waved me into a parking place and accompanied us to Angelica's cottage. "I've seen prisons with less security." I could imagine the security teams patrolling the woods and heard a far-off buzz that I thought might be a drone.

Jay opened the door, smiled, but cast a quick look behind us. "Nice to see you. Come in."

The room was dark, the blinds closed. Our visit had taken Angelica by surprise. Her hair was matted, braided and tossed over one shoulder, and she wore a robe over wrinkled pajamas. She was still in a wheelchair, leg in a cast. Her bruises had yellowed and lightened, but still I felt a jolt of horror at what she'd been through.

Caroline gasped but quickly recovered, extending a quart of rocky road ice cream.

"Caroline! How are you?" Angelica took the ice cream. "Thanks. I needed a bright spot. Jay, please put this in the freezer." He took it into the kitchenette.

Angelica waved to seats. "I know I look like I've gone three or four rounds with the heavyweight champion of the world. And I can't go outside looking like this—well I can't until they get a makeup artist out here. I can't even go on the patio. I don't want pics of me—like this—out there."

"How do you feel?" I asked.

"Stronger. But rehab's hard work."

I couldn't help blurting out, "Have you spoken to the police?"

She took a deep breath. "Yes. The police are building a case against me. They kept asking if Mike and I fought. Then they asked if, I'm sorry, Caroline"—she lowered her eyes—"Mike had ever struck me."

The words hit like a blow, and Caroline recoiled, her hand pressing her chest.

A horrible thought crept into my mind. The bruises were on the left side of Angelica's face. I thought back to Mike throwing a football, something I'd seen him do a thousand times. Mike had been right-handed.

I shook my head, again seeing Mike's face in the barn. He'd had no scratches or bruises, not on his face or his hands. If struck, this athletic, strong, passionate woman would've fought back, I was sure. "Your car crashed and fell onto its left side, the driver's side. That would account for the bruising."

Tears coursed down Caroline's cheeks. No matter what, this was hard for her to hear.

Angelica's eyes welled as she pressed Caroline's hand. "I'm sorry, Caroline, to say things like this in front of you. Of course, Mike never struck me."

Caroline sniffed. "It's okay. I want to know everything."

"One thing they kept asking: Did I take sleeping pills. I don't, never have. Did Mike?"

Caroline shook her head. "I don't know about now, but when he lived at home he always said he slept like a log."

My mind jumped from question to question as I followed this thread. Mike had no defensive wounds. Angelica said she'd had a headache after drinking the wine. Had the killer slipped sleeping pills into the wine bottle?

Caroline and Angelica talked, their voices blurring as I remembered what I'd seen at the Love Nest. I suddenly realized what had bothered me about the wine bottle. I'd seen the trash. I'd seen the bottle and the glasses.

But there'd been no cork.

Mike hadn't opened that bottle of wine. It had been waiting for them.

But who left it?

I pulled myself back to the conversation.

"Angelica, did you see Mike open the wine?"

She shook her head. "I remember him saying how nice it was that Caroline left wine for us and left it open to breathe."

Caroline blanched. "But I didn't leave any wine."

My heart dropped. "Did you tell the police that?"

"Yes," Angelica whispered. Her horrified expression told me that she'd come to the same realization I had. The police would think that Caroline had left the wine.

And her scarf in the barn. . . . I winced. We'd have another visit from Detective Voelker, but it wouldn't be a friendly one.

Chapter 28

Neither Caroline nor I spoke on the drive back to Udderly. I barely saw the road in front of me and had to snap myself to attention when I pulled into Farm Lane, which was jammed with people and cars. I pulled up to the house.

Caroline said, "Riley, what do they say in old movies? I feel the net tightening around me."

"Don't be so dramatic, Caroline," I said, but the words died in my throat. A Penniman police SUV pulled in behind us. Voelker got out and walked up to the passenger window, his eyes hidden behind his mirrored sunglasses. "Miss Spooner, will you please come with me?" he said. Now she was "Miss Spooner."

"I'm coming too," I said, scrambling from the car.

"Not necessary, Ms. Rhodes."

"Detective Voelker"—Caroline's voice was barely a whisper as she got out—"do I need a lawyer? Are you arresting me?"

"No, I'm not arresting you," he said, more gently, as he shut her door. "But you may wish to have a lawyer present while you're questioned."

Caroline looked to me in a panic. "Riley, I don't have a lawyer."

"I'll ask Dad." I knew what she was thinking. Kyle was Mike's friend, but there was no way she'd trust him after learning about his duplicity in the real estate deal.

I felt numb watching Voelker take Caroline away. Heads turned as the police SUV inched through the crowds. Pru ran up to me and put her strong hands on my shoulders. "What happened?"

I told her what Angelica had told the police. "Pru, Caroline needs a lawyer."

"Wasn't Kyle Aldridge just here?" Pru said.

"She wants someone else."

Pru's eyebrows knitted together, then she pulled her phone from her pocket. "I know someone. I delivered her twins. She and her husband are lawyers. I'll call and see if one of them can help Caroline."

The focus of the police investigation had shifted to Caroline. *Voelker's being thorough,* I thought. *You expected this, didn't you?*

Pru squeezed my arm. "Riley, you're pale. Let's get you something to eat and drink. The shop will be fine." She dragged me up the steps of Buzzy's house. I fished in my bag for the key, unlocked the door, and we went into the kitchen. Pru placed some calls as I paced, Rocky at my heels.

"I texted Caroline and told her to expect my friend." Pru brewed tea and gave me some cheese and crackers from the refrigerator as I picked up Rocky and nuzzled him against my chest, glad he allowed me this comfort. Sprinkles sat at the window, surveying the crowd, resigned to the invasion of her kingdom. She always gave Pru space—one queen recognizing another.

I spilled everything that had been happening and Pru's eyes grew wide as she listened. "So Angelica's innocent and was the victim of the same person who put the sleeping pills in the wine?" Pru asked. "Did Caroline take sleeping pills?"

"No. Wait. She told me she took one the night of the funeral." I remembered seeing a bottle in the house. "Buzzy took them." I dashed upstairs, grabbed the bottle from Buzzy's nightstand, and brought it downstairs.

I poured its contents into a dish. "The bottle says twenty pills but there are only ten."

Pru checked the label. "These expired a year ago!"

"I know that and you know that, but everything makes Caroline look guilty."

I paced the dull linoleum floor, Rocky pouncing at my heels thinking my pacing was a game. Caroline's fight with Mike. The wine. The pills. Her—I stopped. I wouldn't mention the scarf to Pru. Why, when I was certain Mike must've picked it up accidentally when he left the kitchen that night?

I remembered the oil painting Caroline had worked on. "Pru, Caroline started a landscape before the funeral. The next day it was almost finished. She couldn't have done that much if she'd been up at the Love Nest." Some alibi. Voelker would never buy it, but I knew my friend was a slow and deliberate painter.

My biggest worry of all was that Caroline had a motive to kill Mike. "The night Mike died, Caroline and he argued. When he left she said, 'I could kill him.'"

Pru squeezed my hand. "Darwin said those exact words, too, and I know he wouldn't have done it either."

The killer wanted to make sure it would be easy to kill Mike by drugging him. That might have ruled out Darwin. I couldn't see him doing something sneaky like poisoning wine.

"My head hurts." I texted Caroline but she didn't answer.

Willow knocked on the doorjamb as she walked in. "Mom, the cash register at the stand isn't working and no one can figure out how to fix it."

Pru stood. "Duty calls. We'll talk when Caroline's back home."

Chapter 29

I fed the cats and gave Rocky a good nuzzle. "Sorry, I have to run."

When I got to Udderly, a line of customers looped around the building. Good. Being insanely busy would keep me from worrying about Caroline.

In the kitchen, Brandon, his ears covered with headphones, bopped at the chiller, adding candy by the handful to a tub of ice cream colored a deep, toxic red. I pulled up short. *What on earth?*

I lifted one of his headphones. "What flavor is this, Brandon?"

He startled. "Penniman Penny Candy?"

I remembered the flavor as having a light pink color. Had Buzzy changed the recipe? I whipped through the pages of the *Book of Spells*, looking from the book to the ingredients and measuring cups he'd set out. "Brandon! You've added twice as much candy!" I picked up a bottle. "Strawberry syrup? That's not in the recipe."

Brandon blushed. "I thought it would taste good?"

I turned away and took a deep breath. Brandon was a good kid. He'd just picked a heck of a time to get creative.

I looked at the mess coming out of the chiller and put on my poker face. "Let's try it."

We each dipped in a tasting spoon and tried the concoction. The texture of gummy candy and crunchy whatever-it-was he'd added was deeply unsettling. I forced myself to swallow.

Brandon closed his eyes. "Oh, that's good."

Irrational laughter bubbled inside me.

Flo joined us and peered at the ice cream over her glasses. "What's this?"

"Brandon has invented his own flavor," I said.

"That's wonderful, Brandon!" Flo smiled sincerely and Brandon grinned.

I scanned the ingredients. It probably wouldn't kill anybody. "Let's get it hardened, then we'll put it in the case and see how it sells," I said. Or, I thought, whether anyone's crazy enough to order it.

Locals always came to see the sunflowers on Friday because they knew to avoid the crowds on the Saturday and Sunday of Sunflower Festival weekend. Customers poured into the shop and the hours flew by. I checked my phone but there was no message from Caroline.

When it had hardened to the correct consistency, I put Brandon's creation in the case. A little boy immediately pointed to it and said, "I want the red stuff." I served him the first scoop. As I readied a cookies-and-cream cone for his dad, the little boy took a bite. His eyes flew open and he took another. "Whoa!" He looked at the cone in wonder then held it out to his dad.

His dad took a bite and grimaced, grabbing a napkin from the counter. "What do you call that one? Makes my teeth hurt."

"It doesn't have a name yet," I said. I'd forgotten to ask Brandon what he wanted to call his creation.

The little boy licked his cone, then made airplane noises and spun in circles. His dad pulled him close and said, "Call it Sugar High." Dad sat at one of the small tables, his son bouncing at his side.

Aaron walked in, McGillicuddy at his heels, and joined the line. The Hermit of Penniman *did* leave his house. A few minutes later I waited on him. "What can I get you?" He peered over his glasses and pointed at Brandon's creation. "What's that newfangled red ice cream?"

"Candy Explosion!" shouted the little boy, the red ice cream now smeared on his cheeks and shirt.

Aaron snorted. "I'll stick to vanilla with sprinkles."

After Aaron left, I went into the kitchen and checked my phone again but there was still no message from Caroline. Out the window, I saw Pru talking with Dandy at the farm stand. Aaron cut through the crowd, McGillicuddy trotting at his heels. He greeted Dandy and then the two of them walked up the lane together. Pru's smile faded as she watched them go.

At six o'clock, Caroline came into the shop's kitchen. I rushed over to her. "What happened?"

Caroline's thin shoulders slumped. "They asked me so many questions, over and over. I was starting to believe I'd killed Mike."

I wrapped her in a hug.

"I'm just drained, Riley. I'm going to make ice cream. That's my therapy." She washed her hands and put on an apron. "I have to thank Pru for recommending her lawyer. He's really nice and was so helpful."

"What happens next?" I asked, shocked at her wan expression.

"I don't know."

After we closed, Caroline's lawyer came to the house and they conferred at the kitchen table. He was a young guy, with serious black-rimmed glasses and a thick old-fashioned leather briefcase.

I stepped outside, breathing in the soft night air. I thought about going for a run, but decided to save my energy. Saturday would be a long day.

Only a single light burned at the Brightwood's farm, in Pru's office. Was she okay? I followed the light to the farmhouse, through the basil-perfumed air of Pru's herb garden.

I could see into Pru's office window. Several open boxes were on the floor in front of a bookcase with empty shelves. She sat at her desk, turning the pages of a thick old book, her expression so far away I sensed a grief that didn't welcome intrusion.

Since my mom passed when I was so young, Pru and Darwin were my model of a happy marriage, their relationship steady as the seasons following one another. Whatever they were facing, I hoped they could weather it together.

I went home and locked the door.

Chapter 30

The sound of voices woke me before the sun. With a groan, I rolled over and squinted out the window. The farm interns were stringing a banner across the barn—Welcome to the Sunflower Festival. Darwin parked a gleaming green tractor by the stand, a photo op for kids to climb and their parents to share the cute images with the world. A gentle sea of nodding sunflowers framed the peaceful scene.

Several photographers had set up cameras on tripods to capture the sun rising over the sunflowers. I flopped back onto my pillow. At the end of the day, there would be photographers capturing the sun setting over the sunflowers. Sunset was past eight this time of the year and we wouldn't close the shop until ten. What a long day it would be. I reached out to stroke Rocky's fur, but his side of the bed was empty. I closed my eyes and wondered what he was peeing on now.

The more I tried to sleep, the more sleep eluded me. I showered and dressed, then went downstairs following the sweet scent of waffles.

Sprinkles was at the window giving a plaintive yowl.

Caroline was already at the table, sipping a cup of fragrant chai tea. "I couldn't sleep. I went over to the shop to make more ice cream then came back and made tea and waffles." She'd sliced some strawberries, whipped real cream, and scrambled eggs. All my favorites. All Caroline had was the mug of tea. "Aren't you hungry?" I poured myself some tea.

"Riley, I wish I could tell you how much—"

I held up my hand. "Caroline. It's not necessary. You'd do the same for me."

"Take over your work? Your travel blog, maybe." She laughed. "Well, in a minute if you went to Spain again."

I knew what was coming. "You're heading back to work, right?"

"Tuesday, this week." She smiled ruefully. "If the police don't arrest me first."

"I haven't changed my mind. I love being in Penniman." I filled my plate and sat down. "And I think the police will arrest Angelica." That last part wasn't as true; I still feared for Caroline. I took a big bite of eggs.

Caroline gripped her mug. "They took my fingerprints, to see if they match some on the wine bottle. That's what Tillie said."

I almost choked on my eggs. "Tillie shouldn't be telling anybody anything." But that was exactly why I wanted to talk to her. She'd spill stuff about the investigation I'd never learn any other way.

Sprinkles made a forlorn chirrup sound. I scanned the kitchen. "Have you seen Rocky?"

Caroline shook her head. "Probably exploring. I found him in my closet yesterday, inside a shoe box."

"Well, whatever he gets himself into, I hope he can get himself out of."

With only Caroline, Brandon, and I working, Saturday morning at Udderly was nonstop with the festival crowd. At lunchtime, I arranged for pizza to be delivered, and Pru sent over a vegetable tray for us to snack on. We needed the energy.

The chiller sat idle. I'd been so focused on making ice cream for the festival, I suddenly realized an inescapable and sobering fact: the shop would be open on Monday and every day after that until the end of October. I needed to keep making ice cream.

Through the window I saw a powder blue trailer with Magic Minis painted on the side pull into the lane. "There's the miniature horse lady. I'll be back."

I showed the driver, an older woman with two braids dyed a Cinderella blue that matched her trailer, where to park. She skillfully maneuvered the vehicle up to the pen, opened the back of the trailer and set down a ramp. A crowd gathered immediately.

The woman put on a matching blue baseball cap with Magic Minis embroidered on it then swept her arm to the back of the trailer. "I'm Dale," she announced. "Meet my babies." She made a clicking noise with her tongue and out of the trailer stepped the most darling creatures, tiny horses no taller than my waist. My heart swelled at the sight of such overwhelming cuteness. Dale beckoned her little charges with soft words. The first horse down the ramp was white with a white mane and wore sparkly pink sneakers. "This here's Lady Mirabelle." As one, the crowd sighed as the darling horse took dainty steps from the ramp into the pen.

"And this is Bob," Dale said. A golden brown little horse, even tinier than the Lady Mirabelle, inched down the ramp. Bob wore red sneakers with a Red Sox emblem, and Dale had affixed a baseball cap to his shaggy mane.

The effect of the little horses was immediate. Phones were raised to take photos. Children swarmed the pen and reached out sticky fingers to pet them, but Dale started the horses on a slow promenade around the pen that kept "her babies" out of reach while still giving everyone a chance to see them.

I hated to drag myself away. "Dale, can I get you a drink? Or some ice cream?"

"Thank you. I'll have some when we're all done and the babies are back safe in the trailer," Dale said. A teenage boy slung a leg over the fence as if to climb into the pen. Dale took off her baseball cap and smacked him with it. "*Back off!*" she barked. "I stay with my babies to make sure folks behave."

"I see you have things well in hand," I said as the teen slunk off. "Thanks for coming."

"Your money's as green as anyone else's. And Buzzy was okay," Dale said with typical Yankee understatement. "Didn't think too much of that son of hers. Heard he was trying to sell off his own ma's property and had a girl in every port. Looks like that fancy New York girlfriend of his took care of his wandering eye."

As I walked back to the shop I considered her words. How fast gossip traveled in little towns like Penniman. I liked Angelica, but better that she was arrested than Caroline. Or Darwin. Or . . . me.

What was Voelker thinking now? Would he think that Caroline's friend would kill to protect her? Getting rid of Mike would take the pressure off Caroline to sell the farm. I was Caroline's alibi and she was mine.

I threw one more longing look at the miniature horses

and caught sight of a pink Mini squeezing into a parking spot by the farm stand. Emily got out and swung her long hair as Kyle unfolded himself from the passenger side and greeted Darwin. What were they doing here?

I jogged across the lane as Darwin, Emily, and Kyle headed to the farmhouse.

At the farm stand, a woman held out her credit card to Pru, but Pru's attention was focused on the group going into the house. I took it and swiped the transaction. Pru shook her head, thanked the woman, and handed her a quart of strawberries.

"What's going on, Pru?" I whispered.

Emily looked back just before the door closed, smiled, and gave us a wave.

Pru frowned. "Darwin won't tell me, Riley."

I returned to the shop, deeply unsettled. As I reached the kitchen door, I noticed something on the step.

Half a dead mouse.

"Not again!" I grabbed a shovel and threw the carcass in the Dumpster that was tucked on the side of the building away from the parking lot, praying no one saw me.

As I completed that disagreeable task, I heard a small yowl. I looked up. Rocky stalked above my head on the very edge of the roofline.

"How did you get out of the house?" I put my hands on my hips. "You're impossible! Rocky Impossible Rhodes, come down this instant."

He licked his paw casually, then jumped from the low roof onto the dumpster, then onto a stack of discarded crates. The way they were stacked, in three columns, each one shorter than the other, made stair steps for the intrepid climber. I made a grab for him but he was

too quick. He leapt and disappeared into a row of sunflowers.

"One more gift like that and you're grounded!"

I tried to keep watch out the window to see when Emily
and Kyle left, but the shop was too busy, the line too
long. Around four o'clock I glanced out the workroom
window and saw a man laden with camera equipment
setting up a tripod. "Not reporters again," I muttered.
"I'll be right back."

I stepped outside, but to my relief it was a professional photographer, not a news cameraman. Two of his
helpers held up a banner that read "Penniman Is Bloom-
ing: For Smart Growth Vote Aldridge."

Caroline leaned out the workroom door. "I forgot to
tell you, Kyle asked if he could shoot a campaign photo
here."

Kyle, Nina, and a woman stepped from an SUV. Kyle
and Nina looked casual in jeans, Kyle wearing a blue
button-down shirt, and Nina in a white denim jacket over
a red T-shirt. The woman adjusted Nina's collar while
Kyle shook hands with the photographer. The shot had
been angled so the field of sunflowers provided the
backdrop to the campaign sign. Even from a distance, I
could tell this image was a winner.

I rejoined Caroline inside and half an hour later, Kyle
and Nina greeted us as they came into the shop to order
ice cream.

Nina beamed as she took a small cup of vanilla ice
cream from Caroline. "The sunflower field's a perfect
backdrop for the photos. The farm just says Penniman,
doesn't it?"

"Thanks for letting me do the shoot here," Kyle said.
Caroline smiled. "You're welcome. Speaking of

photos, I have Mike's phone and there's a great pic of you and him on it, I think from Block Island. I'll send it to you."

Kyle dripped ice cream on his shirt and laughed. "Whoa, I'm a slob. Text it to me, okay?" He grabbed a napkin and swiped at his shirt.

"I will." Caroline turned to Nina. "I saw your watch. It's beautiful. Is it vintage?"

Nina grabbed a napkin to wipe her lips, showing Caroline her sports watch. "Nope. It's got all the bells and whistles to track my workouts."

"Oh, I meant the other one in the pictures. It's lovely," Caroline said.

Nina blinked.

Nina didn't know what Caroline was talking about. The thought hit me with a jolt.

"Thanks again, Caroline, Riley." Kyle handed me some money. "Keep the change." They both headed for the door, Kyle shaking a few hands on his way out. I watched them through the window. Once they were outside, Nina tossed her ice cream in a bin and folded her arms.

Caroline shot me a puzzled look. "What did I say?"

"I'll be right back," I ran to the window in the kitchen and watched the two make their way to their SUV. Kyle stopped to chat with the photographer and crew, but Nina got into the SUV and slammed the door.

That wasn't Nina in the picture on that trip to Block Island. Kyle was going to have some explaining to do.

M y arm ached from scooping ice cream. I massaged it, convinced that my right bicep was getting bigger than the left. Still it was a good day—the festival had brought in a ton of money.

As we locked up and headed home, Caroline and I talked about the uncomfortable exchange with Nina. "I wonder who the woman in the photo was," Caroline said. "How sad. Kyle and Nina have been together since high school. I wonder if they'll get a divorce."

"I imagine they'd want to avoid any negative press in an election year." A memory surfaced. "Wait a minute. I've seen that watch before. When we went to Kyle's office. His secretary had that beautiful diamond watch." I remembered too the photo of Nina and Kyle's family, their beautiful vacation home. "Poor Nina. Kyle having an affair with his secretary. What a cliché."

I realized that Rocky was trotting at my heels and I scooped him up. "There you are!"

"Wait a sec. I'm sure he was in the house when I left," Caroline said.

I gave him a nuzzle. "Little escape artist."

Caroline stopped at the mailbox before we went inside. "I didn't have time to pull in the mail yesterday."

Once inside, Sprinkles glared at me from the powder room. I sighed and flushed.

While Caroline busied herself washing some dishes, the cats slunk into the parlor. I followed and checked outside the window. No fire—for now. I hoped Stretch, or whoever was making the fires, would take a night off. I couldn't wait to take a shower and fall into bed.

I caught sight of the trash I'd found earlier and picked up the wastebasket to empty it. In the brighter light of the kitchen, I looked closer.

"Caroline, look at this." I pulled out the scrap of paper I'd tossed the other day. To my shock, it was half of a check, torn on the diagonal.

She took it in a soapy hand. "That's Mike's signature. Twenty thousand dollars!"

I took it back. "Dated the day Mike died."

"Where did you find it?"

"The parlor." Where Mike and Darwin had argued.

"Wait." Caroline dried her hands. "We don't know who it's made out to. It only has the signature and the amount."

"Who else would it be?" I said. "Mike and Darwin were in there arguing. Mike was trying to bribe Darwin. No wonder Darwin was so mad."

"But bribe Darwin to do what?" Caroline said. "Darwin doesn't own the farm."

I considered. "Caroline, if Darwin told you he couldn't run the farm any longer, or couldn't afford to stay, what would you do? Truthfully?"

After a moment, she sighed and rubbed her forehead. "If Pru and Darwin left? Without them here, it would feel so empty. Lonely. Maybe I would sell that half of the farm and try to keep the house and Udderly? I don't know."

Exasperation with Mike filled me. At the funeral, he'd seemed like the loving brother. That's the problem with people living a double life. You can never take things at face value.

Caroline turned back to the sink, scrubbing a plate with more force than necessary, soap bubbles flying. "Mike sure wasn't good at reading people. Bribing Darwin Brightwood was never going to happen." She dropped the dish back into the dishpan, tossed the sponge into the sink, and flung herself into a chair. I sat next to her.

"Mike knew you'd say no. He was working all the angles." I told Caroline about Emily and Kyle visiting Darwin at the festival. "And they're still working angles."

Caroline took off her glasses and rubbed her eyes. "What other angles are there?"

I recalled Aaron the Hermit's expression when I

asked if he'd been approached to sell. "What if the neighbors sell?"

She shrugged. "They don't own that much property. Besides I don't see the Gravers ever selling."

"But what if? Would it matter to you if they did?"

She threw up her hands. "I don't know. If there was a big development at the top of the hill, it sure wouldn't feel the same here."

Aaron had certainly acted squirrely when I'd talked to him earlier. "Did you know Aaron's last name is Tuthill? Do you know anything about him?"

She shrugged. "He's been there forever. I know he has a little dog named McGillicuddy that's the light of his life and he usually orders vanilla ice cream with sprinkles."

Aaron's property was directly across from the Love Nest. He'd mentioned security cameras. If anyone had seen what happened near the Love Nest on the night of the murder, it would be Aaron. I couldn't believe for a minute he'd forgotten to turn on his security system. How could I get the truth out of him?

Chapter 31

Sunday was a beautiful repeat of Saturday, except that we had even more customers and there were baby goats in the petting pen instead of miniature horses. Udderly's door never fully closed because the line streamed out of the shop into the parking lot. It was testament to my fatigue that when I glanced up to take the next order, it was Flo's handsome honcho, Cadillac Ranch. I hadn't noticed him come in. His warm smile gave me a burst of energy. "Hi! What will it be today?"

"Good afternoon." He touched the brim of his hat and my knees went weak. How did the man do that? "Busy day?"

"Yes, busy but fun." It took me a moment to register that Stretch was beside him. My smile froze. My pick for most likely to be the firebug was also right in front of me.

"I'd like to try a scoop of sunflower and a scoop of strawberry in a cup, please." Cadillac Ranch's voice was music. I served him, then Stretch ordered the same thing.

"Fresh from the farm, right?" Stretch said.

Another customer leaned over to Stretch and said, "If

you think the strawberry ice cream's good, you should taste the peach."

I found my voice. "I'm afraid we don't have peach yet, Stretch. Maybe next week. Will you be around next week to have some?" *Smooth, Riley.*

"Ice cream made with fresh fruit is labor intensive but worth it," Stretch said.

I couldn't keep the surprise off my face. Stretch made ice cream?

"You surprised the lady," Cadillac Ranch said. "May I present my friend, Zach—"

"Just Zach." Zach aka Stretch, pulled his hat tighter over his ears.

"Right now he looks like something the cat dragged in, but he's a very good cook." Cadillac Ranch grinned.

Having seen what Rocky dragged in for me, I had to agree. Zach hadn't shaved and was well beyond any fashionable five-o'clock shadow. He wore a wrinkled polo shirt untucked over baggy cargo shorts and hiking boots, plus that ski cap that made me think of burglars. What an odd combination for a warm summer day. "And I haven't introduced myself properly. I'm Jasper Yeaton."

"Nice to meet you. I'm Riley Rhodes. And that's Caroline and Brandon."

"Nice to meet you." Cadillac Ranch gave each a polite nod of the head. "And Zach's here—"

"For a while." Stretch hunched his shoulders.

The line behind them stirred with impatience.

"I've got this." Zach peeled a twenty off a thick roll of crisp bills. I kept my expression friendly as I gave him change but thought, *Where did he get all that cash?*

Jasper touched the brim of his hat, and they stepped outside. I didn't know if I could call him Jasper now. I'd thought of him as Cadillac Ranch for too long.

Now I was really confused. The guy I thought of as

the camper had a name, Zach, and was friends with Cadillac Ranch?

Two women sitting at one of the tiny indoor tables nudged each other. They took their ice cream and followed Jasper and Zach outside. Through the window I watched the women approach the two men. Jasper was his usual courtly self, greeting them with a slight bow. Zach looked like he wanted to bolt, but Jasper tugged his sleeve. They posed for a selfie. *I guess Jasper is better known than I thought. How odd that he was hanging out with someone like Zach.*

Jasper took a guitar from the back seat of his Cadillac and started strumming, his warm voice streaming in through the open door.

Caroline leaned over to me. "I didn't think I liked country music, but now I do."

Pru burst into the shop, breathing hard. "Houdini escaped!"

"Who?"

"Willow's goat," she said. "Hairy Houdini! He got out of your pen!"

I ran outside. Visitors crowded around the pen but they weren't looking at the goats in it—they were looking up. The little black and white baby goat named Houdini strutted on the shop's roof.

Pru shaded her eyes as she followed his movements.

"What's he doing on the roof?" I gasped.

"Goats like to be up high," she said.

Cars stopped in the middle of the lane as a crowd gathered and held up their cell phones to shoot video. This caused traffic to back up onto the main road.

"Will he come down by himself?" I asked. "He's causing a traffic jam."

Just then Houdini disappeared over the peak of the roof. I remembered how Rocky had gotten down by jumping onto the dumpster and the stack of crates on the other side of the shop. "Quick! He's going around." I ran to the front of the building, and the chattering crowd followed.

Willow ran up to me, shading her eyes as she followed the tiny goat's movement. "I'll get him. Don't worry. I can climb up the dumpster."

Pru tugged Willow's arm. "No, don't go up there, Willow. I don't want you getting hurt."

"There's a black cat up there!" A man pointed. "Bad luck for the goat!" Many in the crowd chuckled.

Rocky sat at the very edge of the roof grooming a paw, unconcerned with the clamor from the crowd. When Houdini clopped over to him, he turned tail and disappeared from sight. I knew he'd jumped onto the stack of crates. Houdini picked his way over to the spot where Rocky had disappeared. My heart jumped into my throat. Goats were surefooted, but Houdini was just a kid. He paused as if deliberating, his little tail wagging.

Someone shouted, "He's going to jump down the pile of crates!"

Willow and I ran, edging through the spectators. As I passed Jasper, he tilted his hat back to follow the action on the roof, then popped the trunk of his Cadillac and reached in.

"Come on, Houdini!" Willow called as we pushed our way to the front of the crowd. The goat teetered on the edge of the roof, then leapt down onto the dumpster, then onto the crates. I didn't see Rocky, but I was sure he was watching. Willow raced forward to catch Houdini as he jumped from the last crate, but a burly man pushed her aside, calling, "I've got him!"

He didn't. Houdini spurted from his arms and zipped into the parking lot.

Shouts and shrieks of laughter spread as the goat

zigzagged through the crowd, but my heart leapt into my throat. I hoped he wouldn't head into the road. Traffic was at a standstill, but if Houdini ran very far away, a moving car could hit him. Willow and I again pushed our way through chattering customers.

As Houdini cleared the crowd and dashed for the road, a circle of rope whirled through the air. In a blink, the circle landed around the little goat's neck. Houdini pulled up short and gave a puzzled bleat as Jasper Yeaton pulled the rope taut and raced up to him.

Jasper knelt next to Houdini, calming the little guy with soft words. Zach aka Stretch doubled over, laughing. Willow ran up and threw her arms around Houdini. The crowd cheered and applauded.

I realized my mouth was hanging open. Flo stood at the shop window, hands clasped by her cheek. I felt the same way. Damn, that man was full of surprises.

I thanked Jasper and returned to the shop, shaking my head. This day was full of surprises. Good surprises. What a nice change.

At closing time, I washed the empty tub that had held Brandon's toxic red experiment. "It sold out in one day. How is that possible?" I dried my hands and flicked off the lights.

Caroline laughed. "No idea."

We headed up to the house. "Pru's bringing over some interns to work in the shop tomorrow night so we can have a nice dinner to celebrate getting through the festival. And you're taking tomorrow off, Riley. I insist."

I rubbed my sore right arm. "No argument from me."

In bed later that night, I thought I'd fall asleep instantly, but I tossed and turned for an hour. I couldn't even lose myself in a book. My mind was like the broken chiller—I couldn't turn it off.

Making lists always calmed me. There's nothing as satisfying as crossing a task off my list, except, perhaps, a hot fudge sundae. I pulled my notebook from my bag, a beautiful handmade leather creation with marbleized endpapers I'd bought in London. I flipped to the last written page, my packing list for Italy.

Rocky slunk into the room and climbed into bed next to me.

I turned to a fresh page and clicked the pen. The notebook had quotes at the top of each page. This page had a quote from Louis Pasteur: "Luck favors the prepared mind."

Think, Riley. Organize your thoughts.

I wrote "Who Killed Mike Spooner" at the top of the page. Who had something to gain by killing Mike? I wrote "MOTIVE—GAIN?" Well, "gain" wasn't the right word. Caroline and Darwin would retain what they had. Eliminating Mike would eliminate the chance of losing their beloved farm. Neighbors who wanted to stop the development? I couldn't believe any of them capable of murder, but added "NEIGHBORS" to the list. I had to keep an open mind.

CAROLINE

DARWIN

NEIGHBORS

I hesitated.

My friends in the military talked about "unknowns" in a way that other people didn't. In the military and intelligence fields, one talked of "known knowns," "known unknowns," and "unknown unknowns." What you knew, what you knew you didn't know, and what you didn't know you didn't know.

"X" was what I didn't know, who I didn't know.

I added "X" to the list.

But "gain" didn't seem like the right motive. Mike's death had been brutal. Emotional. Angry. A crime of passion. I wrote MOTIVE—PASSION. Who fit that profile?

ANGELICA

DARWIN

EMILY

Again I added "X".

I realized that if the crime was driven by emotion, I'd have to put my name on the list. I'd want to help Caroline. "RILEY." After a moment I wrote "PRU" and added her to the "GAIN" list. Pru loved Darwin. Darwin loved the farm. Would she kill Mike to keep Darwin on the farm? Again, I had to keep an open mind, and I remembered how distracted Pru had been after Mike's murder, how fraught with worry and disbelief the conversation I'd overheard.

I remembered Gerri's impassioned speech at the planning meeting. That woman was passionate about stopping the development. I added her name to my list. "GERRI." I laughed. Gerri would lecture someone to death, but hefting that pitchfork? Then I remembered Mike had been drugged to make him an easier target. That made me think the killer was someone who wasn't confident of their strength. I shook my head. Anyone would have to drug Mike to even the odds—he was strong, big, athletic.

Who had opportunity? Anyone could've driven up to the Love Nest, or even walked there, maybe someone camping nearby in the cemetery. "X." The camper, who I felt in my gut was Stretch. What was his story? He was odd, but was he a killer? I added "STRETCH" to the list.

The only person who wanted the development to go through was Aaron. Great. I just proved the most suspicious and squirrely person in the neighborhood was most likely innocent.

I put the notebook on the nightstand and turned off the light. Beside me, Rocky was already asleep.

Chapter 32

Monday morning came too soon, but I'd slept well. Now I had a whole day for sleuthing. I had places to go and people to talk to, but first, a cuddle with Rocky. I reached out, but the spot next to me on the bed was empty, the sheet cool.

Rocky sat at the window with his paw on the screen. His head jerked around and he gave me a guilty look.

"Rocky, what are you up to?"

He jumped to the floor and trotted from the room. I rose from the bed and looked more closely at the spot on the screen where Rocky's paw had been. When I pressed, it gave way and a whole flap opened. The space was just big enough for one determined little cat to squeeze through onto the roof of the porch. I looked down. An old lattice was angled against the porch and next to that was a trash can. Altogether they made stair steps for a determined feline.

Rocky wouldn't be fenced in. Maybe I shouldn't try.

After breakfast, Caroline headed to the shop as I jogged up the hill. I turned west and ran through a row of sunflowers. The bright yellow of the flowers' petals made a dazzling contrast with the bright blue sky.

At the end of the row I looped back, then jogged toward the Love Nest. The crime scene tape across the porch and the barn door sagged. Mike's car was still parked by the door and I peered inside. It was pristine, the complete opposite of Buzzy's hoarder-on-wheels car.

Hoarding made me think of Aaron. His yard was completely hidden by a solid line of woods that faced the road, and most of the trees were choked with vines so thick they blocked the sun. As I ran, I noticed with alarm that barbed wire was strung between the trees, making a nasty, almost invisible fence around his property.

I ran farther up Farm Lane to the narrow opening in the trees that was the entrance to Aaron's domain.

I scanned the yard as I walked up his rutted driveway. There were two decrepit vehicles in the driveway, what New Englanders called "beaters": one a van, one a Buick with Florida plates. A stone patio with flagstones to one side of the house had probably been a pleasant spot years ago, but was now crowded with broken patio furniture, a splintered wooden picnic table, and plastic chairs speckled with mold.

Dozens of rusted hulks of old cars on blocks crowded the other side of the yard. I recognized the bodies of several vintage models, including a Mustang, now reduced to an empty shell.

My skin prickled; I felt watched. I looked up and noted floodlights and cameras on the eaves of the house, another camera by the front door. A wire crossed the yard. With my eyes, I followed it up into the leafy canopy of trees. More cameras.

How many did he have? And why? I knocked on the front door.

The blinds were drawn except for one window, where McGillicuddy barked. I waited but there was no further sound within the house. I turned and jogged away, eager to leave.

Aaron had mentioned that his security cameras weren't on the night of Mike's murder. Though with all these cameras, I doubted if he was telling the truth. But why would he lie?

I recalled the extra security camera in my office at the embassy, the one even Paolo the IT guy hadn't know about, how it had exonerated me. I wondered if the cops would get an order to search Aaron's security footage anyway, despite what he'd told them.

As I left the yard, I thought one thing was certain. It looked like Aaron could use some money. He'd be receptive to a pitch to sell his property. He'd said everyone has a price. If he sold, there might be a domino effect with other neighbors following suit.

The thought of Emily or Kyle trying to coerce Caroline into selling, taking advantage of her fragile state of mind, made my blood boil. I took a deep breath, wiping sweat from my brow. I decided to talk to Emily and tell her to stop bothering Caroline once and for all.

I showered and dressed, then got into Sadie and chugged down Farm Lane. How I missed the Mustang.

In Penniman, all the parking spaces around the town green were taken. That was the trouble living in a tourist destination. Many people stayed in the area after the Sunflower Festival to take advantage of Penniman's lake, organic restaurants, antiquing, and hiking. I swung around the green and parked in the driveway at Dad's house. It would be a quick walk to the green. As I passed the shop, Dad waved from the window, so I went in.

"Riley! You survived the weekend!" Dad grinned.

"It was super busy, but the shop did really well."

"I'm so glad. So did we," Dad said. "I heard you even had music from a famous country singer?"

"Famous? Cadillac Ranch, I mean Jasper Yeaton?"

Dad chuckled. "JD Yeaton. Paulette's gaga for him."

"Really, Riley, you have to keep up." Paulette put a stack of books on the counter and took her cell from her pocket. She had the newest and most expensive model in a prettily decorated gold case. She turned the screen to me.

Someone had posted on social media: "JD Yeaton at Penniman's favorite ice cream shop. Sweet tunes and sweet treats."

Paulette said, "That would be a good slogan for Udderly: Sweet tunes and sweet treats."

"I had no idea he was this well known," I said. "Everyone at the shop calls him Cadillac Ranch."

"He's staying at Moy Mull. He also paints. He came here because he wants to be viewed as just another painter." At first I was surprised that Dad had this scoop but then I remembered he was vice president of the Arts Guild. "We'll oblige him."

It was true. Penniman's peaceful isolation plus the Yankee propensity to mind one's own business made the village a perfect escape.

"How's Caroline?" Dad said.

I filled him and Paulette in, lowering my voice as customers passed by. That reminded me of my errand.

"I'm going to talk with Emily Weinberg right now," I said. "She and Kyle are pressuring Caroline to sell, and I want them to lay off. They're even pressuring Darwin to try to influence Caroline."

Dad said, "Darwin's a man who knows his own mind."

"That might be true." I didn't say it out loud, but maybe the pressure was getting to him. Pru was worried and she knew him best.

A customer approached with a stack of books. I waved goodbye and headed to Emily's office.

Chapter 33

My footsteps slowed when I saw Emily's pink Mini Cooper in the parking lot of Penniman Properties. What was the only thing Darwin remembered about the car that passed him the night of the murder? It was small. Not much to go on. Still . . .

I walked up the sidewalk lost in thought, hardly seeing the charming building. It would be very convenient for Emily if Darwin came under suspicion of murder. It would be hard for him and Pru to live in the area, with the talk, the looks, the gossip. I knew what it felt like to have people gossip about you. Maybe he'd want to move away.

What was Emily doing on Farm Lane the night of the murder? I remembered her flirtation with Mike after the funeral. Was it business or pleasure she'd had in mind? Both? Or just plain murder?

She was my top suspect, but as I climbed the porch to her office, I hesitated. I needed answers, but was a direct confrontation the best way to get them? *Think, Riley. If she's guilty, confronting her would put her on the defensive.*

I decided to take a walk around the green. As I did,

I fell into my old habits, scanning for security cameras and surveillance tails, and checking license plates. I saw nothing besides my favorite tea shop, Lily's; specialty stores, many sporting sunflower shaped flags in honor of the festival; and lots of window shoppers. *Relax, Riley. You're in Penniman now.*

I stopped on the sidewalk to let a group leave a coffee shop. "Good morning, Riley," Gerri's voice boomed.

"Hi," my voice trailed off. I still couldn't bring myself to call her anything but Mrs. Hunt.

"I know it's difficult to change ingrained habits, but you must try to remember to call me Gerri, now that we are colleagues at Udderly." She adjusted a gauzy yellow scarf that matched her linen tunic. "Day off? You deserve one."

"You too. The weekend wouldn't have been so successful without your help."

Gerri slid on jeweled sunglasses, and I had to stifle a smile. How could I have put this woman on my list of suspects?

"My pleasure. The ice cream shop is a Penniman institution and Buzzy was like a sister to us. Well, with all the intermarriages long, long ago, we *are* related, albeit distantly."

"Your family goes way back."

We walked past the war memorial. "Founders, with the Baldwins. Many in our family served. Yours too. Many of our neighbors. They all did their duty."

"The Baldwins?" Baldwin was Nina's maiden name. "Nina Baldwin Aldridge?" I said.

Gerri nodded. "Beautiful girl. Her family owned much of the land here for generations and the thread mill too. Of course, that's closed now." She rearranged her scarves. "She's very active in the community, though I imagine she'll pull back while working on her husband's campaign."

I remembered Nina telling me about organizing the Sunflower 5K and the Memorial Day Run. Memorial Day. That's when Angelica had sailed to Block Island with Mike, running into Kyle and his secretary.

Gerri leaned closer. "Are you okay, Riley?"

"Oh, sorry." Perhaps I didn't have to dig too far for information. This talkative woman knew everything about everyone in Penniman. Instead of asking questions, sometimes it was better to simply let people talk and listen closely.

"I was wondering"—I still couldn't bring myself to call her Gerri—"about Aaron Tuthill. What do you know about him?"

"Aaron? Sit here for a bit." She pointed to an empty bench with her cane. Flo had told me that Gerri had started using the cane after a knee replacement. She didn't need it now, but liked having another accessory.

"The Hermit! I know that's what people call him, but he's no more a hermit than I am. His house is a fortress, not a hermitage. He goes out to the casino often enough. Flo's seen him down there several times when she goes on her church bus trips."

Gerri nodded to a guy pushing a baby jogger. "He might not go out much, but he has lots of unsavory characters visiting him. Florida plates. Dropping off or picking up boxes. And those cars in the yard and that house"—she sniffed—"what a disgrace. His family would be distraught if they could see its current state."

"Has his family been in Penniman long?" I asked.

She shook her head. "The Tuthills came to Penniman in 1920. Newcomers."

"Newcomer" was a relative term.

"And the Aldridges, well, they don't acknowledge him." Gerri waved her hand. "He's the black sheep of the family."

This was a surprise. "He's related to the Aldridges? Kyle Aldridge?"

She took a deep breath. "A distant cousin. Well, his mother was the original black sheep of the family. They disowned her for marrying against her father's wishes. Aaron worked at the family's Ford dealership, but was fired ages ago by Kyle's uncle Nick." She made a gesture that looked like she was sipping from a teacup.

"Drinking?"

She raised her eyebrows and adjusted her scarves.

"Does he have a job now?" I asked.

She shrugged. "He says he works with computers."

"The night of Mike's murder," I began. She turned to me, light glinting on her sunglasses. I had the unsettling sensation of talking to two of myself, one reflected in each dark lens. "What did you do after we finished at Udderly?"

She lifted her chin, gathering her thoughts. "After we left—and wasn't that wonderful, I felt like that was a proper send off for Buzzy—Flo and I returned to the house and ate a light supper. I worked on the genealogy club presentation. Flo watched *Real Housewives*. We had our nightcaps, Manhattan for me, vodka martini for Flo. Nothing out of the ordinary."

"Did you see any unusual cars on the road? A pink Mini?"

She shook her head. "That night? No. But I've seen a pink Mini on the lane the last few days. Emily Weinberg's car. She's been at Aaron's house several times." Gerri's voice warmed with sympathy. "She was always a driven girl, always wanted her father's approval. He founded Penniman Properties, you know. I'm sure a psychologist would have a field day. Her father always favored her older brother, and she's always tried so hard to prove herself."

"Are you thinking of selling?" I asked.

Gerri's look said, *Are you insane?* "Heaven forbid."

Gerri said she had an appointment and walked to her car. The bench where we'd been sitting faced the war memorial, and behind it, Penniman Properties and Kyle's law firm.

I thought of my list of suspects. My pick was Emily, but was it mostly because I didn't like the way she was pressuring Caroline?

A red Mini turned into the parking lot behind the law office. Moments later, I saw Kyle emerge from the car.

Darwin had said he'd seen a small car. I jumped to my feet, ran across the green, and waved Kyle down.

His eyebrows raised as I dashed across the street to him.

"Hi, Riley," he said. "Everything okay?"

"Yes," I said, trying to gather my thoughts.

"How's Caroline?"

"She's well, thank you." I flashed onto the papers in the box Kyle had brought over. "She was puzzled about one thing in the mail. The DNA report for Buzzy."

Kyle chuckled. "Oh, Mike was always helping Buzzy with things that were online. Tech wasn't her strong point." His smile faded. "Well, if Caroline has questions about anything, she can call me."

He wasn't going to tell me anything. I wondered if he knew that the police had taken Caroline in for questioning and that she'd hired another lawyer. I wasn't going to tell him.

"Great car," I nodded toward the Mini.

"Yeah, my wife's. Mine's in the shop. Well, if that's all."

"Yes, bye now." I kicked myself as I walked down the sidewalk. Sleuthing was harder than I realized. I hadn't put Kyle on my list at all. Why would I? He and Mike were longtime friends. . . . Weren't they?

Nina? The Mini was her car, but maybe I was making too much of it. Why would she want to kill Mike? If Nina wanted to kill anyone it was probably Kyle, now that she'd learned he'd been having an affair with his secretary.

I searched my memory. In high school, Nina, Kyle, and Mike had all been part of a tight group of football players and cheerleaders. Caroline and I hadn't moved in that orbit. Mike and Kyle had been best friends since high school. They'd seemed tight at Buzzy's funeral, but could they have been covering up a rift? Who could I talk to about Mike and Kyle?

Everyone knew Penniman High School's beloved football coach had opened a sporting goods store when he retired. It was a block from the green. I changed direction and walked on tree-shaded streets to a more commercial strip where Penniman did its banking, filled its prescriptions, and had its oil changed.

Penniman Sports was situated in a brick building on a busy corner. A little bell jangled as I pushed open the door. I was certain this was a wild-goose chase. *Do the math.* Their football coach had been in his sixties when they played, almost twenty years ago. Would he still be working?

The walls were painted in Penniman High's colors—forest green and white—and a bobcat, the school's mascot, was captured in mid leap across the back wall of the shop, ready to pounce on unwary shoppers.

I admired some high-tech running gear then approached a woman at the counter. Her spine curled forward, but she was tanned and wiry, her white hair cut in a shag, her blue eyes friendly. "May I help you?"

"I'm trying to find Coach—" I hesitated. What was his name?

"Coach Valeri. My husband. He passed two years ago." Her kind look was sympathetic.

"Oh, I'm sorry," I said.

Her smile and voice were gentle. "Many of my husband's former athletes come in looking for him. It's nice to know so many young people looked up to him."

I introduced myself and told her I was a friend of the Spooners.

"Mike was something special." She pointed to a plaque on the wall. "He was quarterback on my husband's first championship team. Tell Caroline I'm very sorry. When is the memorial?"

"She's planning something in the fall." I shifted gears. "I just ran into Kyle Aldridge."

Her gentle grin broadened. "He's a lovely man, still does so much for the school. Oh, he and Mike were inseparable, but both, of course, very competitive. That competitiveness drove them both to succeed. If one did something, the other had to, although honestly, it was always Kyle following Mike's lead. Mike was larger than life, even then. I remember they'd race everywhere. They'd even race to the cafeteria, or see who could chug a bottle of sports drink fastest. My husband told me they raced up the flagpoles in front of the school one day." She chuckled, so did I.

The bell jangled as customers came into the shop.

"Thank you for your time." As I walked out, I smiled. The whole school had watched Mike and Kyle's race up the flagpole. Mike had won the climb, but by a hair. Gerri had given them both detention for a week.

Chapter 34

As I walked back to the green, the warm feeling of nostalgia from my conversation with Coach Valeri's wife evaporated.

Emily fit so perfectly into my theory of spurned high-school love. Her interest in Mike and her jealousy at Angelica had been so obvious. I had to talk to her.

I ran up the steps of Penniman Properties and asked the receptionist if I could see Emily. She escorted me to Emily's office, a room with high ceilings, a carved wooden fireplace mantel, and a charming window seat. A modern desk with a single white orchid was set into a corner, facing gray chairs with pillows in Emily's trademark pink. Emily wore a navy blue suit and was stuffing papers into an elegant leather briefcase.

"Riley!" She smiled as if we were friends. "I saw you chatting with Kyle out my window. How's Caroline?"

"She's fine," I said carefully. "I'm sorry, you look busy." I'd planned to come in with guns blazing, but now I could hardly think of what to say.

"I have to go to a closing. Maybe you can come back later? I hope you're here to talk about Caroline. That deal for the farm would really benefit her, but she has to act."

There was one thing I was comfortable saying. "Emily, please stop asking her. She doesn't want to sell."

She shrugged. "Changes are coming whether Caroline wants them or not."

I crossed my arms. "You mean because Aaron's selling?"

Her voice took on the tiniest edge. "He's not alone."

Who? Not the Gravers or the Brightwoods. *Dandy? She's the only one Emily could mean.*

I remembered Emily and Kyle going into the Brightwoods' house. "Leave Darwin alone too."

Exasperation flared in Emily's voice. "Mike was trying to help those people. Now Kyle and I are."

I didn't like the way she said "those people," and my words flew out before I could stop them. "Mike was only helping Mike. Emily, what were you doing on Farm Lane the night Mike died?"

"How did you—" Tears sprang to her eyes with a speed that took me aback. "Mike meant a lot to me, okay? Ever since high school. But I was always second." She blinked her tears back, then met my eyes, her look defiant. "I'd been drinking, okay? I thought I'd just drive by. I saw Mike's car. Angelica's car was gone so I knocked but he didn't answer. He wasn't there." We both knew what "He wasn't there" meant. She ripped a tissue from her bag and pointed at the door. "You'd better go now."

Emily's emotional outburst threw me off balance. I expected opposition or lies, but not tears. I needed to talk to someone, preferably with Rocky curled up on my lap.

My footsteps led me blindly around the green back to my car. I drove home, trying not to notice the crowd at the shop. Pru waved from her herb garden as I drove past. I parked and walked down to her.

"Hey, you're supposed to be taking the day off, young lady," she said.

I blew out a breath. "I've made a mess, Pru."

She patted my arm. "We all do from time to time. Step into my office. Have you eaten?"

I shook my head as I followed her inside.

"I have some sandwiches in the fridge." She put one on a plate and poured me a glass of lemonade, then we went into her office. The walls were painted a soothing pale yellow and the wooden floors and shelves behind her gleamed. Another bookcase, empty, stood in the corner, hemmed in with cardboard boxes. Framed quilts covered the wall and the shelves behind her were filled with photos of smiling families and children. She sat behind her desk and pointed to the comfortably upholstered chair across from her.

"You just missed your friend Detective Voelker." Her voice was light, but I could see the worry in her eyes.

I froze. "He was back? What happened?"

"More questions for Darwin. Questions for me. At least he didn't take us to the station." She forced a smile that said the subject was closed. "Eat."

Pru's desk was clear except for a vase of purple coneflowers, a laptop, and a large leather ledger. I settled in the chair and took a few bites of the sandwich, but soon I pushed away my plate. An open cardboard box behind her was full of books. "New books?"

"Darwin built me some more bookshelves," she said. "I don't know where that man found the time. Now I have to get these books on them."

"Remember I was a librarian," I said. "I'm happy to help."

"I'll take you up on that." Pru leaned forward. "What's troubling you, Riley?"

"I went to see Emily Weinberg to tell her to stay away from Caroline. She's been pressuring her to sell the farm. But when I was talking to her, she started crying." I swallowed. "I'm sure she called the police on Darwin, and I'd even convinced myself that she'd killed Mike"— Pru's eyebrows shot up—"but now I'm confused and I feel terrible."

Pru shook her head. "Even without Emily's tip, the police would've questioned Darwin and me. I found this." She took a scrap of paper from her pocket and handed it to me. It was the other half of the check I'd found, made out, as I expected, to Darwin. "I found it in Darwin's pocket when I was doing laundry the day after Mike was killed."

I put the scrap on her desk. "We found the part with the signature."

"Darwin told me he tore it up and threw it at Mike," Pru said. "I don't know why he stuffed this piece in his pocket. He was probably so angry he didn't know what he was doing. You know how he always puts his hands in his pockets. When I showed it to him he told me not to worry. But he's been a wreck. He can't sleep."

"I saw Kyle and Emily here," I said. "So they've been bribing him to leave?"

Pru rubbed her arms. "Easier than that, and in a way, worse. They want him to convince Caroline the development's a good thing. They said he can stay as a consultant, managing the smaller footprint farm, that Caroline can't run Udderly and the farm from Boston. But you showed up and complicated things. Then they found a way to make Darwin even more vulnerable."

"How?"

Pru's hands twisted. "Mike told Darwin that the

check was for Willow's college fund. We don't have much money in savings. Mike, and now Emily and Kyle—they've found the chink in Darwin's armor. Willow."

I couldn't imagine a more painful choice for Darwin. We sat silently together for a few moments, then Pru ran her hand over the old leather book.

"What's that?" I asked.

"A record book that belonged to my friend, Martha Woodley. It's a diary of all the patients she served as a midwife." Pru's voice warmed. "She was a mentor, she taught me everything I know."

"Flo told me you went to a memorial for her."

"Yes, her friends gather every year to remember her." Pru gray eyes held mine. "Well, since we're telling truths today. Riley, something has been bothering me, but it's not anything to do with the farm or Mike." She took a breath. "It's about Brooke Danforth."

Brooke Danforth?

"It's so long ago." She patted the book. "I had many of Martha's books packed away because I had nowhere to put them. Now that Darwin built my shelves, I took these out of storage. I was being self-indulgent, missing Martha. So when I found this book in one of the boxes, I started paging through."

Voices came in through the open window and Pru got up to shut it. "I don't want anyone to hear us. Martha was very good at keeping secrets, even from me."

Pru tucked a tendril of silver hair behind her ear as she resumed her seat. I remained still, not wanting to break her train of thought.

"Before I got pregnant with Willow, Martha told me that she knew a girl who might want to give up her baby. She knew we were desperate for a child. The girl was just a few months along and wasn't married. I got my hopes up"—she sighed—"even started thinking of that baby as mine. But about a month later, Martha told me that the girl wanted to keep it."

"Brooke Danforth was the girl?" I couldn't keep the surprise from my voice. Brooke had been an elite-level gymnast. A cheerleader. She'd spent most of her time training and traveling to competitions. Plus, her mother had been so strict. "I'd always heard she wasn't allowed to date."

Pru turned the ledger so I could see it. "Martha took very good notes."

Careful penmanship covered the lined pages, the ink faded to gray. In the far-left column were dates, then a column with names. Martha Woodley had listed every meeting, every event, one after the other, followed by short notations, lists of weights, temperatures, and measurements.

Pru turned the pages to each of Brooke's entries.

"June 5: Rain this morning. When it stopped, I saw a rainbow looped over the lake.

Brooke Danforth. 5′ 1″ 90 lbs. Brooke came to see me today. I wasn't surprised. I'd seen her walking with a boy by the lake a few times. She's not sure if she wants to keep the baby, but if she does, I have someone in mind who wants to adopt.

July 18: Brooke was back. She wants to keep the baby herself. Hasn't told her mother yet. Asked me if she could stay here if there's trouble when she does. I said yes. It will start a war with her mother, but what else can I do? Poor girl has nowhere else to turn."

I lifted my eyes as Pru flipped past Brooke's entries to blank pages. She raised her eyes to mine. "Brooke died from an overdose July twenty-fifth and my friend Martha died a week after."

Chapter 35

"Did Martha Woodley note the father's name?" I said. Pru shook her head. "No, and Martha didn't tell me either. Brooke might not have told her. It wouldn't have been like Martha to pry."

Mike, the Romeo of Penniman High lived right down the road from Brooke's house. "Did you ever see Mike and Brooke together? Near the barn?" *The usual place.*

Pru said slowly, "I don't remember him with Brooke. We hardly ever saw her, even though she lived up the hill. That doesn't mean they didn't date. Teenagers are very good at keeping secrets. And the barn? I had no idea it was a rendezvous place."

Maybe it was only Mike who knew about his rendezvous place. Well, Mike and the girls he met there. My mind flew back to Emily, how unhinged she'd become, how quickly. Was she reliving her past? I heard her words, *"I was always second."* Had she felt a surge of anger because Mike had chosen Angelica instead of her? Had Mike once chosen Brooke over her?

Pru cleared her throat. "Sorry, it brought back so many emotions."

Flo had told me Martha Woodley was killed by a hit-and-run driver. "Where did Martha die?"

"On the road by the lake." Pru's voice was thick with tears. "They never found out who did it."

Never found out who did it. That wouldn't be the end of Mike's story. Not if I could help it.

Her look told me that she was wrestling with the same feeling I was, a feeling of helplessness. We were both searching our memories, grasping for the truth, even though those memories caused pain. How much worse for Pru, now knowing that Brooke's child might've been her own.

"I was just going," Pru said, "to visit the spot where Martha died."

"Do you want company?"

She nodded.

Pru ran her fingers through her hair and captured the mass of pewter ringlets into a scrunchie at the top of her head as I drove Sadie to the lake. We turned onto a road that narrowed between towering trees, the green canopy of leaves thickening as we went. At the end of the road we stopped across from the small sandy public beach on Penniman Lake.

"Turn here," Pru said. I slowly drove the narrow, twisting road that ringed the lake. At one point, I stopped to allow a small parade of children and moms, arms laden with inner tubes, towels, and coolers, to cross in front of us.

As we drove into dappled sunlight around a tight curve, Pru twisted her hands on her lap. "Here."

I pulled the car as far as I could onto the shoulder of the road and we got out. Pru walked into a blanket of golden daylilies that carpeted a sunny patch not far from the base of a gnarled oak. She absently deadheaded a couple of flowers.

"You planted them, didn't you?" I touched her arm.

She didn't seem to hear me. "Hit-and-run. They never caught the driver who did it."

We stood silent for a few moments. "Who found her that night?"

Pru shook her head. "No one ever said. Someone who lived nearby, I guess." We stayed for a few more minutes, listening to the far-off sound of children playing at the lakeshore. Pru turned and we got back in the car.

Chapter 36

After dropping Pru at home, the librarian in me asserted itself. I was curious. I googled "Martha Woodley." As I suspected, there wasn't much information available about her. She'd died seventeen years earlier, before it became commonplace to list obituaries online. I'd have to look at old newspaper records.

I drove to the Penniman Library and parked behind the gray stone building. Research was a way to calm my mind, to channel the restless energy that was surging in me since my disastrous conversation with Emily. Maybe I could find some answers for Pru.

I almost forgot the stack of Buzzy's library books. I gathered the books, ran up the stone steps of the library, and slid them into the Return slot. How I loved this old building! Every time I pulled open the door, I flashed back to being eight years old with my own library card and a *Sailor Moon* backpack Dad let me fill with books.

The librarian, a woman in her twenties with jagged-cut, purple-streaked hair and a raven tattooed on her bicep, set me up at the microfiche reader. Microfiche is a flat piece of film containing microphotographs of the pages of newspapers, magazines, catalogs, and other documents. "Only way to access those old newspapers," she said.

After she left, I scanned Martha's obituary in the pages of the *Penniman Post*, but there wasn't much there that Pru hadn't told me.

Martha May Woodley, seventy-two, daughter of John and Octavia Woodley, was born in Hartford, Connecticut . . . moved to Penniman after retiring as a nurse from the Charter Oak Maternity Hospital. . . . opened an office and offered her midwife services to, the paper said, "the hippie scene in the Penniman hills." She'd also sung in the choir of the Penniman Congregational Church and in the Gilbert and Sullivan Society.

She was survived by a sister in Colorado. I checked for records of the sister. She'd died ten years after Martha.

News reports didn't have much more information beyond what the obituary said and what Pru had told me. Except one detail: Martha's body had been found by a "summer resident of Penniman Lake."

Puzzled, I rewound the microfiche and searched for more news stories. Although some articles mentioned that a "summer resident" or "visitor" had found Martha's body, that person was never named. Why would that be kept secret?

Was the "summer resident" someone who was important enough, influential enough, rich enough that the newspaper would withhold their name from the public? A police report should have that information.

I knew who I had to talk to. Tillie. Did I have the energy? I rubbed my temples, and then my earlobes, an energizing move taught to me by a yoga instructor in Mumbai. Maybe I'd stop at Lily's Tea Room for sustenance first.

I thanked the librarian, stepped from the cool building into bright sun and slid on my sunglasses.

"Riley!"

That voice. I turned.

"I saw you inside. I was just picking up my holds and thought, that's Riley Rhodes!" Behind her red-rimmed chunky glasses, Tillie's eyes shone. *She wants to ask me about the murder,* I thought. Tillie O'Malley was eager to pump me for a scoop. I was happy to pump back. Perfect.

"How about a cup of tea, Tillie?"

We took a table under a black-and-white-striped umbrella on the brick patio behind Lily's Tea Room. Tillie stowed her tote bag quilted with a bright pattern of pink and white kittens under the table. She zipped the top, but not before I caught sight of a stack of paperback books.

"What are you reading?" I asked.

Her eyes gleamed. "The newest by Nicole Vickers! I like my thrills." She showed me a book, then tucked it in her bag next to a romance with a cover featuring a hunky half-dressed guy. Thrills, indeed.

"Hello, Tillie. Hello, Riley, my dear." Coleman Hennessey, a trim man with a short gray Afro and crisp white button-down shirt with Lily's embroidered on the chest pocket lay a warm hand on my shoulder.

"My condolences." His voice was deep with a rich British accent. "Zara and I have been thinking of you and Caroline."

"Thanks, Coleman." I gave his hand a squeeze. "Thank you for sending that nice fruit salad."

"I know Caroline likes it." Coleman and his wife, Zara, had moved to Penniman after he retired from a career teaching music. Soon after, they opened their tea shop, modeled after one Zara's family had owned in Reading, England.

Lily's was one of my favorite spots. Set in a pink and teal Painted-Lady Victorian, its parlor wallpapered with soft William Morris designs, with velvet couches deep with pillows, it had an overall air of cozy gossip. In the winter a fire crackled in the fireplace, and in the summer the patio was hung with baskets of flowers. The restaurant was named for Coleman and Zara's white West Highland terrier, Lily, the only creature in Penniman possibly as spoiled as Sprinkles. My favorite touch was the portrait of Lily over the fireplace.

"Zara took scones out of the oven just a minute ago. I'll bring them out. Earl Grey, Riley?" Coleman said.

"You remembered!"

Coleman smiled. "And for you, Tillie?"

Tillie perused the menu. "Today I'll go for a shandy."

Even more perfect. The shandy's half beer half lemonade would be just the thing to loosen Tillie's loose red lips even more.

Within moments, Coleman set a flowered three-tier tray piled with golden scones and tea sandwiches in the center of our table. Zara bustled out of the kitchen with a tray holding my pot of tea, a matching teacup, and Tillie's frosty shandy, and set them in front of us. Then she engulfed me in a hug.

"Caroline's lucky to have you here, Riley," she murmured.

How Zara could bake and look so cool was a mystery, but there she was in a pristine white apron over a yellow shirt dress, her hair sleeked into a chignon, small white pearls in her ears. "Do you know what she'll do with Udderly? I hear you're the new manager."

News traveled in Penniman. "Caroline's not making any big decisions right now, but I agreed to keep it running."

"I'm glad! If you need anything, let us know." She bustled back to the kitchen.

"Cheers." Tillie's eyes glowed as my cup clinked her glass. "So, what's new with the Mike situation?"

"You probably know more than I do, Tillie." I decided to butter her up. "After all, you're working right there in the middle of everything at the police station."

She cut to the chase. "I heard you visited Angelica."

I bit into a coronation chicken sandwich. *Heaven.* "She's remembering more every day."

"Suspect Numero Uno." Tillie rolled her eyes as she slathered cream on her scone. "You found the body, right? Impaled by a murderous maniac?"

I gulped and coughed, and took a sip of tea, but Tillie calmly licked her fingers and reached for another scone.

"Did you read the forensics report?" I said.

"Yep. He'd taken sleeping pills. Mixed them with alcohol." She waggled a red tipped finger. "Big no-no."

This confirmed my suspicion but I shuddered. If he'd been conscious and someone had come at him with a pitchfork, he would've fought. I didn't remember any defensive wounds on his hands, but I'd verify. "Defensive wounds?"

She shook her head. "He was knocked out by the pill-and-alcohol combo. When I first heard about it, I figured maybe his girlfriend, the tennis player, you know? She's strong."

I hated to admit it but I had too. "Great upper-body strength."

"Like I said, Suspect Numero Uno." Tillie sipped her shandy. "And Caroline's Numero Two-O."

My throat went dry. "Dos."

Tillie's eyes glittered. "They questioned her but I don't think Jack's buying it. You're her alibi, right?"

She tsked. "Not a very good one. I remember hearing you talking about her scarf. The one that was found at the scene."

I took another sip of tea, remembering how Tillie had been listening when Caroline and I discussed if I should mention the scarf. I changed the subject. "Fingerprints on the wine bottle?"

"Mike's and some smudgy ones." Tillie knocked back the rest of her shandy.

"Pitchfork?" I remembered seeing some farm implements when I went into the barn. Had the killer used one of them? Of course, Buzzy never locked the doors and anyone could've gone into the barn. But the killer would have to know the pitchfork was there to use. Despite the overstuffed cushions, I shifted uncomfortably in my seat. Anyone could've gone in, but who even knew the barn was there? Neighbors. Locals. Campers.

Tillie burped quietly and shook her head. "No prints on the pitchfork. Angelica probably wore gloves."

"Gloves point to premeditation," I mused. Any scenario I could imagine for Angelica would be unplanned, a crime of passion after finding out about another paramour. The note . . . *Meet me at midnight. The usual place.* "Where are the gloves?" I hadn't meant to speak aloud.

Tillie regarded me shrewdly. "Good question. Angelica probably tossed them out the window as she drove away."

A glimmer kindled in me. Where on earth would Angelica have gotten gloves? I was sure she'd been drugged too. Were there old gloves in the barn? Maybe, but how would she know where to find them? Angelica was a passionate person. If she was going to stab someone with a pitchfork, I couldn't see her taking the time to put on gloves first.

"So what were you doing at the library, Riley?" Tillie said.

Tillie could get me the police report of Martha Woodley's death. "Tillie, do you remember Martha Woodley?"

Tillie closed her eyes for a moment, treating me to a view of her purple eye shadow. "The hippie midwife? She died years ago. Probably when you were still in high school. You were what five, ten years behind me at Penniman? It was a hit-and-run."

It was now or never, I thought. "Could you show me a copy of the police report? There's something strange about her death."

Tillie's eyes glittered. I'd hooked her.

I lowered my eyes, to hide my satisfaction.

I knew that police reports were public record in our state but going through any official channels could take months. Plus I knew there were some exemptions to the information in public records—for example, the identity of informants. If that was the case with Martha Woodley, I'd never see the report. However, Tillie could get me what I needed ASAP if it piqued her interest.

Tillie's eyes gleamed. She patted her lips with the pink linen napkin. "I can get it for you. Come on."

Chapter 37

I offered to pay and Tillie graciously accepted. We gathered our bags and walked around the corner to the low brick building that housed the police department.

A genial-looking man at the reception desk greeted us. "Isn't it your day off, Tillie?"

She fluttered her fingers. "It's okay. I'm helping Riley here with a question about that hippie midwife."

I tilted my head away, hoping Tillie wouldn't make any further announcements.

The man scratched his head. "Pru Brightwood?"

Is that how people thought of Pru? Hippie midwife?

Tillie shook her head. "No, the hit-and-run years ago."

"Oh, Martha Woodley. She delivered my cousin! That was sad when she died."

My stomach churned. Memo to self: Never tell Tillie anything you don't want broadcast all over New England.

Tillie opened a door labeled Records at the end of the hall. Inside were ranges of metal shelving stuffed with cardboard boxes. Fluorescent lights hummed overhead as she led me to a shelf, craning her head. "There." She pulled down a box and muttered as she flipped through manila folders with yellow labels. "They're organized and cross-referenced by case file number usually, but because there was a death, she'd be in here by last name." She pulled out a folder labeled Woodley, Martha.

I felt a pang—the poor woman's death boiled down to papers in a folder.

"So what did you want to know?" She leaned a hip against the table and popped a stick of gum into her mouth.

I took a deep breath. "I heard about her death—a hit-and-run—and was wondering who found her body."

Tillie opened the folder and took out a sheet of paper. "Here are maps and sketches of the scene where the body was found." I peered over her shoulder. A quarter mile past the curve in the road where Martha had been struck was a waterfront property labeled Point O' Woods. I blinked. That was Kyle's family's home.

She leafed through the papers. "Here's the narrative. Body discovered by a man walking his dog. Mr. Nick Aldridge, a visitor from Hartford." Tillie cracked her gum.

Nick Aldridge. Kyle's uncle. "Thanks, you've been a big help," I said.

"Any time."

I hurried back to the street, sick with the thoughts churning in my mind. Had Mike been the father of Brooke's child? Kyle? I shook my head. He'd always been with Nina. Was Nick Aldridge just a well-connected man who didn't want his name in the paper? Was it an awful coincidence that Martha was killed shortly after Brooke died and that her body had been discovered by a member of Kyle's family? Or had there been a conspiracy to silence Martha Woodley? Had Kyle silenced Brooke to save his friend Mike from scandal?

Driving back through Penniman's rolling farmland, I realized that I didn't know what to tell Pru, or even if I should tell her what I'd discovered. It was nothing that would ease her mind about Brooke Danforth. Pru had enough to deal with now.

My mind spun with questions as I turned into Farm Lane. As I drove past Udderly, I could see the interns working so we could have our celebratory dinner. Willow was going up the steps of the farmhouse, holding a platter.

I needed facts, something solid. I had one more stop to make, a test to prove a theory. I pulled into Aaron's driveway, noting the closed curtains on his windows. The thought of entering that nightmare yard made me shudder, but I parked and walked toward his door. I could only imagine what roosted in the rusty hulks of the cars and piles of trash.

As I approached, Aaron opened his front door.

"Riley! What brings you round here this fine evening?"

I froze for a second then smiled. There was no window in his door, and curtains and blinds were drawn tight across his windows. I'd learned what I wanted to know. He'd seen me on a security camera.

Little McGillicuddy barked at Aaron's heels as he moved slowly out the front door.

"Nice night," I said.

"Ha? What's that?" he bellowed as he adjusted his glasses.

I raised my voice. "You had footage of the night of the murder."

"Nope. Nope. But between you, me, and the lamppost, I didn't see anyone on the road anyway." He shrugged and picked up McGillicuddy, evading my eyes.

He was lying.

"Please, Aaron," I said. "I'm trying to help Caroline."

He spoke louder. "I want to help Caroline too. Best way would be to convince her to sell. The real estate gal told me the developers have a good plan and it would even keep the ice cream shop for the new residents."

"But you've lived here so long—"

"Going south in the winters now," Aaron said. "My old bones can't take the winters no more. We're snowbirds, right McGillicuddy?"

This was going nowhere. "Good night, Aaron."

I drove back and parked in front of Buzzy's house.

The sound of conversation flowed out the door as I entered. Caroline, the Brightwoods, and the Gravers were gathered around a buffet spread on the dining room table. As usual, Sprinkles ignored me, but Rocky laced himself around my ankles. I picked him up and he let me nuzzle his soft head under my chin. "You're home, you beast! Please always come home, Rocky, okay?"

"Come home?" Caroline said. "He was waiting for me when I came in."

I told her about the ripped screen. "Hairy Houdini's not the only escape artist on this farm."

Only last week we'd gathered in a similar way. Now Mike was dead and Angelica hospitalized—gone from a golden athlete to a suspected murderer. Suspect Numero Uno. My head and heart were filled with sadness from the things I'd learned today, but I pushed them away.

I wanted things to go back to normal for a while, forget my scene with Emily, forget Martha Woodley, forget Brooke, forget Aaron's deviousness. I forced a smile. "How were things at the shop today?"

"Great! Everyone here was such a help." Caroline smiled, but her eyes were worried. I remembered that she was returning to Boston tomorrow. I decided to hold off on telling her what I'd discovered about Brooke.

"Everything's going to be fine," I said.

Our meal was surprisingly relaxing. As if by unspoken agreement, no one spoke of Mike or the investigation. The conversation was light, and laughter flowed. Even Sprinkles allowed a few pats on the head. It was as if, without words, we'd all decided to have one normal night, before whatever happened tomorrow happened.

Tomorrow came sooner than I thought.

Chapter 38

A soft touch on my shoulder woke me. My eyelids flew open to the dark.

Rocky gave a long, drawn-out meow, then I heard him drop to the floor. He called again.

"What is it, you infernal beast?" I groaned and sat up. As soon as my feet touched the floor, my skin prickled and my senses went on high alert.

Rocky led me across the darkened hallway to the window in Buzzy's room. Sprinkles sat up on her royal bed, her eyes gleaming and her head swiveling as I crossed the room. Here I could see to the north, up to the Love Nest and the far end of Farm Lane where the orange gleam of fire pulsed. The pungent smell of smoke rode a soft breeze that gentled the curtains.

Unlike the previous nights, the flames were bigger, much bigger.

"Caroline! Get up! Fire!" I shouted.

I threw on clothes and shoes, grabbed my phone, and raced down the stairs and out the door.

I stopped for a few seconds to dial 911. "Farm Lane— north end. Fire!" I gasped as I ran toward the glow that silhouetted the Love Nest. As I approached, I could see the cottage wasn't on fire. The fire was behind it— Aaron's house. I thought of all the trees and vegetation there . . . the fire could catch and spread everywhere.

As I ran full out, I remembered at the last minute the almost invisible barbed-wire fencing around Aaron's property. The only way in was up his driveway.

The heat made an almost physical wall as I hurtled toward the house. I held up my arms to protect my face from the scalding heat. Flames consumed the front door, and the pungent scent of gasoline assailed my nose. Over the roar of the flames that consumed the house, I could hear McGillicuddy barking. I raced left, but flames ringed that side of the house. I retraced my steps, skirting a thread of fire that made a barrier around the house. In one spot, at the stone patio, this wall of fire was broken. I skirted heaps of trash, following the sound of McGillicuddy barking, almost drowned out by the crackle of the flames shooting up the side of the house. A blast of heat stole the air from my lungs. A far-off siren added to the cacophony, hyping my adrenaline.

I looked up. Aaron was at a second-story window, his hands working at his dog's collar. "Take McGillicuddy!" he shouted. He flung himself over the sill, leaning out to hand the struggling dog out to me.

"You have to get out. Come on!" I yelled.

"The doors are blocked," he rasped.

"Lower yourself out the window."

He dropped McGillicuddy and I somehow caught the wriggling dog, gathering his trembling body against my chest.

"Riley!" Darwin ran from the back of the house and grabbed my shoulders. "Come away now! It's not safe!" He dragged me back through the opening in the flames, shielding me with his body. Pru, Willow, and some of the farm interns ran up and gathered around us.

"There's a man in there!" I shouted to the firefighters. Darwin led them to the side of the house. McGillicuddy struggled, yelping madly. Trying to soothe him, I stroked his neck, my fingers tangling in the tags hanging from his collar. Suddenly, he nipped me.

"Ow!"

Gentle hands touched my shoulders. Dandy's concerned face loomed out of the dark, yellow in the reflection of the flames. "We can put McGillicuddy in my front yard. It's fenced, he won't be able to get out." Police officers pushed us back as the fire crew aimed hoses at Aaron's house.

Dandy steered me to her yard then touched my hand. "My goodness, McGillicuddy broke the skin. Come in, you can sit down."

"Riley! Thank God you're safe!" Caroline ran up and threw her arms around me, setting off another round of barking from McGillicuddy. In the glare of a cruiser's headlights, I saw the Gravers, Gerri in a flowing ruby velvet robe and turban, and Flo in green sweats, hurry toward us. Emergency vehicles created a wall between us and the fire, and we huddled together in Dandy's yard, unable to stop watching the flames.

"Riley, you're hurt," Dandy said. "Let's wash that bite."

Rocky threaded my ankles, hissing up at McGillicuddy.

"McGillicuddy was so scared. I can't blame him." I tried to make sense of what I was seeing: Aaron's house encircled by flames, like a noose being pulled tight.

An ambulance pulled up as shouts rang from the yard. EMTs pulled a stretcher to the road, Aaron's form limp on top. I held McGillicuddy tighter.

When I looked down again Rocky was gone. I hoped his survival instincts would keep him from the vehicles and the fire.

Radios squawked: "He was trapped in the house . . . both doors blocked by fire . . . if the stone patio hadn't been there . . . some woman got the dog out."

Next thing I knew, the Gravers surrounded me in Dandy's kitchen as Dandy washed and bandaged my finger, then we crowded into the living room. Outside the picture window, I saw Darwin, Pru, and Willow huddled together, their faces orange in the firelight; the interns, chattering and trying to film the fire on their cellphones; Voelker's stern face, looking down at Caroline; ambulance lights receding down Farm Lane. The last thing I remembered was the jingle of McGillicuddy's dog tags as he ran across Dandy's living room floor, mournfully calling for his master.

Chapter 39

"Riley, I brought you some breakfast."

I peeled my eyes open. Dad sat next to my bed, Rocky serene in his lap. There was a tray with a teapot, a glass of orange juice, and golden brown toast on the bureau. I sniffed. "Is that Paulette's cranberry walnut bread?"

He set Rocky down and got the tray. "You bet."

Yellow sunlight streamed through the window. I sat up and he settled the tray on my lap.

"What time is it?" I yawned. "Did I pass out?"

He sat again and Rocky blinked up at him. Dad took Rocky back into his lap. "It's ten o'clock. You were wiped out when Darwin and Pru took you back here and put you to bed. Caroline called me this morning. She had to go to Boston for meetings. She wanted me to tell you that Pru was running things at the ice cream shop and you're not to get out of bed until you feel ready." He squeezed my hand. "I wanted to check in on my hero daughter."

I gulped some tea. "Hero?"

He put Rocky on the bed with me and turned his phone so I could see the screen. The heading on the

Penniman Post website read "Fire Ravages Farm Lane Home" and under that "Hero Ice Cream Shop Manager Rescues Dog from Flames."

I shook my head, sorting through disjointed memories. "Darwin pulled me away from the house. *He's* the hero." I rubbed my eyes and noticed my bandaged finger. "Aaron saved his dog. All I did was catch McGillicuddy and look what I got for my trouble."

Dad chuckled, but his eyes were serious as he patted my arm.

"Aaron put his dog's life before his own," I said. "Is he okay?"

"He's being treated at the hospital and Donna Danforth is watching McGillicuddy." Dad frowned. "People are wondering if the fire was started by whoever's been camping around here."

Had the camper escalated to arson? Stretch's face materialized in my mind. Was Cadillac Ranch unknowingly hanging out with an arsonist? It didn't feel right. "The camper's only made cooking fires, and tidy ones at that." Or had a cooking fire simply gotten out of control? I recalled the ring of fire circling Aaron's house, the pungent smell of gasoline. That was no accidental fire.

Dad nodded toward a plastic bin next to the closet. "Paulette thought you'd like another box of your things." It was my turn to chuckle. Forget the hero business, Paulette was determined to move the rest of my stuff out of the house. Dad and I chatted for a few more minutes, then he gave me a kiss on the cheek. "Off to the bookshop. Glad you're okay, honey. Check in when you can."

Dad went downstairs, trailed by Rocky.

After I finished Paulette's delicious toasted bread, I showered, the warm water soothing my tense muscles and releasing the smoky smell from my hair. I dressed in shorts and a pale blue linen shirt. Now what?

Answers. I wanted answers. First, I'd see how McGillicuddy was doing and then check out the scene of the fire.

The driveway to Aaron's house was blocked by the Fire Chief's SUV. Two vans with state police decals parked along the street and I could see the investigators conferring in the clearing in front of Aaron's house. Smoke seeped from the singed lawn and weeds that ringed the foundation of the structure. The exterior was charred, the windows gaped open, and part of the roof had collapsed.

I kept walking, my mind reeling. Faint barks came from inside Dandy's house as I opened the front gate into her rose-filled yard. I knocked at the door but there was no answer.

Her van wasn't in her driveway. I walked down her driveway to the sagging garage. Beige curtains covered its front windows but through a side window I saw old lawn furniture, bicycles, and a kayak. No van.

She must have gone out. I couldn't believe she'd left McGillicuddy alone. I wondered if he was tearing her house apart.

I walked up the lane and saw Gerri leaving her house. "Riley!" she called as she rushed toward me. She power walked, doing a little hop every few feet, as her scarves trailed her. I almost laughed when I realized Gerri was running.

"Riley, what an ordeal you've been through!" She gave me a quick hug and I melted at her concern.

"It was nothing anyone else wouldn't have done," I said.

"Hardly," she scoffed. "You wouldn't catch me

risking my life for Aaron." She arranged her scarf around her shoulders and jutted her chin toward my bandaged hand. "I'm glad you're unscathed—except for where that ungrateful dog bit you."

"Where's Mrs. Danforth?" I asked as we walked past Dandy's rose-filled yard. "It looks like she left McGillicuddy alone in her house."

"I'm sure it wasn't something she wanted to do. She does like things just so." Gerri looked at the garage and sighed. "Except for that garage. What an eyesore. It ruins the view from my pergola. Well, we all have our blind spots. Here, she left a note for you—I was bringing it down just now. She had a golf match in Providence this morning and had to leave early. That's probably why she couldn't make other accommodation for McGillicuddy." She pulled a note from a pocket in her tunic top. "She left this before Flo or I woke up. It has the number of the vet on McGillicuddy's dog tag. She said you should make sure he doesn't have rabies."

"Rabies!" I couldn't imagine Aaron's well-loved pet wasn't vaccinated, but still I reeled as she handed me the note.

"It's the same vet Flo uses for Mr. Cuddlesworth." I glanced at the note and the name Liam Pryce jumped out at me.

A silver lining. I stuck the note in my pocket. "Mrs., ah, Gerri, Aaron told me that some neighbors were planning on selling. You haven't changed your mind?"

"Aaron?" She snorted. "You can't trust a word he says. I'll never leave the homestead. You'd have to take me out—what is that vulgar saying?—feet first. No matter what that hussy in the pink car offers."

"I guess he meant Mrs. Danforth?"

She reared back. "If Donna's moving, that's a big surprise to me. A very big surprise indeed. But," Gerri paused, "she is retiring next year and things are very different from when you were in school, Riley. The things students do now. They just broke up a drug ring in the high school last week."

We stopped at the driveway into Aaron's property. Gerri sniffed. "I didn't think it was possible, but Aaron's place is now even more of an eyesore."

"Did you notice anything unusual last night?" I asked.

Gerri's dark eyebrows knit. "I did notice, well, it's nothing unusual really. We're all women of a certain age here on the lane. We all have trouble sleeping. Donna must've been quite upset by all the goings-on. I noticed the light on in her shed very late. Sometimes she goes there when she can't sleep."

"Before the fire?"

"No, I was sleeping like a log until I heard the fire engines. This was after we all went back home and most of the emergency vehicles left, very early in the morning. Three or four a.m.?" She adjusted her scarf. "Your actions really were quite heroic, Riley."

I watched the investigators inspect the foundation by the charred front door. "Darwin's the hero. He pulled me away from the house."

"Darwin's a good man." Gerri waved and called out to the investigators but my mind drifted.

Darwin hasn't been himself, Pru had said. Darwin was behind Aaron's house last night. I'd run up and he'd been there before me.

I pushed the uncomfortable thoughts away as the fire chief obeyed Gerri's summons. He didn't tell us anything we didn't know from watching the previous night. "I smelled gasoline," Gerri said, as if accusing him. He shook his head. Even if he'd learned anything, I'm sure he couldn't divulge any information.

When we entered the shop, everyone dropped what they were doing and surrounded me. "Are you okay?" "How's your finger?"

I was overwhelmed by everyone's concern. As Pru hugged me, I felt tears well. "I'm fine really." I blinked them back and said, "I have to make a phone call and then it's back to work for me."

I went into Buzzy's office and read the note from Dandy. "I don't want to disturb Riley. Please give her this number from McGillicuddy's collar. It's for Dr. Liam Pryce. She must make sure McGillicuddy's rabies vaccination is up to date."

Well, that was one good thing about the morning: I had an excuse to see Dr. Pryce. But no time. A phone call would have to do.

After I told the receptionist what I needed, she put me on hold. To my surprise, Dr. Pryce's warm voice came on the line. "Riley, I wanted to reassure you. McGillicuddy has been well cared for and is up to date on all his vaccinations."

My heart rate picked up at the sound of his voice.

"I want to commend you for your bravery. Not everyone would've run toward a fire to help like that."

He said something else about watching for redness or other signs of infection, but I only heard the end. "And if you have further questions, please call me anytime, or stop in." Oh, how I wished I could think of some further questions.

Brandon knocked on the open door.

I managed to say, "Thank you, Dr. Pryce."

I floated for a moment then turned to Brandon. "Yes, Brandon."

"We're out of mocha almond fudge?"

I tried to focus on my work, but so many customers asked about the fire or congratulated me for saving

McGillicuddy. Their concern felt good, but I couldn't shake the unsettling memory of Darwin running from the back of Aaron's house.

At one o'clock Pru handed me a covered dish. "I made you lunch. You've been through something very stressful, young lady, and you need to rest. We'll close tonight."

I felt fine but I needed answers. "I'll head up to the house. Thanks, Pru."

As I headed out the door, I saw Darwin in Pru's kitchen garden.

He ran over to me. "Riley, how are you?"

I gave him a hug. "Darwin, you may well have saved my life and McGillicuddy's."

He laughed softly as he rocked back on his heels and jingled the change in his pockets. "McGillicuddy. Take my advice, Riley, next time don't risk your life for a spoiled little dachshund. That's not a good trade for the rest of us."

"You were up there before I was." I watched him intently, my stomach churning. "How did you get there so quickly?"

Darwin ran a hand along his short white beard. "I wasn't able to sleep, so I took a walk. I walked up to Town Road, then turned and came back. That's when I saw the flames. Had my phone, thank goodness, and called it in. When I saw the front door was blocked by fire, I ran to the back because I thought I could get in that way. But whoever set the fires blocked the back door too." He shook his head. "Who could do such a thing?"

I hated that my first thought was it would be easy enough to check if Darwin called in the fire. I'd ask Tillie. But I'd never met a man who looked so honest.

Darwin seemed more relaxed than I'd seen him in a

while. "The fire helped me put some things in perspective, Riley. I know Pru told you that Emily and Kyle offered us scholarship money for Willow. But I made a decision last night. Their scholarship was just another name for bribe. I have faith that things'll work out in the end."

Detective Voelker pulled his Penniman Police SUV up to Buzzy's kitchen door. If he turned his head, he'd see me. He turned his head.

Sigh. "I'd better go."

"Good luck, Riley. Before I forget, peaches are in. Time to make peach ice cream?"

"Yes, absolutely." *How will I get all those peaches peeled with my hand bandaged?*

I walked up the hill. "Detective Voelker!" He waited by the steps. I remembered last night, how he'd stood close to Caroline, his posture protective, concerned. Was he married, I wondered? I threw a careful look at his left hand—no ring—but I knew several married guys who didn't wear a wedding band. I felt my wariness warm into something close to friendliness.

"Would you like some lunch?" I peeled back the cover on the dish. Pru had made a beautiful grain bowl, full of veggies and cheese, enough to feed a family of four.

"No, thanks," he cleared his throat. "How are you?"

My approach had thrown him off. I waved my bandaged finger. "Just a scratch."

"I need to take your statement about last night."

"Do you mind if I eat this while I talk to you? I'm starving."

We went inside and I asked him to sit down at the kitchen table.

"Coffee?" I said.

"No, thank you." He pulled out a pen and notepad.

Without Caroline here, he was all business. Sprinkles and Rocky sauntered into the kitchen. Sprinkles yawned and settled into a patch of sunlight. Rocky watched us, his eyes hardly blinking, tail swishing. He was sizing up Voelker. So was I. As I related my experience the previous night, I wondered: How much did I share of my own investigations? Could I get any information from him?

Voelker glanced down the hall.

"Looking for someone?" I took a bite of Pru's delicious salad.

His neck reddened and he scratched his throat. Ah, his tell. "I'm aware that Miss Spooner has gone back to work in Boston. I asked her to keep me apprised of her whereabouts."

"She'll be back this weekend," I said.

His face shut down, the professional cop back, but not before I saw his lips curve. Maybe he was human.

As I answered his questions about the fire I struggled with my decision to keep my thoughts about Darwin to myself. Darwin's explanation made sense, right? Why would Darwin want to harm Aaron?

A thought chilled me. Maybe it was because Aaron had Darwin on surveillance tape the night of the murder?

"Do you believe him?" The words were out before I could stop them.

Voelker's eyes leveled a keen look. "Him, who?"

"Aaron said he didn't have his security cameras on the night of Mike's murder." Why would Aaron say that if it wasn't true? Was Aaron protecting someone? A thought sprang to mind: Was Aaron blackmailing someone?

Blackmail? Aaron had mentioned "the real estate gal"—Emily again. She'd admitted being at the Love Nest the night of the murder. Did his security tapes capture evidence that she'd killed Mike? Would Aaron protect Emily—for a price?

I wondered if those tapes were ashes now.

Voelker was silent as he gathered his papers. "That's all for now. Thank you."

We went to the door. Some interviewer I was—I hadn't learned anything from him. Even Rocky and Sprinkles shot me disdainful looks as they stalked away.

I decided to throw caution to the wind. "When did you start working here in Penniman?"

Voelker pulled up short, and gave me a puzzled, but good-humored look. "Last summer."

"Are you married?" *Asking for a friend.*

He laughed, shaking his head. "Goodbye, Ms. Rhodes."

I ran upstairs and rustled through the box of clothes Paulette had sent over. I slipped into a blue dress made of one of those no-wrinkle wonder fabrics. It fit! It was a miracle. I tied a scarf around my neck and put on lipstick. I was the hero of Farm Lane. I hoped the hospital would let me talk to Aaron.

But when I asked at the hospital Information Desk, the receptionist told me that he was in ICU. Her desk was ringed with photos of a German shepherd. "Come back tomorrow. I'm sure he'll talk to you. You're the girl who saved him and his dog, right?"

"Just his dog," I said.

She patted my hand. "His most precious possession."

I headed back to the shop where crates of peaches were stacked by the back door. Buzzy's voice rang in my ears: *"Fresh fruit must go into the ice cream within twenty-four hours."*

Flo greeted me. "Riley, you're supposed to be resting."

"While you have all the fun?" I tied on an apron,

fumbling the strings with my bandaged hand. Flo took the strings and tied them for me. "I have to get going on the peaches."

She pursed her lips. "With your finger bandaged?"

McGillicuddy had to bite me on my right hand. Could I still use a knife? "No worries."

Gerri called my name from the front of the shop. Flo and I went to the counter, where Cadillac Ranch was taking a massive double-scoop cone from Gerri's hand.

He touched the brim of his hat. "Ladies. I have a proposition."

Three heart rates ticked up simultaneously.

"Word is that you have a lot of peaches. Peach ice cream's my favorite. I'd like to offer an exchange. I've been getting a little rusty and playing would help me keep my fingers and voice in shape. Singing here the other night was a pleasure. If you'd let me play again, you could pay me in peach ice cream."

"That's a deal," I said. "I'll do my best to get the ice cream ready but I'm a bit slow right now." I raised my bandaged hand.

His deep brown eyes radiated concern. "What happened?"

Flo launched into a highly embellished description of my rescue of McGillicuddy.

"My buddy Stretch knows his way around a kitchen. I have it on good authority that he's free this evening," Jasper said. "If you like, I could bring him to help."

Stretch? My stomach fell. Stretch, the strange guy who I thought was the firebug? But . . . this was an opportunity to question him. We wouldn't be alone in the shop. Plus, Jasper vouched for him. "Can I pay him in ice cream too?"

"I think he'd like that. We'll be back around seven." He touched his hat and went outside.

"Stretch the vagabond used to work in a kitchen?" Gerri sniffed. "It must've been before whatever misfortune befell him and sent him onto the streets."

I shrugged. "If he can make ice cream, I'm happy to have the help."

Chapter 40

When Darwin brought us dinner, I noticed that he and Pru were easier together. I was relieved, but then I remembered Pru's face when we talked of Brooke and Brooke's child. If only I could discover who was driving the car the night Martha Woodley was killed, it would ease Pru's mind, just as bringing Mike's killer to justice would ease Caroline's.

Who had answers? I was pretty sure the answer to Mike's murder was on Aaron's security tapes, which were probably destroyed in the fire. But Gerri said that Aaron worked in computers. Maybe the video was stored on some distant server. Or . . .

My mind flashed back to the moment Aaron dropped McGillicuddy, his most precious possession, into my arms. You save your most precious possessions in a fire. Isn't that what people say?

Aaron had been fussing with McGillicuddy's collar before he handed him out the window. I was sure there were charms or dog tags on McGillicuddy's collar, but could it have been something even more essential? Something like a flash drive?

I had to check. "I'm going to walk up to Dandy's and see how McGillicuddy's doing."

"I'll hold down the fort," Pru said. "But don't take long. We have to get the peach ice cream going."

"I'll be quick." I jogged up the lane. Dandy stood at the side of the Fire Chief's SUV, McGillicuddy straining on his leash. As I approached, the Chief gave her a wave and the SUV moved down the lane.

"Riley, how are you?" Dandy smiled but McGillicuddy growled low in his throat. Dandy picked him up and gave him a tight squeeze. "McGillicuddy, this lady saved your life. Behave!"

"I came to see how McGillicuddy's doing."

"Right as rain, not a hair was harmed. That nice veterinarian Dr. Pryce came over to see him, can you believe it?" Dandy said. "A house call. Aaron must be one of his best customers."

"When I was holding McGillicuddy last night, I thought there was something attached to his collar. Something like—" Suddenly I felt foolish, like I was confessing to a nutty conspiracy theory. "Something like a charm, or tag. Is it there?" I tilted my head to look.

She turned McGillicuddy so I could see a single bone-shaped charm with Dr. Pryce's name and phone number. "No other jewelry for McGillicuddy. Must've been your imagination."

My heart fell. I was sure there'd been more than one tag on the collar. "Maybe it dropped off."

"I'll keep my eyes open for it," she said. "Did you get my note and call Dr. Pryce?"

"I did, yes, thank you. Everything's okay."

"Good." She gave McGillicuddy a cuddle. "I'll check for another charm when I go back to the house."

"Thanks. Well, I have to go back and make ice cream."

"We'll have to stop by for ice cream, won't we, Mc-Gillicuddy?" She set him down again.

"Yes, please do. Good night." McGillicuddy and Dandy slowly crossed the street.

I turned to the smoldering hulk of Aaron's house. One of the fire department vans was still parked in the driveway and investigators were moving around the yard. I vowed to go back and search when they left.

As I headed back to Udderly, I was surprised to see Rocky by the side of Dandy's garage. He slipped around the corner like a shadow.

Chapter 41

*B*ack at Udderly, a party had started without me. Music flowed from the front parking lot, drifting over conversation and laughter from what sounded like a big crowd. I went in the back door of the shop and pulled up short.

Stretch was at the stove, stirring a pot. He was clad in jeans and a pressed denim button-down shirt, the sleeves rolled up to display colorful sleeves of tattoos. He wore black high-top sneakers in place of his heavy boots but still had his black cap tugged low on his forehead. I took a deep breath. Cadillac Ranch said he was a good cook and I needed help. Plus I wanted answers. Despite Buzzy's saying that beggars can't be choosers pinging into my mind, I gave him a smile.

"Hi, Stretch."

"Hi, Riley. Thanks for letting me help." Instead of giving off his usual skittish vibe, he now seemed relaxed. "I love making ice cream."

"Glad to have your help." As I washed my hands and slipped a plastic glove over my bandaged hand, he moved to the *Book of Spells*.

"It's exactly the same!" he marveled.

"What's the same?"

He looked up, his face open, and I could see his bright hazel eyes, his aquiline nose, his broad smile with slightly crossed front teeth. A curl of red hair escaped from his cap. "Your friend Buzzy's recipe's the same as mine. Same with some of the others." He flipped through the book. "She and I were culinary soul mates. I wish I could've met her."

"Me too." I looped on my apron and reached for the ties. Before I could tie it, Stretch was there tying it for me. Before I could thank him, he was back with the peaches, holding a knife. Before I could begin to feel uncomfortable, he started cutting peaches.

"Better if you stir, with your finger bandaged. I'll be okay with the peaches." His hands flew—I'd never seen anyone slice anything so fast, so deftly, and he cut every piece into uniform size.

I took up the spoon at the stove, stirring a fragrant custard. "Cadillac, er, Jasper tells me you're a chef."

He hunched his shoulders. "Yeah, yeah. Taking a break."

I backed off. If he remained comfortable I'd get more information out of him. Applause flowed into the work-room. "How did you and Jasper meet?"

He sliced another peach, tossed a piece into his mouth, and sighed. "I went to Texas to learn how to cook BBQ. Jasper has a ranch where he let me live alongside his cattlemen. I love traveling and trying the local cuisine. He told me he was coming out here to recharge his creative batteries, and I decided to come out too." His words sparked a memory. I'd seen a cooking show about a chef who traveled in disguise to different parts of the country to learn about regional foods. A chef with red hair.

Then it hit me. This was Chef Zach Coppola. If I mentioned knowing his identity, would he bolt? He had a reputation for being talented, but also quirky and mercurial.

I needed those peaches prepped. I shifted gears. "I know what you mean. When I was in Thailand, I discovered Thai stir-fried ice cream. I became obsessed with making it."

"Stir-fried?" he said "No way. Tell me more."

I told him about the street vendors who make ice cream treats on a chilled metal plate, adding different fruit, nuts, and flavorings, then "stir frying" the mixture together across the surface. It looked like stir frying, except the mix was being chilled by the super-cooled metal. When the mix became the consistency of ice cream, the cooks used special spatulas to push the ice cream into pretty rolls, put the rolls into cups, and top them with even more delicious fruits, nuts, candy, and cream.

"Thailand." His eyes became dreamy.

"Peaches." I pointed at the peaches.

He met my eyes for the first time and smiled.

After we'd finished the ice cream and cleaned up the kitchen, we sat outside at a picnic table away from the lighted parking lot. The crowd was heading home and a peaceful silence settled around us.

"I couldn't have done that without you. Thank you, Stretch." I thought the moment was relaxed enough for the question I was dying to ask. "Do you like being called Stretch? What's your real name?"

"I kind of like having a nickname. My real name's Zach. Zach Coppola." He took off his cap, his trademark curly red hair spilling out. "This thing gets hot." He scrubbed at his hair. "I like to kind of go undercover when I immerse myself in a place."

I couldn't wait any longer. I had to know, but again I approached cautiously. "Where are you staying? At Moy Mull?"

He looked down. "Well, I did some nights."

"You've been camping," I said.

He took a breath and raised his eyes to mine. "I didn't start that house fire. You have to believe me."

"I do believe you. But you *have* been camping?"

"I want to . . . live a place fully, right?" he said. "Become part of the landscape, the *terroir*."

I'd heard that word before, at a winery. "The earth?"

"The land, the weather, everything that makes a place distinctive. I got interested in local food and then foraging. That's what I've been doing here. Foraging. Living off the land. Wild mushrooms, greens, onions, berries . . . it's all there. I even got a wild turkey one day."

The knives I'd found in Dandy's yard. "You lost your knives."

He leaned toward me. "Do you have them?"

"No, the police do."

"Great," he raised his hands. "I don't want to get arrested for trespassing."

I considered. "You were camping on Caroline's land. I'm sure she won't press charges."

He held his head in his hands. "Yeah, that night I lost my knives, I was off my game. I'd found a great spot by the cemetery but I heard the cops come. I figured that crazy lady I'd seen earlier saw me and reported me."

Crazy lady? "What crazy lady?"

"I had cleared some ground there at the cemetery a few days before." He pointed up Farm Lane. "The dead have a great view on the side of that hill."

I shuddered, but remembered that Chef Zach was known for being eccentric.

"Anyway, it was late at night—not sure what time, but your shop was dark for hours. I saw a lady digging up flowers on a grave. I thought, that's strange, but what do I know? I'm pretty weird."

"Do you mean planting flowers?" I'd noticed fresh flowers on Brooke's grave. I shuddered. Did Dandy plant them at night?

Zach said, "I'm not sure what she was doing exactly. I didn't stick around."

"Do you remember what day that was?"

He shrugged. "Last Friday?"

The night of the murder. "Did you hear anything else? See anything else?"

"No, I took off when I saw her. I went back a few days later, but that's when the cops came and I lost my knives. Then last night . . . I heard about that fire. But it wasn't me." He put his cap on, tucking his hair underneath. "You've got to believe me."

I searched my feelings. I did believe him. "Where were you last night?"

"I stayed at Moy Mull, the art colony. I have a room there, where I keep my stuff. Jasper can vouch for me. We were up till all hours talking. He's a get-up-late, stay-up-late guy."

"What time did you guys turn in?" I asked.

"Two-ish? You can ask Jasper."

Rocky had woken me up at one o'clock. Stretch had an alibi. So who set the fire at Aaron's house?

Chapter 42

After I said good night to Stretch/Chef Zach, he walked down Farm Lane to Fairweather Road, insisting that he'd enjoy the walk back to Moy Mull.

I ran into the house, my body aching for a hot bath and a few hours with my feet up, but after flushing for Sprinkles and giving her and Rocky a treat, I grabbed a powerful flashlight from the mudroom and hurried outside.

All was peaceful as I walked up the hill, but I was troubled. I was certain that object I'd felt on McGillicuddy's collar was important. If Dandy didn't have it, it must've fallen off.

I swung my legs over the police tape at the end of Aaron's driveway—so sue me—and followed the flashlight's broad beam. At one point I pulled up short, stopped by the gleam of light on metal, but it was only a crushed beer can. The smell of smoke and wood doused by the firefighters' hoses grew stronger as I crossed the stone patio and approached the house. Bits of trash—wrappers, a pie tin, a length of chain, an old watering can—all caught the beam. I brushed aside the singed weeds at the foundation under the window where I'd caught McGillicuddy, but found nothing.

I walked back to the driveway entrance, stepped over the tape, swung the beam from side to side as I crossed the lane to Dandy's house, retracing my steps from the previous night. Her house was dark, except for security lights on the driveway and by the front door. I pushed the front gate, but it was locked.

I considered climbing over, but I couldn't bring myself to do more than scan with the flashlight. No gleam of metal, only glorious roses in lush summer bloom. Still, the object could have fallen off McGillicuddy's collar into one of these flower beds or the house. I'd come back tomorrow and search.

Chapter 43

The next morning, I slept late. I dashed down to Udderly, but Willow was already there with three interns. She'd drawn a ripe golden peach and the words "It's Here!" on the flavors chalkboards.

A half hour before opening, a line formed outside the shop. Word spread fast in Penniman.

My cell rang. "Riley!" Caroline spoke in a strained whisper. "I just heard about the fire on the news! Are you okay? Why didn't you call me?"

"I've been so busy. Don't worry, I'm fine. Aaron's in the hospital but I think he's okay. I'm going to go see him. I have a lot to tell you."

We promised to talk later and I hung up.

Three interns took the morning shift at the shop. Pru had been out late delivering a baby and was sleeping. I did a quick inventory. With Chef Zach's help, I had enough peach ice cream to last the week.

At lunchtime, Pru came over and shooed me out the door. I was glad to have her relieve me because I had to make a bank deposit. I'd taken to Buzzy's not-very-secure method of locking cash in the bottom drawer of her desk. I stuffed stacks of wrinkled bills in a grocery tote and prayed it didn't look like I was carrying several thousand dollars in cash.

After stopping at the bank, I drove to the hospital. The same receptionist from yesterday was at the Information Desk. Before I could speak, she announced to her coworkers, "This is the woman I was telling you about. She ran into the flames and saved Aaron Tuthill's dog from the fire!"

They applauded and I felt a blush warm my cheeks.

The receptionist told Aaron I'd stopped by yesterday and he'd left instructions that I could visit. She gave me directions and I headed up the elevator.

Aaron had been moved out of ICU to a single room in the step-down unit. I followed the sound of a talk show blaring at an alarming volume. In the sunny hospital room, Aaron lay against the bright white sheets, his metal glasses slightly askew, his gray hair wild.

I took a deep breath and spoke as loudly as I could. "Hi, Aaron. How are you feeling?"

Aaron fumbled for the remote and turned off the TV. He sat up, wheezed, and took my hand in his. "I feel fine. Wish I was out of here," he rasped, then his eyes reddened. "You saved McGillicuddy! Thank you, Riley. How is he?"

I raised my voice. Thank goodness that other bed was empty. "I'm glad I could help. McGillicuddy's fine. Doctor Pryce even made a house call to see him."

"Doctor Pryce." He sighed with relief and sank back on his pillows. "He's a good man."

"Yes, he is." On that we could agree.

Aaron said he felt fine, but his skin was gray against the hospital sheets and his breath came in short gasps. I knew I had to talk quickly. "Aaron, did you put something on McGillicuddy's collar before you dropped him out the window? A flash drive?"

His bushy gray eyebrows flew up. "Do you have it?"

Bingo. "No. I saw it when I caught McGillicuddy."

"So you don't have it?" He struggled upright. "How could it fall off?"

"I checked your yard and I'll check Dandy's, er, Mrs. Danforth's—"

"Donna Danforth?" His voice rasped. "What about her?"

"She's watching McGillicuddy."

He inhaled with a sharp gasping sound. "I thought *you* were watching McGillicuddy?"

"No, she is."

He shut his eyes and his head fell back against the pillow. He took several gasping breaths, and the panel on the wall over his head lit up and started beeping.

"What's wrong?" Panic rose in my chest, and I turned, frantic, as a nurse strode in.

"Sorry, you'll have to leave now," she said.

Well, I almost killed him. My heart hammering, I waited by the door for the nurse. When she emerged, she patted my arm. "He'll be fine, he just got overtired. He needs rest."

On the drive back to the shop, I took several deep breaths, trying to calm my jittering nerves. I'd saved McGillicuddy but almost killed Aaron.

But I was filled with a sense of determination. I was right—he did put something on McGillicuddy's collar.

I drove down Farm Lane past Dandy's house and noted that her blue van was parked in the driveway. Aaron's reaction when he learned that Dandy had McGillicuddy was so extreme it made me certain that I didn't want Dandy present when I searched for the flash drive.

Ice cream opens doors. I ran into Udderly's kitchen

where Pru stood at the sink washing scoops. "You wouldn't believe how many people have been asking for a flavor called Sugar High," she said.

I stopped short. "Brandon's flavor? Are you kidding?"

"It's popular with teenagers. I think it's a dare to eat it." She turned off the water and faced me. "Riley, seriously, what are you doing here? The interns and I are doing fine. I heard you were up all night making ice cream with Stretch."

"Remind me to tell you about Stretch." I grabbed a to-go cup and packed it with peach ice cream. "Pru, I'm going to check on McGillicuddy at Mrs. Danforth's."

"Really?" Pru folded her arms.

I winced. The woman could read me like a book. "Yes, I have ulterior motives." I just didn't have time to tell her all of them.

I had to search for that flash drive and . . . how did I tell Pru that ever since I heard that Brooke had been pregnant, I had to know for certain who the father was, that I feared it was Mike? As I walked back up the lane, I remembered Brooke's bedroom, the diary on the nightstand. No girl ever left her diary on her nightstand for her family to find. Dandy must have found it and read it after Brooke's death. All her daughter's secrets laid bare. What if Brooke had named Mike as the father of her child?

Wait a minute, Riley. Dandy had access to that diary ever since Brooke died seventeen years ago. If she'd wanted to confront the father of Brooke's baby, she would've done it years ago. If she'd thought it was Mike, surely Buzzy or Caroline would've known and told me about it.

I shook my head. Maybe there were clues in the diary

that a mother wouldn't understand. I needed to read it myself. What I planned was a violation of privacy, no doubt, but I needed answers and this was the only way I could think to get them.

Chapter 44

To my surprise, Dandy's white picket gate was open when I arrived. I searched under the rose bushes for Aaron's flash drive but I saw nothing but well-tended earth. I squared my shoulders and rang the doorbell.

Barking commenced inside and I heard a harsh "Quiet!" as the door opened.

"Oh, hello, Riley. How are you?" Dandy was dressed in her usual matching tennis skirt and top—navy blue with white trim—with a visor holding back her shoulder-length gray hair.

"Hi, Mrs. Danforth. I'm doing well, thanks. I was thinking you might need a break from watching McGillicuddy." The little dog's barks were now interspersed with a high-pitched whine. "I'd love to take him for a walk." She hesitated in the doorway with the door almost closed behind her, her hand on the knob.

I'd prepared for this situation. I held out the pint of ice cream. "I thought you'd like some peach ice cream. We just made it."

Her face brightened. "Oh, thank you, I do like peach. I'll put this in the freezer. Come in." My eyes swept the living room floor and hallway as I entered. No sign of any flash drive or dog charm on the gleaming hardwood floors, or particle of dust for that matter.

Dandy had put up a barricade in the kitchen to keep McGillicuddy from exploring the house. She stepped over it and I followed. In the corner was a cut-down cardboard box lined with a threadbare bath towel, not the digs the beloved pooch was probably used to. From the way Aaron coddled him, I figured McGillicuddy's standard of living was close to Sprinkles'.

"There he is!" I said.

The little dog yipped and approached, but thank goodness didn't seem excited enough to bite me again. I stroked his soft head.

"I told Aaron when I saw him at the hospital I'd take McGillicuddy for a walk. I thought you needed a break from dog sitting."

"How thoughtful." She put the ice cream in the freezer. "You saw Aaron?"

"Yes, I just came from the hospital. He's fine but he looked lonely." He certainly hadn't looked fine when I left him, but I hoped the lie was enough to lure Dandy away from her house.

She tilted her head. "Perhaps I should go see him."

"I'm sure he'd appreciate company. Is it okay if I take McGillicuddy for a walk while you're gone?"

"Yes, that's a wonderful idea. Let me get the leash. I left it outside on the patio. I'll be back in a moment."

As soon as she stepped out, I hurdled the gate and dashed down the hallway to Brooke's room, unlocked the window, and pushed it open slightly. McGillicuddy yipped wildly from the kitchen.

I dashed back and was in the kitchen petting McGillicuddy when Dandy returned. Too late, I wondered if she had an alarm system, but I didn't see a keypad by the door. I craned to see the front door, but saw no keypad there either. If she had security cameras, I didn't know what I'd do. But I hoped her issues were confined to gardening in the cemetery at midnight, like Aaron's was on surveilling the neighborhood.

"Go for a walk with Riley," Dandy said in a singsong voice as she clipped on McGillicuddy's leash. "It'll be good to tire him out." We went into the backyard, where she'd made a run for McGillicuddy out of chicken wire.

Dandy got into her van and pulled out of the driveway. McGillicuddy and I trotted after her. I watched the van head toward Town Road. The hospital was less than five minutes away. I had to move fast.

"C'mon McGillicuddy, back we go." I hustled back up the driveway, but McGillicuddy's little legs couldn't keep up. I picked him up, struggling to hold his wriggling body. I had to get to Brooke's diary.

I turned the knob on the kitchen door, but as expected, it was locked. The window would have to do. I unclipped McGillicuddy's leash and put him in the run. He barked, short, insistent yips that said to anyone listening: *Something is wrong!*

I dragged a patio chair under Brooke's window, climbed up, then hooked my fingers under the sash and lifted. I boosted myself onto the ledge. It was easier than I thought. All that scooping and toting tubs of ice cream had made my arms strong.

I heard a car in front of the house and froze as it passed by. McGillicuddy barked a few more times, then plopped down on his belly to watch me. This was more excitement than he was used to. It was more than *I* was used to. I wiped my sweaty hands on my shorts. What was wrong with me? I shouldn't be doing stuff like this, but I was tired of waiting for answers, tired of being unable to help Pru with this sorrow about Martha Woodley, and tired of being unable to give Caroline answers about

Mike's death. If there was a chance I'd learn something
that'd help, I'd take it.

I prayed I wouldn't get caught.

I pushed the thought away. After slipping off my
shoes, afraid dirt would cling to the pretty pink and
yellow rug, I dropped into the room and crossed to
Brooke's nightstand. I noted the position of the diary, so
I'd remember exactly how to replace it.

As I picked up the denim-covered book, a special
kind of quiet suffused the room. I imagined Dandy
in here every day, lying on her daughter's bed, paging
through this book, looking for answers, for some clue
she'd missed, some warning she should've heeded.

I opened the diary. Brooke's entries were written
in blue pen, with some words in different-color ink for
emphasis. I skimmed, looking for Mike's name, but I
stopped short when I saw Emily's in a passage from the
October before Brooke died.

*Emily's so jealous. I can't do anything right with her.
She wants to be cheer captain, she wants my clothes, she
wants my boyfriend. I know she does. She's pathetic. She
could have any guy she wants why does she want him
too?*

All these years later, Emily was here, in Brooke's
diary.

I scanned more pages but didn't see Mike's name, or
any guy's name for that matter. Only "him." I remembered Dandy had forbidden Brooke to date. Perhaps
Brooke knew her mother would read her diary and she'd
wanted to keep any "him" from her mother's prying eyes?

*June 5: I told him about the baby. He's worried
about his precious family finding out. I told him it was
my decision and he had to decide if he wanted me too.*
My heart dropped—his girlfriend had needed him—

how could Mike do that? This corroborated the notes in Martha's ledger.

I flipped pages. The penultimate entry was dashed off, the ink smeared.

July 18: I hope Martha Woodley remembers what she said about me staying with her. Because I'm leaving. I told Mom. I thought her head would blow off. She wants to know who the father is, but I'm not telling. Not yet. He called and said we'd figure it out. I knew he wouldn't let me down.

With trembling fingers, I turned to the next day, the last entry.

July 24: Nina's coming over. She wants to bake together like we did when we were kids. Mom says it's so nice. Ironic much, mom? She's always been on me about my weight. She's always nice when Nina's around. Now Mom says she'll help me with the baby. I don't care. I know what I want and she can't tell me what to do.

The next page was empty.

The blare of a car horn and voices from the street made me jump and I set the diary back in place. As I turned to go, I noticed a rocking chair against the wall by the doorway, which was out of my line of sight when I'd stood there the other day. Several well-worn stuffed animals were heaped in a pile on the seat, including a teddy bear wearing a stained white T-shirt with the words "Sugar Bear" written in sloppy magic marker.

A car pulled in the driveway and McGillicuddy yelped madly. I jumped across the room, jammed my feet back in my shoes, and slid out the window onto the chair. My hands slipped as I grasped the window and jerked it down. I jumped from the chair and placed it back on the patio, my hands trembling so badly I almost knocked it over.

I raced over to McGillicuddy seconds before Dandy
rounded the corner of the house. My chest heaving
and sweat pouring down my back, I bent to stroke Mc-
Gillicuddy and realized the chair had left marks in the
soft earth beneath the window. With another jolt, I realized that Dandy would surely discover that though the
bedroom window was closed, it was now unlocked.

"They wouldn't let me see Aaron," Dandy said
shortly, swinging her keys into her palm with a thwack.

"That's too bad." I headed for the driveway, fighting
an urge to run. "McGillicuddy was a good dog. Look
how tired he is. I'd better get back to the shop. Bye!"

I ran down Farm Lane and up the steps of Buzzy's
farmhouse, my mind whirling with two facts I'd learned,
answers to two questions I hadn't thought to ask.

Brooke hadn't noted any boyfriend's name in her
diary.

Nina had visited Brooke the night before she died.

What had happened to make Brooke take a handful
of sleeping pills? She had a safe place for herself and her
baby and still she took her own life? *Think Riley, despite
Brooke's confidence, she was a teenager.* I thought back
to when I was eighteen, tried to imagine living with a
woman who made her students shake in their boots.

She's always been on me about my weight.

On the bookshelf in Mike's room, I'd noticed yearbooks. I pulled out the one from his senior year, and
curled my legs under me on the bed as I turned glossy
pages to Mike's senior photo. He grinned from the page,
handsome, brash, the world at his feet. A list of activi-
ties was printed under every photo. His read "Football,
State Champions. Business Club. Swimming. Tennis."

I paged to Kyle Aldridge's photo. While Mike had
been handsome, Kyle had been cute, still hadn't grown

out of his boyishness. "Football, State Champions. Tennis. Student Senate. Class President. Spring Play: *Brigadoon*."

In her photo, Emily Weinberg dipped her chin at the camera, a look perfected, no doubt, by many hours in front of the mirror. "Cheer. Student Senate. Fashion Club. Tennis."

I flipped back to the *B*s. Nina Baldwin. Nina's swan neck, pearl earrings, and square jaw were elegant, even in a class photo. "Cheer. Student Senate. Tennis."

I turned to Brooke Danforth's photo. How many people looked that good in their yearbook photo? She exuded confidence, charisma, a girl who knew what she wanted. "Cheer Captain. Gymnastics Team, State Champions. Fall Festival Homecoming Queen. Spring Play: *Brigadoon*."

I flipped to the photos of the prom. A banner across the school doors proclaimed the theme: "Truly, Madly, Deeply." The cheerleading team was photographed in front of a pink stretch Hummer. I wondered whose idea that had been.

I remembered the photos Rocky had knocked off the bureau. I jumped to my feet and stood them up, first the photo from the pie eating contest. In October, Brooke had written, "she wants my boyfriend." Next, I turned over Mike and Emily's formal portrait from Senior Prom, his bow tie coordinated with her pink gown. Emily had gotten Brooke's fall boyfriend, Mike. I was sure that Brooke wouldn't let a guy go unless she wanted to let him go.

I scanned the shelves and found another photo, a group shot at the prom with Mike and Emily in the same pink-accented clothes, standing together; Nina and Kyle at the other end of the group; and Brooke surrounded by girls in the center of the photo. A few guys in the back and kneeling in front mugged for the camera, flashing hand signs.

I went back to the yearbook and paged through dozens of prom photos; Brooke was always in a group of girls—she hadn't gone to the prom with a date. I turned to the section with photos of the spring play, *Brigadoon*. The cast danced in swirling plaid kilts, Brooke in the foreground, Kyle in the background, holding a bouquet of heather.

I flipped the heavy yearbook cover closed.

Spring Play. Brooke was pregnant in June. I closed my eyes, picturing her desk. She'd saved the program from the play and a tiny bit of dried heather, put them on her desk so she'd see them every day when she did her homework.

I also saw the teddy bear with the ridiculous homemade T-shirt, the words "Sugar Bear" in big black letters, relegated to the pile of cast-off, formerly loved stuffed animals. I imagined Dandy, sitting on her daughter's bed, paging through the diary, looking for clues, seeing that bear every day. And suddenly, after so many years, hearing someone say those very words: Sugar Bear.

What exactly happened the day Brooke died? How to find out? I didn't dare ask Dandy. There must've been a police report on Brooke's death. I knew how to get one.

Tillie met me at Udderly after she left work. I had promised her a free peach ice cream cone in return for information. With all the thoughts I had swirling in my head, I'd hardly been able to keep orders straight.

Tillie and I sat at a picnic bench in front of the shop. In the gathering twilight, I silently read the report as Tillie munched her ice cream cone.

Deceased found in bedroom. Mother stated deceased had taken sleeping pills on occasion under doctor's supervision. Mother found girl in the morning when she didn't come to breakfast. Empty bottle of sleeping pills found by deceased's bed.

The medical examiner's report corroborated Martha Woodley's records. Brooke was pregnant.

Decedent's mother has no knowledge of the identity of deceased's boyfriend.

The sleeping pills had suppressed her breathing.

Stomach contents . . . blueberry pie.

Tillie sat across from me enjoying the warm night air, savoring her delicious creamy treat.

"Do you remember when Brooke Danforth died?" I asked.

Tillie cocked her head. "Yes. No. What I remember more was that it was the first time I heard about eating disorders."

When she finished, Tillie thanked me, got into her red convertible Beetle, and took off. I sifted through the papers again and realized that something was missing. Not something, someone. There was no mention of Nina Baldwin. I guess she'd gone home after baking the pie with Brooke.

On my phone, I searched "bulimia" and found this: "an eating disorder in which a large quantity of food is consumed in a short period of time, often followed by feelings of guilt or shame."

If you knew your friend had bulimia, would you bake them a pie?

Chapter 45

The windows of Buzzy's farmhouse glowed with warm light. Why were the lights on? A car I didn't recognize was parked by the kitchen door, a Zipcar with Massachusetts plates. Caroline was home?

"Riley, is that you?" Caroline called as I entered. Sprinkles lunged from under the kitchen table and I just managed to avoid tripping on her.

"I thought you were staying in Boston all week?" I said.

Caroline put a takeout salad on the table. She was still dressed in her work clothes, a conservative black skirt and simple white blouse. The jacket of the suit was on the back of her chair, and its lapels were already covered with Sprinkles' fur.

"With that firebug on the loose? I didn't want you alone," she said. "I got a Zipcar and came down."

My heart warmed. Petite Caroline, my protector. "We don't have to worry about the firebug." I paused. "Well, we don't have to worry about *one* firebug."

Caroline shook her head as if trying to clear her thoughts. "What are you talking about? There are two? Here, eat something." She put some salad on a plate and set it in front of me, her concerned brown eyes magnified behind her glasses. "What is it? You look like you're going to burst."

I was too jittery to sit, unsettled by what I'd learned and what I now believed. Sprinkles' head swiveled as I paced and told Caroline what I'd done and what I suspected.

"You broke into Dandy's house and read Brooke's diary? Have you lost your mind?" Caroline's voice rose. "What does Brooke's diary have to do with Mike's murder?"

"I think the seeds of Mike's murder were planted seventeen years ago . . ."

Caroline slowly lowered herself into a chair.

". . . when Brooke got pregnant with Kyle Aldridge's baby."

Caroline gasped and her brow knitted. "What?"

"I'm pretty sure Kyle was the father of Brooke's child." How would Caroline react to my next words? "At first I thought it was Mike's."

Her eyes widened but she shrugged. "Mike dated a lot of girls but I don't remember him with Brooke. She never seemed into him."

I took a deep breath. "Caroline, when we were at the funeral, remember Emily came up to us and Mike couldn't recall her name? He called her Sugar Bear. Brooke has a teddy bear in her room with a Sugar Bear T-shirt."

"So?"

I rubbed my forehead, trying to gather my rushing thoughts. "Let's start at the beginning. Brooke kept secrets from Dandy. Dandy forbade her to date, but Brooke did. When Brooke died, suddenly Dandy had access to her diary. However, Brooke never named boys' names. She just wrote "him." Picture Dandy in Brooke's bedroom, every day after Brooke died, paging through that diary, looking for clues, wondering who the father of Brooke's baby was.

"I realized something when I, ah, broke in. If Dandy sat on the bed, she'd see that teddy bear. Since Brooke never named boyfriends in her diary, I think Dandy put that bear together with Mike at the funeral. Dandy must've had the shock of her life hearing someone speak the words she'd seen every day in her daughter's room. She'd stumbled when she heard them. I thought she'd simply been distracted by Emily's outfit. Plus—" I stopped, certain now.

Caroline whispered, "Yes?"

"I don't think Brooke's death was an accident."

"Not an accident? You think someone murdered Brooke? Who?" Caroline whispered. "Kyle?"

I gripped the back of a chair. I'd considered so many scenarios. What did the diary say? *He's worried about his precious family finding out. Martha Woodley noted that she'd seen Brooke walking with a boy by the lake—where the Aldridges lived.* I remembered the football summer camp photos over Mike's bed. I shook my head. "No. Brooke died in July, when Kyle and Mike were at football camp in Indiana. No, it was someone who wanted to keep Kyle for herself."

Caroline searched my face. "Oh my god. You think Nina killed Brooke? But they were best friends."

I said slowly, "The diary says Nina was at Brooke's house the night before she died. Nina wanted to bake a pie with Brooke. She must've known about Brooke's eating disorder. She knew Brooke took sleeping pills. All she had to do was grind some of the same brand of sleeping pill, add them to Brooke's pie, then make sure Brooke's own bottle was empty so it looked like she'd taken them all."

Silence fell on the kitchen and I met Caroline's eyes.

After a moment, she said, "There's no way to prove that now, is there?"

I shook my head and fell into a chair. Rocky emerged from the parlor, threaded around my ankles, then padded softly to the door, where he sat down and groomed a paw. Sprinkles flopped onto the floor, batted a toy mouse, and yawned.

Though the night was warm, a chill ran through me and I rubbed my arms.

Caroline spoke softly. "So you think Dandy killed Mike because she blamed him for the pregnancy and for Brooke taking her own life? Mike was killed because Dandy assumed, incorrectly, that he was the father of Brooke's baby?"

I shook my head. "No. I think Dandy told Nina what she believed and that she intended to confront Mike."

Caroline picked up Sprinkles and stroked her fur.

My thoughts and words tumbled. "Careful Nina was covering her tracks. All these years everyone assumed Brooke had died by an overdose. Then when Dandy had this realization, incorrect though it was, that Mike was the father of Brooke's child, killing Mike was a way to cement that belief.

"Dandy must've been"—I could only grope for words—"shaken to her core. She and Nina are close. She'd probably told her what she'd figured out, and that she was going to confront Mike.

"Nina had to act. What would Mike say? Had Kyle ever told Mike that he'd gotten Brooke pregnant? The diary said Brooke and Kyle were talking, perhaps making plans. Maybe Kyle had planned to make a life with Brooke." *Had he ever told Nina any of this? Had he told Mike? It didn't matter. What mattered was what Nina believed, what she feared she'd lose. Poor Nina, all these years living a life that looked perfect on the outside, but suffering betrayals by Kyle—in the present with his secretary, and in the past with her best friend.*

"The only course open for Nina was to make sure Mike couldn't answer any of Dandy's questions. Letting Dandy think that Mike had been the father of Brooke's child added a layer of camouflage to the fact that Nina had killed Brooke, giving credence to Brooke's suicide and hiding Kyle's role in her pregnancy.

"This was an opportunity for Nina. Kyle's starting on the campaign trail. If Dandy was convinced that Mike was the father of Brooke's baby and Mike was silenced, that messy chapter of Kyle's life would be closed forever."

The paper bag with Mike's effects was still on the table. I picked it up. It was lighter than I remembered. I opened it and looked inside. The phone was gone.

"Caroline, did you move Mike's phone?"

"What?" She looked inside the bag then up at me, her face stricken. "Someone took Mike's phone!"

"And left a heavy gold class ring and keys to an expensive car?" I thought back to that uncomfortable moment with Kyle and Nina at Udderly. "Caroline, do you remember Nina's face when you asked her about the diamond watch? She had no idea Kyle was on Block Island with another woman. I should've realized Nina wasn't there—she was here doing the Memorial Day Fun Run." Another memory surfaced. "Do you remember after the funeral, Nina came up to talk to us? Angelica was there. Do you remember what Nina said?"

Caroline rubbed her forehead, then her eyes widened. "Nina was so excited to meet Angelica. She said 'I'm so pleased to meet you.'"

"Nina hadn't met Angelica before," I said. "But they all—Kyle, Mike, Angelica, Kyle's secretary with the fancy watch—had been together on Block Island."

"How on earth did Nina find Mike's phone?" Caroline said. "It's in the bag."

"She probably called it. Kyle must've had Mike's number." Caroline didn't even have to mention that the door was unlocked. I'd forgotten to lock it.

Still, that was desperate, breaking into this house. Nina's back was against the wall.

Caroline's voice seeped into my consciousness. "We have to call Detective Voelker."

"So I can tell him I broke into Dandy's house?" I chewed my lower lip. How could I corner a killer without mentioning that? I had no evidence except old photos, a diary, a sprig of heather, a typewritten note, and a missing phone. I couldn't believe Voelker would take any of it seriously.

I grabbed a flashlight from the mudroom and checked that the beam was strong. Its solid weight was comforting. "Stretch said a crazy lady was digging at Brooke's grave the night of the murder. I'm going to the cemetery to check it out."

"You're not going alone. Wait a sec." Caroline grabbed a piece of note paper and a pen, then spoke out loud as she wrote, "We've lost our minds and are going to the cemetery. Come get us if we're not back by breakfast."

Rocky yowled as we ran out and closed the door on him. My stomach churned as we walked up the road and turned onto the narrow lane that ran past the cemetery. "Let's cut behind the sunflowers." In case anyone was watching, the tall stalks would hide our approach to the cemetery.

I thought about Nina as we took slow, careful steps on the sun-baked earth. For as long as I could remember, Nina and Kyle had been a couple. They were both from old Penniman families, perfectly matched.

While I was sure Brooke and Kyle had been as

discreet as high school kids can be—love triangles are a delicate, dangerous business—Nina wasn't a fool. Nina must've seen the sprig of heather in her friend's room, noticed that she'd saved the *Brigadoon* program. When she'd learned about the other woman on the Block Island trip, it must've reopened the wound of Kyle's earlier betrayal.

I wondered if there'd been other infidelities along the way. Nina, neat as a pin Nina, was a woman with so much to lose. She had a spectacular home, beautiful children, Kyle's political career, her place at the top of Penniman society. She'd killed Brooke to keep Kyle for herself. She'd done too much to give that up now, and had killed Mike to keep her secret.

Or was I wrong? Would we find another woman, another crazy lady, at the grave?

Pale light glowed from the cemetery near Brooke's grave and seeped through the curtain of sunflower stalks.

Caroline's breathing was ragged as she grabbed my arm, holding me back. "Don't get too close." Her fear gave me pause. Mike's killer had killed before.

"I'm just going to look," I whispered.

I parted the leaves.

Soft white light created a nimbus around Brooke's gravesite. A woman, tall and thin, crouched at the headstone. The light of a lantern distorted her shadow into something nightmarish, her limbs elongated like spider's legs. She wept as she stabbed at the earth with a trowel.

As Caroline craned to see better, she lost her balance and fell into the row of sunflowers. The rustle of dry stalks carried in the still night air.

The woman's head jerked around, her face contorted by fear. Nina. "Who's there?"

A black form darted past me, brushing my ankles.

Rocky? Caroline cried out. Rocky leapt from the ground to the stone wall, then straight at Nina.

She shrieked and flung her trowel. Rocky sprang aside, hissing as the trowel missed him by inches. Nina scrambled to her feet and ran into the trees, taking the same path Stretch had, the path to Dandy's house.

Caroline and I gasped and clutched each other. "Nina! And Rocky!" Caroline exclaimed. "Sorry I yelled. I felt him brush my feet and I freaked out."

I picked my way through the sunflowers, and after a moment Caroline followed. In the distance, a car engine turned over and sped away.

Rocky peeped around Brooke's headstone and slunk over the disturbed earth.

The grave drew me closer, but I stopped short of the spot where Nina had dug. I crouched, turned on the flashlight's beam, and watched Rocky sniff at the freshly dug soil.

Caroline stepped close to the grave, but I put out my arm to stop her. I didn't want to contaminate the site further. Rocky tested the earth with his paw and started digging.

She whispered, "He's going to find the phone."

I swallowed hard. Yes, but I was pretty sure Rocky would find something else too. Stretch had told me the crazy lady had been at work here on the night of the murder.

Rocky suddenly stopped digging and looked up at me, his amber eyes inscrutable. Just visible in the dirt was the finger of a leather gardening glove.

Police vehicles arrived in minutes, lights strobing over the gravestones. The squawk of radios, the slamming car doors, the jangle of the cops' equipment belts were loud in the dark. We spoke with the officers, then Voelker arrived on scene. After listening to our story, he said, "Go wait at home."

Caroline and I shared a guilty look, then melted back into the sunflowers and watched. Voelker crouched by the grave and shone a flashlight on the glove. The investigators conferred around the site and I heard one say they needed to wait until daylight in order to search and photograph the scene properly. Officers taped off the area.

"I can't wait until daylight," I said.

"So Nina buried the gloves," Caroline's voice was small. "She killed Mike."

I wrapped my arms around her, remembering the loose dirt and plantings I'd seen at Brooke's grave. Did Dandy know what had been buried there? "The police will have to talk to Stretch." I hoped he could positively identify the woman he'd seen burying the gloves. I tugged Caroline's hand. "There's something else I have to do."

"Are you kidding me?" Caroline's voice strained. "What else is there? Nina killed Mike, right? The police have the gloves! She was digging there."

I took a deep breath. We crept to the end of the row of sunflowers, then crossed Farm Lane, moving in the shadows away from the line of police vehicles. We melted into the crowd of curious farmhands gathered there. Darwin saw us and rushed forward. "I was looking for you!" he said.

I turned up Farm Lane toward Dandy's house. Caroline and Darwin followed.

"Nina killed Mike," Caroline said dully.

Darwin put his arm around her and looked at me over Caroline's bowed head. "Is that true? Why?"

"It's complicated," I said.

The scent of smoke still emanated from the burned hulk of Aaron's house. I recalled his thick glasses. He'd seen a tall, slim woman with shoulder-length hair at the barn on his security camera the night of the murder. He'd assumed it was Dandy. He'd thought the knowledge gave him the upper hand, gave him leverage to get her to join the real estate deal, but all it had done was almost get him killed in a fire and put his most precious possession in Dandy's hands.

"Come on," I said. Safety in numbers. Dandy must know the police were just down the road at the graveyard. Had she seen Nina drive off? Surely the police would soon be knocking at the door of Nina's spectacular lakefront home.

I opened Dandy's garden gate, stepped into the lush beauty of her garden, inhaling the soft scent of roses. McGillicuddy barked from within the house. Before I could knock, Dandy pulled open the door, a hand to her chest, panting. "What is it? What's going on?"

I felt a surge of sympathy for Dandy. There was only one way I could help her now.

"I hope you didn't get rid of Aaron's flash drive," I said. "You'll need it to prove your innocence."

Chapter 46

Dandy reared back. She looked from Darwin to Caroline and back to me.

"The police are searching for evidence at Brooke's grave," Caroline said in a quiet voice.

Dandy stiffened, her knuckles white on the doorjamb. Behind her McGillicuddy whined, his nails tapping as he ran back and forth on the kitchen floor.

"You and Nina resemble each other. Your height, your build, your hair, even the way you both dress in athletic wear," I said. "That's why Aaron's been blackmailing you. He saw Nina on his security video and thought she was you. You burned down his house to protect her."

Dandy slumped. I grabbed her arm and Darwin took the other. We helped her into the living room and lay her on the sofa as Caroline picked up McGillicuddy, soothing him with quiet words.

As Dandy's eyes fluttered open, she moaned, "Nina was Brooke's friend."

Did she never suspect that Nina had killed Brooke?

"Where's the flash drive?"

* * *

Twenty minutes later, Caroline and I walked down the lane toward home, with Darwin holding a surprisingly docile McGillicuddy. When we'd left Dandy with Detective Voelker, she was leading him across her yard to her garden shed.

I suddenly became aware that Rocky was trailing us. I scooped him up.

"You crazy cat," I whispered.

Darwin said a tired good night. "We'll talk tomorrow. I'm . . ." his voice trailed off as he walked down the lane toward the warm lights of his farmhouse.

Sprinkles stood at our door, yowling an injured greeting.

Caroline picked her up and held her close. "Riley, do you think Nina would've killed Angelica too?"

I stepped into the familiar warmth of the kitchen and let out a sigh. "One thing that was odd from the start was the note and the wine. I thought the wine was drugged to immobilize Mike, which, yes, it was. He was big and athletic and would be hard to overpower. But the note to go in the barn seemed a bit much.

"Nina was a big fan of Angelica's. I think she wanted to spare Angelica seeing Mike's murdered body. Maybe she thought Angelica would fall asleep first and then Mike would go in the barn and fall asleep there."

Sprinkles yowled and squirmed out of Caroline's arms.

"She was desperate . . ." Caroline's voice trailed off.

Nina wanted to preserve the life she'd built with Kyle. "I'm sure of it." A thought tugged at me, another thread to tie up but I was so tired, it was all I could do to flush for Sprinkles and trudge upstairs. Tomorrow I'd go to Aaron's and tie up that loose end.

Caroline gave me a hug. "I'll see you in the morning."

Chapter 47

After only four hours of sleepless tossing and turning, "haggard" didn't even begin to describe what I looked like. I put on coffee, fed the cats, and slumped into a chair at the kitchen table. A knock at the door made me wince and I pushed myself to my feet. Tillie, a vision in a scarlet jumpsuit, waved through the window. I opened it and she slid inside. "Since we're working together," she said, "I thought I'd let you know what happened at the station last night."

Her words acted like a jolt of caffeine. As she took a seat at the table, I poured her a cup of coffee. Rocky gave her the cold shoulder, but Sprinkles let Tillie pet her.

Tillie filled me in on what had happened after we'd left Dandy's house.

Dandy and Nina had been taken to the police station for questioning. Tillie had heard the call on the police scanner and decided she had some filing to do in the observation room during Nina's interview.

"She was a queen," Tillie said with grudging admiration. "She didn't give them anything."

Tillie also managed to be present when the police viewed the security video from Aaron's flash drive. Dandy had hidden it in her garden shed the night she set fire to Aaron's house. "The footage wasn't great, but you could tell who was who, and it was definitely Nina Aldridge going into the barn," Tillie said. As Tillie recounted what she'd seen on the tape, the scene unspooled in my mind like a movie.

Around nine-thirty the night of the murder, Mike and Angelica walked down the front steps of the Love Nest and went down Farm Lane to join us all at Buzzy's house.

As they disappeared from sight, a tall woman with a slim, athletic build crossed the lane to the Love Nest. She carried a large tote bag. She went into the house for a few moments, then exited, retracing her steps across the lane. She must've parked her car by the cemetery, where she'd have a clear view of the road and the Love Nest.

Angelica returned, then a few minutes later, Mike. After almost an hour passed, Angelica burst from the house, stumbled down the steps and into her car, and roared off. Mike exited the Love Nest and went into the barn. Then, shortly after midnight, the same tall woman crossed the road again but bypassed the Love Nest and went into the barn. She crossed the road again minutes later, this time running, holding a pair of gardening gloves.

"The rest of the footage corroborated Emily's and Darwin's stories," Tillie said. She pointed at Rocky and chuckled. "He was there!"

Rocky looked up from his food for a moment, blinked, then went back to his breakfast.

"What happens to Nina now?" I said. "And Dandy?"

"Lawyered up, of course." Tillie said as she gathered her things. "Gotta go. See you later."

I gave Rocky a nuzzle. "I need to go for a run."

I jogged up Farm Lane, passing police vehicles parked on the road to the cemetery and in front of Dandy's house. I played my role: I'd dressed in jogging clothes and pulled my hair into a ponytail that bounced with each step. I was just another runner and the investigators ignored me.

Perfect.

I darted into Aaron's driveway. I had one more thread to tie. I knew I should wait for the police, but my curiosity got the better of me, as usual.

Once in Aaron's yard, I wished I was wearing work boots with steel toes. I bushwhacked through the weeds to a row of car bodies, hoping I didn't step on any scraps of rusty, tetanus-inducing metal. I realized that I hadn't understood what I'd seen in Aaron's yard. Aaron didn't have parts of cars in his yard. He had car parts, a chop shop.

For many professional theft rings, stealing and stripping vehicles for parts has always been a lucrative business. Parts are often worth more than the intact vehicle and are easier to move and sell, especially parts for rare vintage vehicles.

One rusted hulk drew me. On an earlier visit, my eyes had been drawn immediately to the body of a Mustang, a model that came out when I was in high school. I recalled the photo I'd seen in Mike's bedroom, a photo of Kyle showing off his shiny new car. The rusted shell in front of me was the same model, but there was nothing left of the paint job and detailing that had been the envy of the school–the tires, seats, and engine had long since been scavenged. I edged through waist-high Queen Anne's lace to the front of the car. The bumper was still there, but no buyer would want it. There was a significant dent in the right front corner.

After seventeen years' exposure to the elements, I didn't think there'd be any evidence left behind, but I'd let the police make that determination.

That afternoon, Pru and I walked among the sunflowers. Dark circles ringed her eyes. A delivery the previous night had been successful, but difficult.

I knew from Brooke's diary that she had spoken to Kyle about the baby. She'd probably mentioned Martha Woodley. I remembered how proud Kyle'd been of his new Mustang, and then months later had a new one because he said he'd wrecked the first. No one had questioned it.

I told Pru about the car I'd discovered in Aaron's yard. "I don't know if Kyle planned to kill Martha," I said, but I thought to myself, *How easy to turn the wheel.*

Pru shook her head. "It could've been an accident. He was young, probably scared."

Pru was right, there was no way to know for sure, without a confession from Kyle, and I knew that would never happen.

"Do you think Kyle's family knew?" Pru asked.

That was one thing I was certain of. "I think the Aldridge family covered it up. That was a very expensive car. For it to end up in Aaron's yard, sold for parts? I think the family turned to its black sheep to make the problem go away."

Chapter 48

A few weeks later, Caroline and I took seats at a long mahogany conference table in her lawyer's office. At Caroline's insistence, Pru and Darwin were there, sitting across from us.

Caroline's lawyer gave her a reassuring smile. "No surprises in Mike's will, everything to the family except for a very generous bequest to his fraternity." He slid a paper to Caroline. "Here's a list of his assets. Mike was very good about taking care of his personal affairs."

An unfortunate choice of words, I thought.

He slid another paper in front of Caroline. "He left his sailboat to you, and his car—"

"We'll sell them," Caroline cut in.

The lawyer raised his eyebrows. "His condo?"

I glanced at the paper in front of Caroline, taking in the numbers. Mike may not have been the best brother, but he was certainly financially successful.

"Sell it," Caroline said.

Caroline's lawyer tented his fingers. "Think about the tax consequen—."

"Sell it."

Pru caught my eye across the table and we shared a smile. Shy Caroline was coming out of her shell.

"We'll need some improvements to the farm. We're tearing down the barn and the Love Nest and Darwin will plant a field of sunflowers there. Riley's in charge of improvements to the ice cream shop." Caroline nodded to her lawyer. He handed a check to Pru. When Pru looked at it, she gasped.

"It's for Willow to go to art school," Caroline said.

Pru's eyes glistened as she passed the check to Darwin. "That's so generous."

Caroline said, "I know in my heart that nothing would've made Buzzy happier."

Darwin shook his head. "I don't know if we can accept—"

Pru folded her arms. "Darwin Brightwood, when someone gives you a gift, you take it. Thank you, Caroline. Thank you."

I pulled Sadie up to the kitchen porch. Distant rumbles were all that remained of an afternoon of thunderstorms that had caused temperatures to plunge and kept customers home.

"It's gotten chilly," Caroline said.

I remembered the sweater I found when I'd taken Sadie from the barn. "Buzzy's sweater's on the back seat."

She grabbed the sweater and scurried to the mailbox as I ran up the steps. Once inside, she handed me an envelope with a New York return address. I tore it open and took out two tickets to a tennis tournament. "Center court!" There was a short note. "Come see me play. I miss you guys. I miss Mike. No matter what, we're friends, right? Angelica."

I showed the note to Caroline, knowing that her

emotions regarding her brother were still tangled, wondering what she would say. Her lips turned up. "Let's go see her."

I laughed. "I'm glad you said so, because otherwise I'd have to take Paulette. She's a huge tennis fan."

Caroline put on Buzzy's sweater. "Ah, this is cozy. Glad the meeting with the lawyer's over with. I'm glad it's *all* over with."

Not quite. I could still hear Nina's shriek as she ran from the grave.

Donna Danforth confessed to setting fire to Aaron's house, but she wouldn't talk about anything having to do with Nina, protecting her until the end. I wondered if that would change if she ever let herself believe that Nina had killed Brooke. I'd never think of her as Dandy again.

Though the police examined the shell of Kyle's Mustang, there wasn't enough forensic evidence to prove he'd killed Martha Woodley in that hit-and-run so many years ago.

The life Kyle had known was over now anyway. He was busy shuttering his political campaign. Nina was on house arrest, out of jail on several million dollars bond.

After carefully choosing a few photos and yearbooks to keep, Caroline cleared out Mike's room and had the walls painted my favorite emerald green. I went to Virginia for a few days to close up my apartment so I could return to become the full-time manager of the shop. I had a few flavors I wanted to add to the menu.

On the same day Aaron the Hermit was released from the hospital, he picked up McGillicuddy and disappeared. A Penniman Preferred Properties For Sale sign now hung on a post in front of his burnt-out hulk of a house. I wondered what kind of plans Emily was making, what her next move would be. For now the Preserve at Fairweather Farms was on hold, but the land was too valuable. I knew it wasn't the last we'd hear from her.

Caroline stood at the sink, looking at the front of an envelope.

"Tea?" I put the kettle on. Rocky jumped onto my chair. I picked him up, sat down, and draped him across my lap.

Caroline didn't answer.

"Caroline?"

"This was in the pocket of Buzzy's sweater." She turned the envelope so I could see the words written on it in Buzzy's looping handwriting: *My will.*

"Open it!" I jumped out of my seat, Rocky giving a cry of protest at the quick movement. She tore open the envelope and we bent over the paper.

Though the words on the envelope were handwritten, the letter inside was typed.

Loved Ones,

I'm supposed to say something about being of sound mind and body. You bet I am! Is that legal enough for you?

I've given this lots of thought.

I was born and raised here on this farm. I know the world is changing. I don't want Mike or Caroline feeling like they owe me something. Live your lives, kids. If you live it here on the farm, great. If you live it in Timbuktu, I hope you're happy.

This place is special. I don't want it to change. If Mike or Caroline plan to sell the farm, then I don't want them to have it.

"That's clear," I said.

If neither Mike nor Caroline want to keep the farm, then it is my wish that Fairweather Farms become part of the Penniman Land Trust. No hard feelings. I'd like Darwin and Prudence Brightwood to remain as managers of the farm. I know they love it as much as I do.

Mike and Caroline get everything in the house, whether they want it or not.

One thing: Udderly Delightful is my baby. Please find a way to keep it open. If you have to hand it over to someone, please make sure it's someone who will love it as much as I do.

That's it. Oh, please take care of Princess Hortense Ophelia Tater Tot, aka Sprinkles, in the manner to which she has become accustomed. In other words, spoil her rotten! I've stashed some money for her care in my mattress.

Caroline, sell whatever you want. If you want to change the house, go ahead. I won't mind. Much. LOL.

Love you all,
Mom/Buzzy
Elizabeth A. Spooner

"Is it legal?" Caroline spoke as if dazed.

I laughed. "Who knows? As legal as Buzzy could be. Call your lawyer. He'll get a kick out of this."

A rap on the door made us look up. Sprinkles cast a bored look toward the door then stalked away. Caroline hurried to answer it. "Detective Voelker!"

For heaven's sake, his name is Jack. How long is it going to take these two to see the inevitable? I rolled my eyes, but my heart warmed for my friend.

Rocky groomed his paws, unconcerned, bored even. *You actor!*

Caroline led Voelker into the kitchen. He carried the tip jar and set it on the table. "My apologies. One of our officers left this off the list of your brother's effects and I forgot to bring it over. You'll have to sign for it."

I looked closely at the money in the jar. Most of it was bills, probably enough to cover the repair of the ice cream chiller.

"Good timing, Buzzy," I whispered.

Rocky leapt onto the table and nosed the jar. We all laughed, but I swept him up in my arms. "Why don't you make some coffee, Caroline? I left something in the car. Come on, Rocky, come with me."

"Coffee?" Caroline said.

"Thanks, that would be nice," Voelker replied.

My work here is done, I thought as I stepped outside onto the front porch. I settled on a step, drinking in the view across the sunflowers. Rocky purred in my lap. For the first time in a very long while, I had no travel plans, and that was fine with me.

THE END

Recipe

Buzzy's Ultimate Frozen Margarita

2 cups water

1 cup sugar

2/3 cup freshly squeezed lime juice

3–4 Tbsp triple sec

3–4 Tbsp tequila

1 tsp grated lime peel (zest)

1. Stir water and sugar in heavy medium saucepan over medium heat until sugar dissolves. Increase heat and bring to boil. Pour into bowl.

2. Mix together lime juice, triple sec, tequila, and lime zest. Add to sugar base. Refrigerate until cold—about two hours.

3. Pour mixture into ice cream maker and process according to manufacturer's instructions. Transfer sorbet to container, cover and freeze until firm—about two hours.

To serve, put glasses in the freezer for one hour to chill, then scoop the sorbet into them.

Have straws ready because it's very good as a slushy too.

Makes approximately 4 servings.

Enjoy responsibly!

Recipe

Sunflower Ice Cream

1 ½ cups whole milk

1 cup granulated sugar

Pinch of kosher or sea salt

2 ½ cups heavy cream

½-1 Tbsp pure vanilla extract

Caramel sauce

Honey

Roasted, shelled sunflower seeds

1. In a medium bowl, combine milk, sugar, and salt until sugar is dissolved (use a hand mixer on low or a whisk). Stir in the heavy cream and vanilla. Cover and refrigerate a minimum of two hours (best overnight).

2. Whisk the mixture before adding to an ice cream maker and follow the manufacturer's directions. When the mixture is thickened, remove from machine.

3. Make at least three layers of ice cream. Smooth ice cream in bottom of an airtight container. The size of your container will determine the number of layers and the amount of caramel, honey, and sunflower seeds in each layer. My taste-testers liked a ratio of 2 parts caramel to 1 part honey and 1 part sunflower seeds. For example: Drizzle ½ cup caramel, ¼ cup honey, and ¼ cup

shelled, roasted sunflower seeds on each layer. Add more or less to taste. Repeat until your container is full, leaving room for a decorative swirl of caramel and a sprinkle of sunflower seeds on top. Freeze until hardened, 3-4 hours.

Makes approximately 5 cups.
Enjoy!